JAX RETRIEVED HIS BIKE and rode into the center of town. The streets were empty. The traffic lights were on, but frozen green, red, or yellow.

He thought about zombies.

He thought about alien abduction.

He thought about *Spongebob Squarepants* and the episode where everybody took a bus out of town to get away from Spongebob for a day.

He thought about the old movie where Will Smith and his dog were the last creatures left on earth.

He would have been happy to see even A.J. Crandall, but he saw no people, no animals, no zombies—nothing.

He didn't want to be the last human on earth.

THE EIGHTH DAY

DIANNE K. SALERNI

HARPER

An Imprint of HarperCollins *Publishers*

The Eighth Day
Copyright © 2014 by Dianne K. Salerni
All rights reserved. Printed in the United States of America.
No part of this book may be used or reproduced in any manner whatsoever without
written permission except in the case of brief quotations embodied in critical articles
and reviews. For information address HarperCollins Children's Books, a division of
HarperCollins Publishers, 195 Broadway, New York, NY 10007.
www.harpercollinschildrens.com

Library of Congress Cataloging-in-Publication Data
Salerni, Dianne K.
  The eighth day / Dianne K. Salerni.
    pages cm
  Summary: "Orphan Jax Aubrey doesn't expect much on his thirteenth birthday, but
when he discovers there's an extra day squeezed between Wednesday and Thursday
whose origins are rooted in Arthurian legend, it's clear his life will never be the
same"— Provided by publisher.
  ISBN 978-0-06-227216-4
  [1. Magic—Fiction. 2. Time—Fiction. 3. Guardian and ward—Fiction. 4. Orphans—
Fiction. 5. Arthur, King—Legends—Fiction.] I. Title.
PZ7.S152114Eig 2014   2013037296
[Fic]—dc23   CIP
                                                                                          AC

Typography by Ellice M. Lee
15 16 17 18   OPM   10 9 8 7 6 5

First paperback edition, 2015

To Gabrielle and Gina,
who always asked: "when,"
and to Bob,
who answered: "on Grunsday."

1

JAX PEDALED HOME from the store and muttered in cadence with the rhythm of his bike wheels: *This sucks. This sucks. This sucks.*

The groceries were heavy in his overstuffed backpack. But Riley had let the refrigerator go empty again, and if Jax wanted to eat tonight, shopping was up to him.

Riley sucks.

That was something Jax could grumble with enthusiasm. *Riley sucks. Riley sucks.*

Billy Ramirez was always trying to convince him how lucky he was. "I wish I had as much freedom as you do," he complained at least once a week.

You mean you wish your parents were dead? Jax never said it out loud, thinking Billy would notice his silence and get the hint.

"Your guardian is so cool."

Yeah, living with a guy barely out of high school who forgets to pay the electric bill is so cool. Often Jax was tempted to offer a trade: He'd go live with Billy's parents and Billy could come live with Riley Pendare.

Traffic was steady this late in the afternoon, as people drove home from work. Jax flinched every time an impatient driver veered around him. He missed his old home in Delaware, where they had *bike lanes.* At the end of the block, Mr. Blum was watering his new sod again. Jax swerved to avoid the spray from his hose—*Missed me today, you old fart!*—and diverted onto the sidewalk in front of Riley's house, the smallest one on the street and the one most in need of a paint job. There was an old red Ford F-250 parked out front, so Jax knew who was visiting even before he went inside. This was not good news. He locked his bike to the rain gutter at the side of the house, then slung the heavy backpack off his shoulders and carried it up the front steps.

The door opened directly into the living room, where it was dark except for the television. Thick drapes protected the room from even the tiniest threat of a sunbeam. Jax had once opened them to see if sunlight would shrivel Riley up like a vampire. It hadn't, but Riley had complained about the glare on the TV.

Riley was watching his favorite show right now. ". . . a tunnel running beneath the pyramids lined with mica, which is used today for heat shields on spaceships. It's as if the place were designed for launching alien spacecraft . . ."

"Alien spacecraft? Wrong again, dude." The guy

2

on the recliner threw a crushed soda can at the host of *Extraterrestrial Evidence*. It bounced off the TV screen and hit the floor. Jax groaned under his breath as he closed the door. Wouldn't it figure A.J. Crandall would be here anytime Jax brought food into the house?

"Is that groceries?" Riley Pendare was sprawled on the sofa, still wearing his uniform from Al's Auto. "Thanks, Jax. I was gonna go later."

Yeah, right.

A.J. lifted his shirt and scratched his great, hairy belly. "Did you happen to get cigarettes?"

"I'm twelve," Jax reminded him.

"Darn." Then A.J. hefted himself up on his elbows. "He's twelve?"

"Yeah." Riley got up and followed Jax into the kitchen. "Thirteen in a couple weeks. Right, Jax?"

Jax shrugged. His birthday was tomorrow, but it wasn't like he was expecting a party or a present.

Riley dug through the grocery bags and found a frozen pizza and a package of hot dogs. He ripped open the pizza box and tipped the frozen disc into the oven.

"Almost thirteen?" A.J. hollered from the living room. "You think he's a late bloomer or a dud?"

"What's that supposed to mean?" Jax yelled back.

"Ignore him." Riley found a pot to put the hot dogs in.

A.J. lumbered into the kitchen. "Hot dogs and pizza . . . nice."

"Are you eating here?" Jax complained. They'd be out of food again by this evening.

"Pendare's not supposed to let me starve. We have an *agreement*."

"You don't look like you're starving, Crandall." Riley held out his hand, and A.J. produced a twenty, which Riley stuffed into a flour jar on the counter. *The kitty*, Riley called it, both because it was where he kept the household cash and because it was shaped like a cat.

A.J. located a lone soda in the refrigerator. "This isn't cold," he complained.

"Fridge's threatening to quit again." Riley dumped the entire package of hot dogs into a pot of water and turned up the gas flame. Then he thumped soundly on the side of the old Kenmore.

"Some mechanic you are," Jax muttered.

Riley pushed his hair out of his eyes. "Refrigerator's not the same as a car, Jax."

A.J. snorted. "Just call you-know-who to come fix it."

"Every time I call her, she wants a favor in return."

"Poor you. Wish she'd call in a favor from *me*."

Jax didn't know who they were talking about, and he didn't care. When A.J. reached for the last grocery bag, Jax snatched it away. "That one's not for you." He looked at Riley. "Save me some food?"

"Well, sure," said Riley, as if he hadn't eaten everything Jax brought home on other occasions.

4

With a worried glance at the stove timer, Jax carried the bag out the front door and down the sidewalk to the house of his elderly next-door neighbor. As usual, Mrs. Unger met him with her wallet. "What do I owe you, Jaxon?" She held up cash, like she had to prove she had the money.

"I'll check the receipt." He put away her groceries while she followed him around the kitchen with her cane. "Sorry I didn't buy any eggs," he said, checking the contents of her fridge. "I thought the dozen I bought last time would've lasted longer."

"The eggs are all gone?" Mrs. Unger pushed up her glasses. "I didn't eat them."

Sure you didn't. "Guess it was that ghost of yours again," he said cheerfully.

"Oh!" she exclaimed, as if he'd reminded her. "I found my library card on the kitchen table. It must be time to exchange the books."

"I'll do it this weekend. You want more like these?"

"Whatever these books are, get more of them." Mrs. Unger waved her hand at a stack of books on the counter. "*I* don't read them, you know."

Of course Mrs. Unger didn't read romance novels. She borrowed them for her ghost, the one who stole her eggs, moved the spices in her cabinet, and rearranged things in her closet.

Getting old and senile must be hard.

Jax checked the receipt. "Twenty-four seventy-nine."

"Here's thirty." When he protested, she said, "Take thirty. You saved me a trip."

"Thanks." He folded the three tens into his back pocket. She kissed him on the cheek, and he groaned theatrically even though he didn't mind.

"Anything else you need?" He eyed her kitchen clock. The pizza would be about done. He needed to get back before A.J. ate it all. "Yard work? Pulling weeds?"

Mrs. Unger smiled. "I don't have any weeds."

Jax took a look for himself when he ran back to his own house. Mrs. Unger had perfectly tended flower beds. He wondered how she managed it with her eyesight and her cane. The built-in flower beds along the side of Riley's house were nothing but hard-baked dirt, tough as concrete. Not even weeds grew there.

His timing, for once, was perfect. Riley was just scraping the pizza off the rack with the cardboard box it came in, and Jax scored a couple slices and a hot dog. Riley kicked a chair away from the kitchen table, which was his version of an invitation to sit down. "How's everything at the old lady's house?" he asked.

"Fine," said Jax, walking past the chair and out of the kitchen with his plate. He wasn't going to stick around to eat with Riley and A.J.

His bedroom was dark and cramped, with only one window. A wallpaper border circled the room, patterned with hound dogs wearing Confederate-flag bandannas. When Jax had moved in, Riley said the place had come that way when he rented it. "Change anything you want," he'd suggested.

But Jax hadn't put any effort into redecorating his room, because he wasn't staying long. That's what he'd thought four months ago, anyway.

He flung himself onto the bed and rested the paper plate on his stomach. At first, he stared at the ceiling while he chewed, but eventually his gaze wandered around the room. The trombone he'd given up playing was still propped against the wall. Nearby was the telescope he'd gotten last year and lost interest in after one use. His dad had complained long and hard about that.

Then Jax turned his head toward the photos on the bedside table. There was an old picture of Jax as a pre-schooler on his mom's lap, taken just before she'd gotten sick, and another of Jax and his father at the Grand Canyon last summer. Jax was smiling crinkly-eyed into the sun, while his dad had put up a hand to shade his eyes.

Why'd you do this to me, Dad?

If Jax had swallowed the hot dog whole, it couldn't have choked him worse than his own anger.

Jax knew the accident hadn't been his dad's fault. Someone, a drunk driver probably, had run his father's car off the road, causing it to plummet downhill and into the Susquehanna River. That person—whoever he or she was—had been the sole focus of Jax's anger until Riley Pendare had shown up and stolen him away from the only family he had left.

In the days after his father's death, Jax had been taken in by his mother's cousin, Naomi, and her husband. He hadn't known them really well before the accident, but they were family, willing to give him a good home. Then Riley had appeared at Naomi's with an affidavit, claiming to be Jax's guardian. "Rayne Aubrey signed the guardianship of his son over to me," he'd told them, crossing his tattooed arms across his chest. "This document says so. In the event of his death, I'm supposed to take custody of Jaxon Lee Aubrey."

Naomi called on a friend of the family for help, a lawyer who came to the house and hammered Riley with questions and received little satisfaction from his answers.

Who was Riley Pendare to Rayne Aubrey? Son of an old friend.

Why had Rayne Aubrey chosen Riley Pendare, eighteen years old and a stranger, as a guardian over his late wife's cousin?

Riley had been particularly uninformative here. "It was his wish."

But one answer had been more upsetting than any other.

"When?" Naomi had demanded. "When did Rayne make this arrangement?"

"Three weeks before he died" had been Riley's reply.

The lawyer thought the whole thing was ridiculous—Riley was too young and the situation too strange—and suggested they call Child Services to schedule a court hearing. Jax hadn't liked the sound of that, but it was better than letting this tattooed stranger take him away. Then Riley had a private word with the lawyer, gripping his arm and pulling him aside, out of everyone's earshot. The lawyer called Naomi over, and Riley spoke quietly to her, too, putting his hand on her shoulder.

The next thing Jax knew, everyone had changed their minds. The lawyer said Jax would have to live with Riley while waiting for the hearing, and Naomi agreed it was necessary. "It's just for a little while," she promised him. Jax watched in horror as his belongings were piled into the truck Riley had arrived in—which didn't even belong to him. Turned out he'd borrowed it from A.J. to pick up Jax for the five-hour drive to this little town in western Pennsylvania.

It was during that long, silent drive that Jax's knot of anger began to grow larger. He found there was plenty to spare for Riley Pendare—and his own father.

2

ON JAX'S THIRTEENTH BIRTHDAY, Billy Ramirez tossed him an apple in first period. "Don't say I didn't give you anything."

Jax caught the apple. "Thanks." It was probably the only birthday present he would get.

"We should throw a party. Do you think Riley will let us have one at your house?"

"I don't know who would come." Jax hadn't made many friends, partly because he kept telling himself he wasn't staying and partly because this school was so much bigger than he was used to. Jax had come from a small neighborhood school where he'd known all his classmates since kindergarten. Now he was bused from Riley's town to a consolidated megaschool servicing five different townships. In seventh grade alone, there were more than four hundred students. They included kids like Giana Leone, who came from wealthy McMansion neighborhoods, and wannabe thugs like Thomas Donovan, who was at that moment eyeing Jax's apple as if he wanted to swipe it.

"I don't know if Giana would come," Billy said cheerfully, "but I'm not afraid to ask her."

"Who said I'd want you to?" Jax had smiled at the girl *one* time and Billy wouldn't leave it alone. He hoped Giana, sitting across the aisle, hadn't heard. He was pretty sure the snort behind him meant that Thomas's sister, Tegan, *had* heard. Jax glanced over his shoulder, but Tegan had her head bent over last night's homework, trying to finish it before the teacher passed by. She looked just like her twin brother, with a freckled face and carroty-orange hair. Jax didn't even think Tegan had her own wardrobe. She always wore the same oversized hoodies and baggy jeans as Thomas.

"Ask Riley tonight," Billy whispered.

Jax sighed. He didn't believe Riley would let them have a party. Riley liked his privacy. When Jax had moved in, there hadn't even been internet.

"How can you *not* have internet?" Jax had demanded on his second day in the house.

"Don't want it."

"What, are you like from the Middle Ages?"

Riley barked out a laugh. "Ha! Funny."

"You have cable."

"I like TV. What I don't like is giving anyone with an internet connection the ability to hack my computer."

11

That was the most paranoid thing Jax had ever heard. He stood there, his mouth opening and closing like a fish, holding the ethernet cable to his computer. There was nowhere to plug it in. "I need it for school."

"Use the public library."

Jax was surprised Riley even knew what a library was. "I hate this place, and I hate you!" He flung the cable down, and since that wasn't satisfying, he shoved a box of books off the desk he'd been given in an alcove off the kitchen. "Why couldn't you leave me where I was?"

Riley said nothing.

Jax kicked a chair over, stormed upstairs to his ugly room, and slammed the door.

The following day, when Jax came home from school, he found Riley underneath the desk with a toolbox. "Hey! What're you doing to my computer?"

"Hooking up your internet," Riley replied, screwing a jack plate into the wall.

Jax hadn't thanked him, and Riley hadn't stuck around to be thanked. They'd never spoken of the incident again, although Jax overheard A.J. mention it once.

"I can't believe you got him internet. Living dangerously, aren't you?"

"Yeah, probably. But I know how he feels."

After school on his thirteenth birthday, that internet connection brought Jax a very brief email from his cousin, Naomi:

Happy Birthday Jaxon. Wishing you the best from Naomi, Ted, and the kids.

In spite of the promise she'd made on the day Riley took him away, Naomi hadn't fought for Jax very hard. The court hearing had been canceled with no explanation, and he heard from Naomi less and less frequently. Jax opened a chat box:

Jaxattax: hi naomi can we chat?

He heated some canned chili for dinner while waiting for a reply. Eventually a new message appeared.

Naomi: hi jax. been meaning to call you.

Jax threw himself into the chair and typed:

Jaxattax: do you have news for me?
Naomi: sorry it's been hard since ted lost his job. lawyers are expensive.

Jax ran his fingers over the keyboard, trying to think of a tactful way to remind her she'd get money from his father's estate if she won his custody from Riley.

Naomi: the case worker who met you last month reports you're settling in and happy

so i thought things were better.
Jaxattax: she said what?!?!

What Jax had told the caseworker was that Riley had forgotten to pay the electric bill and almost missed the gas bill; that he only bought as many groceries as he could carry home on his motorcycle; that he could barely take care of himself and was in no way capable of taking care of Jax. Jax had *thought*, from the caseworker's thin-lipped expression, that she was ready to put Jax in her car and drive him back to Delaware herself. How had that turned into "settling in and happy"?

Jaxattax: i told her what i told u. its awful here!
Naomi: she doesnt think its a good idea to move you again so soon
Jaxattax: no it IS. asap
Naomi: honey you know i want whats best for you but i kind of agree with her

Jax swallowed hard, his fingers hovering uselessly over the keyboard.

Naomi: gotta make dinner for the kids. happy birthday jax.

Before he could respond, Naomi left the chat.

* * *

Jax slept poorly and woke up before his alarm the next morning. Flailing out an arm, he flipped the switch before the buzzer could go off and rolled out of bed without looking at the clock. He pulled on jeans and a T-shirt, glanced in a mirror long enough to run his fingers through his tangled brown hair . . . and that was good enough.

Once again, there was nothing in the house for breakfast. The refrigerator didn't hum when Jax opened the door, and the lightbulb didn't light. Had it finally died, or—? He reached out and flipped a switch on the wall. No lights, no electricity. Again. Heaving a sigh, Jax took cash out of the kitty and picked up his backpack. He'd have to buy a breakfast burrito from the corner convenience store before the bus came.

The morning sky was strangely pink and purple when he left the house, like it might storm. Jax ran down the sidewalk, looked both ways before crossing the intersection . . . and then stopped and looked again.

There were no cars on the road in either direction. Although this was the usual time for people to be driving to work, the street was empty, and there was only one car at the corner store, parked in the back by the Dumpster.

Was the place closed? It never closed. He pushed open the door, and the lights were on, if a bit dim, but nobody was in sight. "Hello?" Jax hollered. He helped himself to a breakfast burrito and popped it into the microwave but couldn't get the oven to turn on. *It figures. My life is a cold burrito.*

He took his unheated burrito to the counter and fished two dollars out of his back pocket. "Anyone here?" he yelled. Maybe the clerk was on the toilet. As for everybody else . . .

Jax looked out the windows. There were still no cars passing by. No kids were gathered at the corner bus stop. At the Blum house, nobody was watering the precious sod. His eyes wandered up toward the bizarrely pink and purple sky.

Oh, crap.

It could be tornadoes. Had he missed a siren? Was everyone hunkered down in their basements waiting out the danger while Jax Aubrey bought a breakfast burrito in a store with walls of glass?

He flung the money and the burrito down and pelted for home. Maybe he should have run for the nearest house and begged to be let inside, but he felt a weird responsibility for the one person dumber than himself. "Riley!" he hollered, bursting in the front door. "Riley, are you up there?" He took the stairs two at a time and threw open the door to his guardian's room, only to find the bed empty. *Dude, I ran back here for you, and if you went to the cellar without me . . .*

Jax pounded downstairs, grabbed his phone from his backpack, and ran outside to the wooden cellar door against the side of the house. It was heavy, and he had to hold it over his head with one hand while he clambered down the stairs. When he let go, it felt like the door missed his head by inches. "Riley, are you down here?" Jax called, trying to light up his phone screen. It wouldn't turn on. Resigning himself to darkness, he sat on the dirt floor, faced a wall, and covered his head, just like he'd been taught in school.

He waited more than an hour, he thought. But he heard no wind. No sirens. When he couldn't stand it anymore, he climbed the cellar steps and pushed up on the door. Outside, the sky still looked weird, but it was more pink than purple. Jax heaved up the door, latched it open, and climbed into the yard. This time he *really* looked around.

The neighbors' cars were parked on the street and in their driveways, just as they normally were in the evenings. Jax checked the shed at the back of their yard, where Riley kept his motorcycle, and found the Honda 350 missing. Of all the people in the neighborhood, it looked like only Riley had gone to work this morning.

Jax crossed the yard and banged on Mrs. Unger's door. "Mrs. Unger, are you there?" He made his way around her house, peering in every window and through the kitchen door. When he backed away and looked up, he thought he saw a curtain flutter on the second floor, as if someone had just let go of it. "Mrs. Unger!" he hollered. He stared at the window, but there was no further movement and no answer, so he gave up and ran across the street to another house.

He pounded on every door up and down the block, shouting for help and growing more frantic by the minute. He looked in his neighbors' windows shamelessly, and at every house, it was the same. There were no signs of struggle, hurried packing, or anything out of the ordinary.

But he didn't see a single soul.

Billy Ramirez lived a block down the street, and no one answered his desperate knocking there, either. Jax knew they kept a spare key shoved up the nose of a ceramic tiki head on the back porch, and he used it to let himself in. The house was eerily silent. Calling out again and receiving no answer, Jax tried to turn on the TV, but like his phone, it wouldn't come on. The clocks on the microwave and the DVD player displayed 12:00, as if there'd been a power failure and they'd reset—except they didn't blink.

He almost didn't go up to the second floor, afraid of what he might find there, but after two false starts and a long time standing by the front door with his hand on the knob, ready to chicken out, Jax heaved a deep breath and ran upstairs. He flinched every time he threw open a bedroom door, but there was nothing to see—no bloody horror scene out of a movie. The beds looked slept in, but Billy and his parents were missing.

After leaving the Ramirez house, Jax retrieved his bike and rode into the center of town. The streets were empty. The traffic lights were on, but frozen green, red, or yellow.

He thought about zombies.

He thought about alien abduction.

He thought about *Spongebob Squarepants* and the episode where everybody took a bus out of town to get away from Spongebob for a day.

He thought about the old movie where Will Smith and his dog were the last creatures left on earth.

"Oh, crap!" Jax yelled, braking.

Will Smith and his dog had *not* been alone in that movie. There'd been other creatures that lurked in dark places and came out at night to kill.

It took three tries for Jax to break through the glass doors of the Walmart with a concrete parking block. Inside, only dim emergency lights were on. They provided illumination to see by but left enough of the store in shadow to make Jax skittish.

He filled a shopping cart with supplies he'd seen people grab before snowstorms or hurricanes and during zombie movies. With one hand on his bike and another on the shopping cart, he walked home, keeping an eye out for people and monsters. At home, he carried his stolen items upstairs, thinking that the second floor would be easier to defend. He bypassed the shed as too easy a target and hid his bike and the Walmart cart under a bush behind the house. In apocalyptic movies, there were always stray survivors who'd steal what you had.

Hours passed while he watched out the windows. He

would have been happy to see even A.J. Crandall, but he saw no people, no animals, no zombies—nothing.

The day weighed heavily on him, time passing at a crawl. He wished they had a clock that ticked—or anything that made a sound. Oddly, he felt drawn to Riley's room—as if he missed him, which was impossible. He poked through his guardian's stuff, kicking dirty clothes across the floor, opening drawers, and peering at the photo of an unknown girl tucked into a mirror. But there were no answers here any more than there'd been at the Ramirez house.

He had to force himself to eat a cold can of stew and drink a bottle of water. It was rare for Jax to have no appetite, although it had happened the day his dad never came home . . . and the day they'd found the car in the river . . . and the day Riley Pendare had brought him *here*.

When it grew too dark to see anything outside but the creepy glow of the streetlights, he pulled the curtains shut and curled up miserably on his bed to wait for dawn. In the morning, he'd risk going out to look for other survivors.

His final thought, as he drifted into a troubled sleep, was that he didn't want to be the last human on earth.

3

"JAX, GET UP! You're gonna miss the bus."

The pounding on Jax's bedroom door caused his heart to thump in panic for a reason he couldn't remember. *A bad dream?*

"Jax! I gotta get to work. I can't drive you in."

"Okay, okay!" He rubbed his eyes and sat up. Across the room, his open closet door gave him a view of the water bottles and canned food stacked waist high inside.

Not a dream.

Outside, a motorcycle engine revved up.

"Riley!" Jax shouted. He leaped out of bed and stumbled down the stairs and out the door in time to see his guardian pull away from the house.

Jax stood on the stoop and stared at the neighborhood with his mouth hanging open.

Across the street, a woman stuffed a toddler into a car seat. An old man walked past the house with two dogs. Mr.

Blum watered his sod, which had gone dangerously brown, while overhead a jet cut a white swath across the sky.

Holy crap, it was the Spongebob *episode after all. They all left town for a Jax-free day and now they're back.*

He grabbed hold of the doorknob to steady himself.

I broke into a Walmart!

Jax scrambled upstairs. He pulled on clean clothes and closed the closet door. When he ran down to the kitchen, he found bread on the counter, along with new containers of peanut butter and jelly.

It figures Riley goes shopping when I've got a room full of stolen canned goods.

He made the bus by a hair. All the usual riders were on board and nobody was talking about mass disappearances. Billy was engrossed in reading *The Fellowship of the Ring*, and Jax sat down beside him.

Did it really happen?

Jax looked out the window as the bus passed through town. Walmart employees were nailing boards over the broken glass on their front door.

He sank lower in his seat. *It happened.*

In first-period science class, his hand shook as he wrote his name and the date on a lab paper.

"Is the party on?" Billy slid into the chair beside him.

"Riley said no," Jax lied. He'd never asked.

"Dang it. Well, at least come to my house for dinner tomorrow after school."

"Sure," Jax mumbled. Then he lifted his head. "Tomorrow's Saturday."

"Tomorrow's Friday." Billy tapped the date on Jax's paper. "Today's Thursday, dude."

Jax stared at Billy. *Yesterday* had been Thursday. He looked across the aisle. "Hey, Giana. Is today Thursday or Friday?"

Giana tossed a lock of wavy brown hair over her shoulder. "Thursday. All day." She glanced at her friend Kacey, who rolled her eyes and laughed.

"O-kay." Jax erased the date roughly, almost ripping the paper.

Today was Thursday, the day after his birthday. The day he'd broken into a Walmart *hadn't happened*. Still, when the classroom door opened again, he flinched, expecting cops. But it was just the Donovans coming in late, which they did once or twice a week.

As Tegan walked past Jax's desk, she stopped, and Thomas plowed into her. Jax looked up to find both twins staring at him. Tegan sniffed and glanced at her brother. "What?" Jax demanded. Maybe he hadn't showered this morning—or on the day that no one else remembered— but he didn't think he stank.

Tegan nudged her twin with an elbow, and Thomas nodded, then went to his seat by the window. Normally he pulled his hood up over his head and took a nap during first period, but today Jax was uncomfortably aware of

Thomas's gaze on him throughout class.

It matched the one he sensed on the back of his neck, coming from Tegan.

When Jax got home from school, he verified the date on his computer. They had electricity again, and the refrigerator worked, as did his phone. It really was Thursday, but his closet was full of Walmart goods. The alarm on his clock was switched off, which he'd done himself when he woke up yesterday.

Jax retrieved a plastic storage tub from the top shelf of his closet. Opening this was a last resort when he was miserable, because it was a toss-up whether it made him feel better or worse. Inside were his mother's jewelry, a bottle of her perfume, and a scrapbook she used to keep, which contained photos of the Aubrey family until Jax was six. Neither he nor his dad had kept it up after she died. Four months ago, Jax had added his father's Rolex watch to the sad little collection, along with a wooden box about twelve inches long and six inches wide. Since Jax had been living here, he'd opened the tub only once, to take out this wooden box and make sure Riley hadn't stolen the contents.

Not long after moving in, Jax had come home from school and found Riley and A.J. talking intently in the kitchen. On the table between them lay something Jax recognized. "Hey!" He lunged across the room. "That's my dad's!"

Riley snatched the object off the table before Jax could reach it. "No, it's mine." Then he held the dagger out for Jax to see, hilt up, blade down—the way someone would hold a cross to stop a vampire.

Jax faltered. Riley was showing him the knife like he expected Jax to recognize it wasn't his father's. "My dad had one like that," he said, half in accusation, half in his own defense.

"I know he did. But this one's mine." Then Riley slipped it into a sheath on his hip. It was an odd thing to be wearing, unless he was going hunting. And a decorative dagger like that would be a strange choice for skinning rabbits and gutting deer—or whatever hunters did.

Jax immediately ran upstairs to check the storage tub in his room. His father's dagger was still in its box, where it belonged. It had a five-inch blade and a cast-metal handle engraved with the Aubrey family crest. The carving on Riley's knife was different, but the weapons themselves were very similar.

Seeing the two daggers, Jax had to accept that his father and Riley really had known each other. His dad had often shown this dagger to Jax, implying that it represented membership in a club. Jax assumed he meant something like the Masons or the Elks. He couldn't imagine Riley as a member of one of those clubs, but clearly he and Jax's father had shared *some* secret.

Today, Jax closed the case with a snap. He had his own secrets now. Briskly, he returned everything to the storage tub—except his father's Rolex, which he wound up and strapped to his own wrist.

He didn't intend to lose track of time again.

Jax consulted the watch frequently. Days went by with no hiccup in time, and if it hadn't been for the items in his closet, he might have convinced himself it had never happened.

Monday after school, Riley dumped a stack of books on the desk while Jax was working on his computer. "Are you going to the library?" Riley asked him.

Jax picked up the book on top. It had a girly cover—flowers and a sunset and a woman in a fancy dress. "What, are you dying to read the sequel?" He looked up at Riley. "I didn't even know you *could* read."

Riley crossed his arms. "Did you tell Mrs. Unger you were going to the library this weekend?"

Yes, he had. Jax looked at his dad's watch. He hadn't skipped over time; he'd just been so worried about his secret day that he'd forgotten his promise. He didn't like letting the old lady down, but he liked Riley pointing it out even less. "Is her ghost complaining?" he asked crankily, slapping the book down on the pile.

"Her ghost?" Riley asked sharply.

"Mrs. Unger is a little . . ." Jax made a twirly finger next to his head.

Riley glared at him. "Are you going to exchange the books or not?"

Why do you care? Jax wanted to say—or better yet, *You do it.* But Jax didn't want to see Riley doing good deeds for Mrs. Unger. He preferred to think of Riley as a jerk. "Yeah, I'll go tonight."

"Make sure you do," Riley said gruffly, which made Jax wonder why he *did* care.

Unless he counted Riley's interest in Mrs. Unger's reading habits, nothing weird at all happened for the better part of the week. But on Thursday morning, when Jax's alarm clock didn't wake him and the watch on his wrist didn't tick, he sat up, alert. He guessed what he was going to see even before he pulled back the curtains on his window.

The sky was a pale purple, and no cars passed on the street.

This time, instead of panicking, Jax made an effort to observe everything carefully. His clock was frozen at 12:00 a.m., and it didn't blink or respond to the push of any buttons. The bedroom lights didn't go on when he flicked the switch, and his father's watch had stopped at midnight. Downstairs, the microwave and the refrigerator didn't work, but oddly, the gas stove did. He shrugged and made himself a breakfast of instant oatmeal.

Afterward he biked through the town, which was as empty as last time, and out to the interstate. Just when Jax thought the highway, too, was empty, he spotted a vehicle in the oncoming lane. With an excited whoop, he waved both hands over his head to signal it, but the car wasn't moving toward him. He coasted to a stop near the stationary SUV and hopped off his bike. The driver's seat was empty, which gave him a chill. He reached out to open the door, and a spark leaped from the metal handle to his hand. Using his shirt as insulation, he tried again, but every attempt to touch the vehicle resulted in a shock.

Jax leaned as close as he dared to the driver's window and peered inside. He didn't know what he was looking for until he saw it. The gear shift was set to drive. This car wasn't in park; it was supposed to be moving.

He had planned to bike to the next town and see if the same thing was happening there, but this car answered the question for him. If it wasn't the same every place, there'd be traffic on the highway, and this car would've gotten where it was going with whoever was supposed to be inside.

So instead he headed home. Inside one of the moving boxes that had come from his old house, he was pretty sure, there was a camera. He hadn't used it in years because he had a camera on his phone, but his phone didn't work today and the camera might.

Now that he knew everything would be back to normal tomorrow, Jax was excited. He was going to document this craziness and share the photos with Billy. He leaped up the front steps of the house, threw open the door, and crashed right into Riley.

4

"JAX!" RILEY GRABBED JAX by his T-shirt and hauled him into the living room.

After his first gasp of surprise, Jax felt a surge of disappointment. This fascinating world wasn't his alone. He had to share it with Riley Pendare.

Riley shoved Jax into a chair and unclipped a two-way radio from his belt. "I was so sure you were a dud," Riley said, then spoke into the radio. "Melinda, you copy? Over."

A woman's voice answered. "I'm here, Riley. Over."

Jax sat up. He and Riley weren't the only ones here.

"False alarm. It was the kid. Let the others know. Over."

"Copy that."

"Who's she?" Jax demanded when Riley clipped the radio to his belt. "What others? There are no people here! I looked everywhere! Last week, too."

"Last week?" Riley narrowed his eyes. "This isn't your first time?"

"This is the second time. But you weren't here last week. Nobody was!"

"I was here. I just wasn't *at home*." Riley crossed his arms over his chest. "I thought your birthday was next week."

"It was last Wednesday."

"Why didn't you tell me? I would've been looking out for you if I'd known."

"What does my birthday have to do with it?" Jax demanded. "What *is* today?"

Unexpectedly, Riley grinned. "Today's Grunsday. Well, that's not its name, really. That's just what Crandall's dad calls it, and the name kind of stuck with us."

"Crandall's *dad*?" Jax repeated. "Who's *us*? Was that A.J.'s mother on the radio?"

"No, that was Melinda." Riley sighed. "I wasn't expecting this, but you're here now. Let's set up the generator. You don't want to spend the day without electricity, do you?"

Jax followed him out of the house and into the shed at the back of the yard. "Are you saying A.J. knows about this, too? Or just his dad?"

"The whole Crandall family." Riley wheeled his

motorcycle out of the way, then threw a canvas tarp off two generators and half a dozen gasoline containers. "This is the eighth day of the week—an extra twenty-four hours between Wednesday and Thursday."

"No way." Jax looked at his father's watch, stuck at twelve midnight. "Time is stopped?"

"It's not stopped. The sun still moves across the sky, doesn't it? We're just living through a different timeline." Riley shoved a moving dolly under one of the generators.

"But I saw a car frozen on the highway."

"Objects traveling at velocity during the moment of change *look* frozen from our perspective, but they're moving normally in their own timeline. It all depends on the observer." Riley unbuckled a wristwatch from his arm. "Here. This is a watch I wind only on Grunsdays." Jax leaned close enough to confirm that it was ticking. "Take it," said Riley. "I'll get another one. As long as you only wind it on the eighth day, it'll work in this timeline."

Jax strapped the watch above his dad's Rolex while Riley wheeled the generator up to the electric meter on the side of the house. "So—it's like a parallel universe?"

"No, because it doesn't run parallel. It skips over days. And this is the same universe. Things you do on this day stay done." Riley narrowed his eyes at Jax again. "What'd you do last week? You must've been pretty freaked out."

"Uh . . ." Try as he might, Jax couldn't keep his eyes from darting to the back of the property.

Riley looked too and saw the handle of the Walmart cart sticking out from beneath the bush. "Is that—? Aw, Jax." He ran a hand through his hair. "I should've known a Walmart break-in on a Wednesday night wasn't a coincidence."

"I thought it was the zombie apocalypse!" Jax said. "How was I supposed to know any different? How did you know, your first time? Why *you*, anyway? Why me? What are we doing in a different timeline?"

"We inherited it. Me, from my family. You, from your father."

A shiver trickled down Jax's spine. "You're telling me this happened to my father?"

"Every week, between Wednesday and Thursday. *You* only get it from your father's side," Riley said, attaching cables from the generator to the electrical box, "which is why I wasn't sure you'd be one of us at all."

"One of us?" Jax croaked. "Aren't we human?"

"Of course we're human." Riley looked shocked. "What kind of bad science-fiction movies have you been watching?"

"Where's everybody else?"

"People living in the normal timeline can't see into Grunsday, and vice versa."

"So they aren't here?"

"Oh, they're here. We just can't see them."

"Shouldn't there be some sign of them? Uh, their

clothes . . . ?" Jax imagined puddles of clothes dropped wherever the people were standing, sitting, or lying. Had there been pajamas in the beds at the Ramirez house? He didn't remember.

"Nah. Whatever's on your body goes with you. But that doesn't mean the people aren't still there." Riley pointed at the house across the street. "If that house burned down today, the occupants would die."

"It could burn down *between* Wednesday and Thursday?"

"In the regular timeline, the house would explode into flames. It would be gone in an instant." Riley unscrewed the gas cap on the generator and checked the fill level. "Fetch me one of those containers in the shed." Jax did as he was told, and Riley called after him. "Things you do on Grunsday have consequences in the other time stream. Break stuff, move stuff around, and they stay broken and moved. And it looks pretty freaky to people on the other side."

"That can't happen very often," Jax reasoned, handing him a gasoline can, "or people would notice."

Riley filled the generator. "It happens all the time. Explosions from unexplained gas leaks. Poltergeists. Crop circles—how do you think they appear overnight?"

"Are there a lot of people like us in Grunsday?"

"A few, but not all can be trusted. Your father wanted to make sure you ended up with someone who would watch out for you. That's why I couldn't let you live with your cousin."

Jax clenched his fists, suddenly reminded of why he resented Riley. "You never explained any of this to me."

"I had to wait and see what you were. Since your mother was a Normal, you only had a fifty percent chance of being one of us. Most of us transition for the first time when we turn ten or eleven. For some, it doesn't happen until the twelfth birthday." Riley powered up the generator. Jax expected a loud roar, but it hummed with surprisingly little noise. "It's a late bloomer who gets it on the thirteenth birthday—and a dud who never gets it at all. If your birthday had passed without you having a Grunsday, I would've let you finish the semester here and then sent you to live with your cousin." He added under his breath, "In fact, I was counting on it."

Jax steadied himself against the house, because this really was the final blow. He could've lived with Naomi after all, if this bizarre thing hadn't happened to him.

Except it *had* happened.

And Jax's father had kept it a secret.

"Where *were* you last week?" Jax couldn't vent his anger at his father, but Riley was a handy target. "Why weren't you here?"

"I had to make an overnight trip to meet someone who lives only on Grunsday. I had no choice."

"Someone who *what*?"

"Normals live seven days a week and don't know about the eighth one. But there's a race of people who don't experience the regular seven. And then there's people like you and me, who transition between the two time streams. We call ourselves Transitioners."

"Wait, back up," Jax said. "A *race* of people who live only on Grunsday . . ."

"Right. They exist on this one day and skip over the other days of the week. They can't interact with anyone confined to the normal seven days, although they frequently live in those people's houses." Riley leaned on the dolly. "Any place that's ever been called *haunted* probably has one living there, eating the food and moving stuff around." He looked like he was waiting for Jax to reach some kind of revelation.

But Jax was already there. "Mrs. Unger's ghost . . ."

"Yeah," said Riley. "She's real." Then he looked at the second floor of Mrs. Unger's house and made a thumbs-up sign.

Jax lifted his head.

A girl with long, ghostly-pale hair was watching them from an upstairs window.

5

EVANGELINE DROPPED THE CURTAIN and walked away.

Now there was a second Transitioner living next door—a newly developed one, if yesterday was any indication. New Boy had been terrified, banging on Mrs. Unger's door and peeping in windows all over the neighborhood. Then he'd dragged groceries home in a cart and carried them inside like he was preparing for a siege. Evangeline had watched his antics from the upstairs windows. It would've been funny if he hadn't obviously been scared half to death, and she wondered why the boy had been left so ignorant.

Not that Evangeline could claim to know a lot about Transitioners. Maybe they let all their children discover the eighth day by surprise.

It seemed as if he was getting an explanation now. She'd only caught a few words of the conversation by the shed, but apparently New Boy would be living here. She didn't like it, but no one cared what she did or did not like. And she'd tolerated the other boy for eight months, so what was one more?

Of course, in *their* timeline it had been several years since the first boy arrived. He'd been not much older than New Boy was now—maybe thirteen, with dark-auburn hair in need of a haircut and bruises on his face like someone had beaten him. He'd walked with a crutch. Evangeline had assumed he was a runaway passing through town and thought if she kept herself out of sight for a few days, he might move on without ever being aware of her.

But then he'd stood on the lawn between the houses, leaning on his crutch, and called out her name—her family name. "I know you're there," the boy had shouted at the house. "The Taliesins told me. I don't mean you any harm."

Evangeline's first instinct had been to flee, to dash out the back door and take off running down the street. But if he really did know the Taliesins . . .

Cautiously, she had approached the window. He raised his left hand when he saw her, identifying himself.

"Will you come out?" he'd called.

Rattled by his presence, by him knowing *who she was*, by *who he was*, she'd shut the curtain with a snap of her wrist. He could have been lying, although when her heart stopped pounding and she thought it through, she decided he probably wasn't. By the time she'd reconsidered his offer, he'd given up and gone inside his house.

The Taliesins must have sent him to watch her, although

why they'd done so, she didn't know. Evangeline had been in this house five years by her own counting, and she'd spent the first four utterly alone. This boy was the first person she'd seen since the Taliesin brothers brought her here and left her, so long ago. She didn't count the Taliesins as friends, but they were Kin, trapped in the eighth day like she was, and they had every reason to keep her safe.

By their definition of *safe*, of course.

The day Evangeline's parents died, she'd been running through the woods with Elliot hanging on to her hand and Adelina on her heels when two men stepped into her path. She'd gasped and drawn her younger siblings close before she saw the strangers' pale blond hair and piercing blue eyes and realized they were Kin and not Transitioners. She thought they must be allies of her father's, sent to help her.

But they weren't. She'd learned that when it was too late to do anything about it.

The Taliesins had separated her forcibly from her brother and sister and ordered her to stay in hiding until she received further instructions. That was how she'd become the lonely ghost in this house—her only company, books and the photographs of the Unger children who shot up like weeds, quickly surpassing her. Eventually they'd all moved out, and then Mr. Unger had died, leaving Mrs. Unger a widow.

Five years of her life in this house equaled *thirty-five* to the Ungers and the rest of the world, and she'd received no further instructions from the Taliesin men.

Just the boy who moved in next door.

He hadn't spoken to her after that one time, hadn't threatened her or done anything to frighten her into running away. Occasionally he acknowledged she was there—like with the thumbs-up just now or the snowmen last winter. Once in a while she even acknowledged him back. Recently, he'd started hooking a generator to Mrs. Unger's house on the eighth day, providing her with electricity. He seemed to live a solitary life, but he was in contact with other Transitioners. There was Fat Friend and the two people she thought were Fat Friend's parents. Once there was a Black-Haired Girl who drove an expensive-looking blue convertible.

And now there was New Boy.

His arrival probably had nothing to do with her, but the other one—Red, she'd nicknamed him—had been absent a lot lately, which was a change in habit for him. She sensed trouble afoot. Although she hadn't inherited her mother's talent for prognostication, Evangeline always tried to listen to her instincts. One never knew when a feeling might really be a premonition.

She should renew her protections on this house.

All the symbols she needed for home protection were stocked in the kitchen: salt, basil, fennel, dill weed, bay leaves, and olive oil to bind them together. Once she had the elements gathered in a porcelain bowl, she closed her eyes and rubbed the herbs between her fingertips.

"No harm shall enter here."

She repeated the command over and over, building the potential until she was breathless and gasping. Her eyes flew open, and she looked down at her work. Her ancestors would have ground this mixture into paste with a mortar and pestle. But Mrs. Unger had a Cuisinart, and thanks to Red, Evangeline had electricity.

Minutes later, she was marking every entrance to the house—window and door—with a thin line of paste. "No harm shall enter here." It wasn't a perfect form of protection, but it was the best she could do without making a permanent alteration to the house that would frighten Mrs. Unger and attract unwanted attention. Putting the library card out to request new books was one thing. Painting magical symbols on the walls was a different matter entirely.

She had just finished and was heading for the kitchen to clean up when she heard footsteps on the porch. Evangeline threw herself into the corner of the hallway, where she could see the front door but not be seen from it.

New Boy was at the door. He was a couple of years younger than Evangeline, with an unruly mop of dark-brown hair. He knocked tentatively and peered through the glass.

Evangeline pressed against the wall.

The mail flap clicked open, and a folded piece of paper flew into the house, sailing in a graceful arc before landing on the floor.

Evangeline looked at the bowl in her hands. "Some protection."

6

RILEY HAD TWO RULES regarding the girl next door. "Number one, don't tell anyone about her."

"Of course not." Jax stared up at the window.

"Number two, leave her alone."

"But—"

"Leave her alone."

"What if—"

"What's rule number two, Jax?" Riley growled.

"Why'd you point her out to me, then?"

"You'd wonder why I was hooking up a generator to Mrs. Unger's house. And I wanted her to know she shouldn't be afraid of you."

"Why would she be afraid of me? I just want to meet her."

"She doesn't want to meet you." Riley flipped the switches in Mrs. Unger's electric box. "I've lived here for years, and she's never spoken to me."

Jax's eyebrows shot up. "She's never talked to you, but you're giving her electricity?"

"It's a courtesy. And sometimes, when she feels like it, I get a courtesy thank you. You'll see." Riley motioned him over. "C'mere, and I'll show you how to do this. That way, if I ever have to be gone on a Grunsday again, you can hook up both houses."

Riley talked him through the procedure, and they started up the second generator. "They're quieter than I expected," Jax commented.

"I paid extra to get the quietest on the market. Didn't want to attract attention."

Jax looked around. "Who would hear it?"

Riley didn't answer. "The gas stove works, and we've got public water, so that works. But the only way to have electricity on Grunsday is to supply your own. The power companies are run by computers, and anything with a computer chip is dead today."

"Why?"

"Because processing chips measure time, but Grunsday exists on a timeline they don't recognize. Unfortunately, almost everything has a chip these days. That's why we have to keep the old refrigerator from quitting."

"Ohhhh." Jax nodded. "And that's why your motor-cycle is a piece of junk."

"Junk? The Honda 350 is a classic!"

A classic piece of junk. "But wait," Jax said. "There's

electricity in town. The traffic lights are on, even if they're stuck, and the emergency lights were on in Walmart."

"That's an afterimage of the light that was there at midnight on Wednesday." Riley picked up the gasoline can and walked it to the shed. "The lights in Walmart—did you have trouble seeing by them?"

"Actually, yeah."

"Don't break into a store again. If it's an emergency, there are other ways to get what you need."

"I thought it was an emergency," Jax said indignantly. "I'm not a thief."

"I'm not a thief either," Riley replied. "But I have stolen when I needed to."

As much as Jax wanted to hold himself above those ethics, he couldn't. He had a closet full of Walmart goods that proved otherwise.

Riley spent the afternoon working on his bike. Jax kept his eyes on the windows of the house next door. He wanted to ask Riley what the girl did in there all day, but if she refused to talk to Riley, he probably didn't know. So instead, Jax asked a bunch of other questions Riley couldn't or wouldn't answer.

Why hadn't Jax's father told him about this extra day? Did other Aubrey relatives have the same ability?

"Do you *have* other Aubrey relatives?" Riley asked.

Not that he knew of. His father had been an only child, and his Aubrey grandparents had died before he was born. "Why are *you* my guardian?"

"Your dad knew my dad."

Jax watched Riley check the fluids on his bike. "Your dad's dead, isn't he?"

Riley didn't look up. "My whole family's dead. At least you have cousins."

"Can I still go live with them?"

"Eventually. I was gonna talk to Crandall's dad about it. We were all so sure you were going to be a Normal. Now . . ." Riley stood and picked up his helmet. "We can't let you go without some training." He mounted his motorcycle, then paused. "You can come along. If you want to."

Jax didn't want to go to A.J.'s house, and Riley didn't want to bring him. Jax could see it on his face. "No, I'm gonna ride my bike and look around."

"Stay within the town limits. It's safe for you here."

"And it's not safe outside of town?"

Jax watched Riley's expression. He seemed to be mulling over how to answer that question. "Just stay close," he said finally, turning the key in the ignition and revving the engine. "And leave the girl alone."

The motorcycle was hardly out of sight before Jax whipped off a note to the mysterious girl and shoved it through

Mrs. Unger's mail flap. Then he spent the rest of the afternoon kicking himself for not waiting until he could come up with something less stupid than:

Hi, I'm Jax Aubrey. Maybe we can hang out sometime and have a soda. I'd like to meet you.

He wondered if she would read the note or just leave it lying by the front door for Mrs. Unger to find. Mrs. Unger would think Jax was nuts.

When it was obvious the girl wasn't going to introduce herself—or even come to a window again—Jax took a bike ride through town. It wasn't as interesting as he'd thought. In fact, it seemed like the extra twenty-four hours were going to be pretty dull. He could ride his bike on the empty roads and wander into stores that had been open at midnight. He also could walk out with anything he wanted and snoop in neighbors' houses.

He wasn't tempted. The fact that he'd searched the Ramirez house while Billy and his parents were kinda-sorta there made his skin crawl. And even though he guessed the security cameras at Walmart hadn't been working last Grunsday, Jax still wasn't convinced the police weren't going to pin the burglary on him.

Riley returned in the evening and showed Jax how to disengage the generators. When they shut down the one at Mrs. Unger's house, Jax found a basket of freshly baked cookies left nearby. "She thanks you with baked goods?" Jax rummaged through the basket to check for a note. There wasn't one.

"Not very often." Riley sighed glumly. "I guess I have to share them with you now."

Jax stayed up until midnight to see for himself what happened. A few minutes before twelve, he sat on the front porch with his father's Rolex on his left wrist and Riley's Timex in his right hand.

Riley's watch ticked steadily until exactly twelve o'clock and then stopped.

The Rolex started.

Across the street, a pit bull went berserk, running up and down the length of its fence, barking and growling at Jax. From the dog's perspective, he'd just popped into existence from nowhere.

"You'll get used to it," Riley said from behind him.

Jax held up both watches. "But they're mechanical watches! There's no computer chips in them!"

Riley shrugged. "Every time-measuring device is affected by relativistic change, and, like the car you saw on the highway, a lot depends on the perspective of the observer." When Jax's mouth dropped open, Riley grinned. "Einstein's theory of relativity. What, did you think that because I work at a garage, I'm stupid?"

Well, yeah, actually. He had.

7

THURSDAY WAS DISTRESSINGLY NORMAL, full of teachers and classes and work. Jax wondered how he could have an extra twenty-four hours that bored him silly and still be annoyed by a regular day. Either Grunsday should be more exciting or Thursday should be more satisfying.

When he got home from school, he scoped out the windows of Mrs. Unger's house. If what Riley said was true, the girl wasn't there today. She wasn't *anywhere* today.

A.J.'s truck was parked in front of the house—A.J.'s *old* truck, which, like Riley's motorcycle, had no computerized parts. Hefting a plastic bag of milk and orange juice, Jax went into the house and was greeted with "*Heeeere's* our little Walmart burglar. Went back for more, did ya?"

Jax glared at Riley. "Did you have to tell him?"

"Steal anything I might like?" asked A.J.

"I took canned goods and water and batteries, you jerk. How was I supposed to know Thursday was still coming?" Jax walked stiffly into the kitchen. He wasn't proud of what he'd done. The refrigerator wheezed when he opened the door to put away the milk and juice. It sounded like it had emphysema.

There were two pizza boxes on the counter. With A.J. in the house, he expected them to be empty, but there were four slices left and Jax grabbed them all, piling them crisscross onto a plate.

Riley came in and broke up the boxes.

"I have more questions for you," Jax said around a mouthful.

"I'll bet you do. But that'll have to wait until later, if you feel up to it."

"Why wouldn't I feel up to it?"

"It's tattoo night!" A.J. hauled a leather case into the kitchen and onto the table. He unbuckled it and whirled it around to face Jax. The case was filled with tattoo guns, needles, and bottles of ink.

"You're giving Riley another tattoo? Where?" Riley pretty much had tattoo sleeves up to his armpits.

"No, I'm giving one to you," said A.J.

When A.J. wasn't driving equipment for a strip-mining company, he worked part-time at a tattoo parlor. But that didn't mean Jax wanted the big doofus sticking needles into *his* arm. Just because they shared this weird Grunsday thing didn't mean he liked A.J.—or Riley. "It can't be legal to give me a tattoo," Jax said.

"It is with the permission of your guardian," said Riley. "Trust me, Jax. This is traditional. Your first Grunsday. Your first tattoo."

Jax hesitated. The *idea* of a tattoo was cool, although not the needle part. Jax hated needles. And what would Naomi say, when Jax finally went to live with her? "I'll pass," he decided, and started walking out with his slices of pizza.

Riley stepped into his path and gripped his arm. "Sit down, Jax. You're getting a tattoo."

Jax shivered and sat down.

He looked at A.J.'s equipment.

He was getting a tattoo.

"I'll have a snake," he volunteered.

Riley let go.

A.J. burst out laughing. "You can't have a snake!"

"Riley has a snake. And a tiger, and a bunch of other things."

Riley held up both arms for Jax to see. "These are camouflage. The only reason I have these is so people don't bother to look at this one." He extended his left hand, and for the first time Jax noticed a family crest in blue, gold, and red ink on the inside of his wrist. It was so well surrounded by other, more interesting tattoos that it practically faded into the background.

For a moment, Jax felt dizzy. "My dad had a tattoo just like that. Except—"

"Yeah, I know. He had your family crest, and this

one's mine. You have to have it, Jax. We all have it." Riley looked at A.J., who rolled up his shirt sleeve and turned his arm over. He, too, had a crest inked on his wrist. Jax had never noticed that one either, not that he looked at A.J.'s arms that much—or any other part of A.J.

"All Transitioners are marked this way," Riley continued, "and you're never going to reach your potential without it."

A.J. leafed through his stencil paper. "Do you have the Aubrey crest for me to copy?"

"Jax has it. Go get your father's dagger, Jax."

Jax was out of his seat, up the stairs, and into his room before he realized it. Only when he was halfway down the stairs with his father's dagger did he pause. He didn't want to put this in A.J.'s hands, and he wasn't sure he wanted a tattoo.

Instead, he wanted to know what Riley meant by "potential." He wanted to question how there could be an extra day and scientists not know about it. He wanted to know more about the girl he'd seen in the window of Mrs. Unger's house.

Jax looked at the dagger.

He wanted to know if his father was expecting to die when he signed Jax's custody over to Riley.

"Jax," hollered Riley. "Bring the dagger."

Jax ran down the remaining steps into the kitchen, then handed over the dagger.

Billy would've thought this was the coolest thing ever—hanging out with Riley and getting tattooed. Jax watched A.J. copy the design, then extended his arm for the stencil as if it were someone else's arm. When the tattoo gun came out, he squirmed in his seat, but Riley stood behind him and placed both hands on his shoulders. The machine whirred when A.J. pressed his foot to the pedal, and the needles bit into Jax's arm.

They stung, like little hornets. Jax watched the ink sink into his skin and blinked rapidly. A.J. wiped away tiny droplets of blood. "I feel sick," Jax whispered.

"Turn your head," A.J. said.

He did, but the room grew dim.

He heard Riley's voice: "Whoops. There he goes."

And A.J.'s: "Makes my job easier."

Then somebody turned out the lights.

8

THE VOICES FADED in and out, and it took a while for Jax to focus on the words.

"Why don't we all move someplace else? The Emrys girl too."

"Camouflage works best when you stay in one place, Crandall. Start moving, and all bets are off."

"Yeah, but in this case . . ."

"Jax is awake."

Jax could've sworn he hadn't moved. But now he opened his eyes. His left hand tingled, and when he looked at it . . . "Hey!" he shouted, sitting up and finding himself on the living room sofa. "I passed out and you *finished the tattoo*?"

A.J. shrugged. "You were nice and still."

His skin looked puffy and red, but the Aubrey crest was now inked into his wrist. It must have taken hours to finish the job. Was it normal to be out cold that long? Jax looked accusingly at the other boys.

But his eyes were drawn back to the tattoo. It was undeniably cool. A.J. had gotten creative with the design: the eye on the scroll was fancier, he'd made the bird a bald eagle, and the flames were colorfully inked in red and gold. But it was basically the same family crest that Jax's father had had tattooed on his wrist and engraved on his fancy dagger.

"There's one more thing to do." A.J. picked the Aubrey dagger off the coffee table. "Come over here . . . and kneel down in front of Riley."

"No," said Riley.

A.J. frowned. "I know he's young for it, but how else are you going to protect him?"

"Gimme that." Jax stood up and snatched the dagger from A.J.'s hand. He didn't know what they were talking about, but he didn't like the sound of it. Kneel to Riley?

A.J. turned toward Riley. "You said you were going to look out for the kid."

"I will," said Riley. "The oath I made to his father covers that. I don't require anything else from Jax."

"I don't know what you promised my dad," Jax said, "but you've been a lousy guardian."

"Is that what you think?" Riley replied.

"You haven't looked out for me." Jax scowled. "You haven't explained anything to me—*why* we get this extra day, or *who* else gets it, or *how* there can be people who live on only one day a week."

"Those are a lot of questions."

"I've got more." Jax held up his sore arm. "Why do I have to have a tattoo with my family crest, but you *camouflage* yours?"

"You're right. We do need to talk about that, but not tonight." Riley removed his dagger from its sheath and balanced it on the palm of his hand. "Getting marked takes a lot out of you," he said, looking up from the dagger and meeting Jax's eyes. "I might be a lousy guardian, but I know you're tired and need to go to bed."

I am not, Jax wanted to say. Instead he swayed, and his

eyelids got too heavy to hold up. He would've fallen into the coffee table if Riley and A.J. hadn't grabbed his arms. They hauled him upstairs, Jax mumbling protests all the way, and when they dumped him into bed, his eyes closed and stayed that way.

"You'll sleep till morning" was the last thing he heard Riley say.

In the morning, Jax woke with a sense of panic. His arm was sore but not so puffy anymore. He tried to remember why he'd held out his arm to A.J. and all he could think of was: he hadn't wanted to. It made him shudder to remember how eagerly he'd asked for a snake when seconds earlier he'd wanted nothing to do with those needles. He pulled on a long-sleeved shirt and left the house for school without stopping for breakfast.

"Jax?" Riley called out from the kitchen as he passed by. "Hey, Jax!"

Jax didn't answer. He quickened his pace and walked down the street to catch the bus at Billy's house.

The long-sleeved shirt didn't fool Billy, who spotted the tattoo on the bus. Jax had to give a partial explanation, and Billy was hurt. "If A.J. Crandall was doing home tattoos, why didn't you call me? My mom would've *killed* me for getting a tattoo." He said the last as if it were an honor Jax had denied him.

Jax couldn't tell Billy about Grunsday, and he couldn't explain how Riley and A.J. had tattooed his arm against his will. "I passed out, all right?" he finally said. "I would've called you, but I fainted as soon as A.J. stuck a needle in my arm, and I was embarrassed."

"Dude, you didn't."

"Like a girl. I fainted like a girl." *And stayed passed out for the next three hours.*

Billy crowed with laughter. Jax tugged down his sleeve and asked, "Can I stay at your house this weekend?" Suddenly, Jax was afraid to go home—afraid of Riley.

"Sure. Unless . . ." Billy's eyes lit up. "Do you think A.J. would—"

"You'd need permission from your parents," Jax said promptly.

Billy's shoulders slumped. "I said it before and I'll say it again. You are so lucky to have Riley Pendare as your guardian."

9

THE BOYS HOLED UP in Billy's basement rec room Friday night to play video games. Jax borrowed Billy's computer and waited until his friend was fully engaged defending Hyrule against an army of giant spiders before he opened up Google. Searching for *Grunsday* turned up nothing but jokes. *Eighth day* or *eight days a week* unearthed movies and song titles. Jax scratched at the tattoo, which had begun to itch, then tried *extra day between Wednesday and Thursday*.

A site called Between Wednesday and Thursday topped the list. The link led to a message board with a banner that read: *If you have to ask, you don't belong here.* There was only one thing visible on the page:

This is a private group. Potential members know why they belong here. If you wish to join, send a message HERE describing why you deserve membership in 140 characters or less.

Jax hesitated only a moment before clicking on the link and typing a message:

> just had the eighth day for the 2nd time. seeking
> more information.

He included his email address as requested and tapped the send button.

Billy let out a horrible, bloodcurdling cry and stretched his arm over the back of the sofa, offering the controller to Jax. "Just got my brains slurped out of my head. Wanna turn?"

"Yeah." Jax deleted his search history and logged off. He was just sitting down on the sofa when his phone chirped, and he pulled it out of his backpack to check his texts.

> Riley: where r u

Jax's heart lurched. Reluctantly, he thumbed in a reply.

> Jax: @billys house
> Riley: u didn't tell me
> Jax: i never tell u

There was a long pause after that. Then:

Riley: u coming home tonite?
Jax: staying weekend
Riley: WHEN r u coming home?

In four months, Riley had never kept track of Jax's comings and goings. Jax remembered Riley's hand on his arm, pressing him into the chair for the tattoo, and shivered in revulsion.

Jax: depends when will U b @ work?

There was another pause before Riley's final message.

Riley: guess u dont want answers to those ?s after all

Billy's mom let Jax stay the weekend, sleeping on the couch in their basement. "Your guardian says it's okay?" she asked.

"He doesn't care where I am," Jax said, and she nodded grimly, as if that was exactly what she'd expected. Mrs. Ramirez was a lot less impressed with Riley Pendare than her son was. Jax kept his sleeve pulled down over his new tattoo lest her disapproval for Riley spill over onto him. He ate every bit of home-cooked food she put in front of him.

He didn't go home until late Sunday morning, when he

found a blue '58 Thunderbird with its roof off parked in front of the house. He would have assumed anyone with a car like that must be visiting one of the neighbors, except it was a classic car with no computerized parts—and by now Jax was catching on. He scrambled up the front steps and pushed open the door.

Riley was sitting on the sofa next to a very pretty girl with long black hair. When Jax walked in, Riley stood up hastily. "Uh, Jax . . ."

Jax cleared his throat. "I can come back later if you're, um . . ."

"We're not *anything*."

The girl also stood up and smoothed down her short skirt. "You must be Riley's protégé. Aren't you a cutie!" She barely came to Riley's shoulder, even in high-heeled boots, and she wore a short leather jacket that matched a sheath at her hip containing *an engraved dagger*.

Jax gaped at her, and she raised her left hand to show him the tattoo on her wrist. It was delicate and feminine and bordered by red roses. When she walked toward Jax, he smelled the scent of roses in her perfume.

"This is Deidre Morgan," said Riley. "She fixed our refrigerator, and then she was *leaving*."

Deidre ignored him. "I didn't catch *your* name, cutie." Her dark eyes lingered on Jax's tattoo.

"Jaxon Aubrey. You fix refrigerators?" She was like no repairman he had ever seen.

"I fix all kinds of things," she said, leaning an arm on Jax's shoulder. "Machinery's my talent, especially engines of war." Jax froze, suddenly realizing the dagger wasn't the only weapon this girl carried. There was a shoulder holster under her jacket and something tiny and pearl-handled sticking out of the top of her boot.

Nope. Not your typical refrigerator repairman.

Riley rolled his eyes. "Just give him the radio, Deidre."

"Spoilsport." She unclipped a radio from her belt and offered it to Jax. "This is a secure radio for you to use on the eighth day. Channel two is how Riley will contact you, but in an emergency, call for help on channel one, and they'll all get it."

Jax frowned. "They?"

"Riley's raggedy crew." She turned to Riley with a smile. "Anything else I can do for you, sweetie?"

"No, thanks, Deidre," Riley said. "I appreciate your help."

"Say no in haste, regret at leisure."

He laughed. "I've told you what I think."

"Your counterproposal is weak," Deidre said pleasantly. "You've got one thing of value to offer, and if you want my family's manpower and weaponry to deal with the Emrys situation, you're going to have to put that on the line. Think it over, sweetie. Jax, nice to meet you." In a passing breeze of rose blossoms, she was out the door and gone.

"Geez, Riley," Jax breathed. "Is that your girlfriend?"

"Deidre?" Riley laughed. "No."

What, then? His personal assassin?

Riley waved a hand at the sofa. "Have a seat."

Jax felt a surge of panic. He remained standing, bristling from head to toe.

"I'm not ordering you. I'm asking," Riley said quietly.

Was that some kind of admission? "Did you drug me the other night?"

"Drug you? No." He said it with the same amusement as when Jax asked if Deidre was his girlfriend. "Please, Jax. Sit down." Riley sat down in the armchair, as if demonstrating how it was done.

Reluctantly, Jax put the radio on the coffee table and sat down.

"I asked Deidre to set up the radio so you'd have a means of communication on Grunsday. Keep it with you at all times on the eighth day."

"And if there's an emergency"—*what kind of emergency?*—"Deidre would come?"

"No, not Deidre. She just supplies me with these radios because she has access to them and we're old friends."

Old friends. Yeah, right. "She said you wanted weaponry—" Jax began.

Riley interrupted him. "Call on that radio, and you'll raise me or the Crandalls. It has enough range to reach any of the corresponding radios within town limits."

"What if I'm outside town?"

"Don't be. A lot of Transitioners use Grunsday for their own advantage. I'm talking petty thievery, burglary, and some things a whole lot worse. My mother always said that having the extra day was too much temptation for some people. Maybe even most people." Riley ran a hand through his hair and looked away, frowning as if he'd surprised himself by sharing something about his mother.

It surprised Jax, too. He opened his mouth to comment, but Riley sighed and looked up again. "It's better to stay with your own group, where there's safety in numbers. Your father learned that the hard way."

Jax stiffened. "What do you mean?"

"What'd your dad do for a living, Jax?"

"He owned a company called Information Resources."

"Which did what?"

"He always said he 'moved information.' He was a consultant."

Riley stared at the floor for a moment, then met Jax's eyes. "You mean people paid him to get information. Information other people didn't want them to have."

Jax frowned. "Now wait a minute."

"Like plans for business mergers and new products and secret deals . . ."

"No!" Jax leaped to his feet. "You make it sound like he was some kind of spy!" Riley didn't drop his gaze, and Jax glared at him. "My dad wasn't a crook."

"Your dad stumbled across something dangerous," Riley said. "And realizing the danger, he approached me and offered useful information in exchange for my promise to look out for you if the worst came to pass. It did, and here we are."

"What?" Jax demanded. "What did he find out?"

"He knew something that got him killed. If I told you, I really would be a lousy guardian, wouldn't I?"

10

JAX LAY ON HIS BED holding the Grand Canyon photo. In the picture, his father was wearing an embarrassing Hawaiian-print shirt, and the hand he was using to shade his eyes wasn't the one with the tattoo. There wasn't a single thing in this picture to suggest Rayne Aubrey had a secret day of the week or made his living as a corporate spy.

But Jax had to admit, there were things about his father that didn't make sense. The tattoo, for one, which he told people was a leftover from "wild college days." But on more than one occasion, he'd warned Jax to pull up his grades "so you can go to college like I never did."

And then there was the business, Information Resources, which had no employees and no office. Jax had never even seen a business card for it. He'd never questioned this before because, after all, what kids were really interested in their fathers' work?

Riley had refused to answer any more questions about Jax's father or the bargain they'd made. "You want to leave here, and that suits me fine," he'd said. "Once you leave my protection, it's better if you know as little as possible about your father's business—and mine."

But Jax was tired of being surprised. He slammed the framed photo onto the bedside table and went downstairs to his computer.

Buried in his in-box below all the spam, Jax found an email with the subject line: *Between Wednesday and Thursday Admission Granted.*

> Fellow Eight-Day Citizen: Your application for admittance has been granted. The username and password below will access your membership.

Jax entered the ID numbers he'd been given and was prompted to change his log-in information. He chose his customary username, *jaxattax*, and the same password he used for everything. Immediately, he was redirected to the forum, where he found a list of discussion threads.

Introductions
Discussion Topics
   • **Vermin Infestation**

- **Can Duds Be Cured?**
- **Niviane's Enchanted Forest: Was It a Real Place?**
- **Locus of the Spell: Stonehenge or Pentre Ifan?**
- **The Kin Issue**

Youth Camps

Chat Groups

But Jax couldn't get into any of the discussions. Whenever he clicked on a link, a pop-up informed him:

403 Error. Try again later.

Transitioners might have a secret day all to themselves, Jax thought, as he sent an email to technical support, *but they're lousy with computers.*

The kid who smashed Giana Leone's ceramic vase never realized he did it. He was talking to his friend in the hallway and didn't look back when his elbow struck her arm. She lost her grip on the vase, and Jax, passing by, made a grab for it but missed. The vase hit the floor and shattered.

Giana held out her hands in dismay. "That stinks," Jax said. He squatted and started picking up the broken pieces.

"It's just something I made in art class. I don't care," Giana said, although the look on her face plainly said she did. She fetched a trash can from an empty classroom.

Jax picked up shards with one hand and piled them into the other. "Do you want to save the big pieces and glue them back together?"

"What's the point?" Giana gingerly picked up pieces of pottery and cast a sideways glance at Jax's hand. "I can't believe you got a tattoo. Isn't that illegal?"

"Not if your guardian says okay." She was eyeing him like she couldn't decide whether the tattoo made him cool or creepy, so he said, "My dad had a tattoo like this. It's a way to honor him."

"Oh." Giana stood and picked up the trash can. Jax could've kicked himself. Nobody wanted to hear about his orphanhood.

"You had Mr. Gupta's history test this morning, right?" he asked, quickly changing the subject. "I have it next period. How was it?"

"Not too hard, if you studied," she said, starting to walk away.

"Was it mostly on Chapter Fifteen?" He stood up too, desperately wanting to extend the conversation. "'Battles of the Revolution'?"

Giana stopped with a jerk, almost losing her balance. "Yes, but he focused on the Pennsylvania battles." Giana's forehead rumpled. She made a movement as if to walk away, but it was like she'd been welded to the spot. "You better know all about General Anthony Wayne."

"What about the essay? Was it tough?"

Giana pressed her lips together and stared at Jax, then blurted out, "You have to compare the British and Continental armies. I didn't have any problem with it."

"Thanks for the tip." Jax grinned. "D'you like history?"

"It's my favorite subject." Again, Giana made a strange, jerky movement, like she was going to walk away but didn't.

Jax's heart flipped over. It seemed like she wanted to keep talking to him. "They're showing a historical movie at the PTA Fun Night this Friday, aren't they? I mean, it's a ghost story, but set in the past, right?"

"Yes." Her eyes were very wide.

"Are you going?" The bell rang for the next period.

"Yes." Her voice sounded strained.

"Me too." He made that up on the spot. "So maybe I'll see you there?"

"You probably will."

Jax hadn't felt this light-headed since A.J. had stuck the needle gun into his arm. "Okay. Talk to you later." Giana expelled her breath and bolted down the hall. Jax stood there, grinning, until an unexpected blow sent him staggering. He caught his balance and glared at Tegan Donovan, who for no reason had hip-checked him as she walked by.

"That was smooth," she said. "Jerk."

He blinked stupidly. What was wrong with *her*? Why would Tegan care if he was talking to Giana?

Then his grin returned. Giana Leone wanted to talk to Jax Aubrey. Wow.

The rest of his day was a blur, and nothing, not even the history test, could squelch his good mood. But he wasn't exactly sure what their conversation meant. Was he allowed to *wave* at Giana from across the auditorium on Friday night? Hover nearby? Sit next to her?

After the last bell, he tried to catch her at her locker. Maybe he could clarify the situation. Giana glanced his way, slammed her locker closed, and walked in the opposite direction. Jax quickened his pace. "Giana! Wait up."

She whirled, her eyes flashing. "What?"

Jax stepped back, startled by her expression. But his mouth kept going, plunging forward in his convoluted plan to find out her favorite candy and show up with it. "I was wondering, for Friday, if they sold snacks, or if we were allowed to bring—"

"I don't care what you do," she snapped. "Just stay away from me!"

"Uh . . ."

"And don't you *dare* let anyone know I told you what was on the history test."

Jax gaped at her. Students in the hall were turning to watch.

"Freak," Giana hissed, walking away as fast as her legs could take her.

* * *

Girls. Did they take lessons on how to humiliate a guy? Or did it come to them naturally?

Jax replayed the conversation in his head all the way home, but he couldn't figure out what had happened. One minute, Giana had been talking to him and admiring his tattoo—well, sort of—and a couple of periods later, she'd practically spit in his face.

"Pendare?" A.J. lifted his head off the recliner when Jax opened the front door. The host of *Extraterrestrial Evidence* was blathering on about aliens abducting the ancient Khmer Empire.

"No, it's me." Jax stomped into the kitchen and got a soda from the refrigerator, which now hummed smoothly and kept everything cold. He sat at his computer in the alcove off the kitchen and checked his email glumly, still stinging from Giana's last word. *Freak!*

Huh, imagine if she knew how much of a freak he really was.

An automated response from the Between Wednesday and Thursday website suggested Jax "check online assistance between the hours of 3–5 pm." He signed in and found the link for tech support. A chat window opened within seconds.

terrance: yo jaxattax. what u need?
jaxattax: cant access discussions
terrance: reload page

jaxattax: already did

terrance: must b glitch. sign on w/family account till i check

Jax felt the usual punch in the gut he got whenever somebody mentioned *family*. But he was learning to use it to his advantage.

jaxattax: no family. thats the problem

terrance: no family on forum? new members welcome.

jaxattax: no family period. thats why i need forum

terrance: sorry. u newly turned & no family 2 help?

jaxattax: yup

terrance: where you live?

Now Jax paused.

terrance: just the state, not yr address. im not a creep. there r groups 4 newly turned kids. maybe one in yr area.

jaxattax: PA

terrance: ill check PA & work on fixing yr account.

jaxattax: thx

He closed the chat window and looked at the list of discussions he couldn't get into. He was attracted and repulsed by the idea of a group for kids like himself. Part of him wanted to talk to somebody besides Riley; another part screamed, *Don't make yourself more of a freak!* After a few seconds, his attention was drawn to some of the discussions topics.

- **Niviane's Enchanted Forest: Was It a Real Place?**
- **Locus of the Spell: Stonehenge or Pentre Ifan?**

He knew what Stonehenge was but opened up a new window to check out Pentre Ifan, which turned out to be some other standing stones in Wales. Then he Googled *Niviane*, but the name was connected to Merlin the wizard and didn't seem related to the eighth day. He leaned back. Hadn't he overheard A.J. and Deidre mention a name to Riley? *Everett? Emory? Emris?* Jax sat up and started typing.

According to a baby name site, *Emris* meant "immortal, undying." But when Jax tried the alternate spelling *Emrys*, Google took him right back to the site he'd already seen for *Niviane*: Merlin. One of the ancient names for the wizard was Merlin Emrys. And Niviane, depending on which version of the legend he read, had been either Merlin's girlfriend, apprentice, or betrayer. Possibly all three.

Jax stood up and walked into the living room. A.J.'s huge carcass lay sprawled on the recliner, a soda can resting on his belly. This felt like asking *Jeopardy!* questions of a dog, but what the heck? "A.J., what do you know about Niviane?"

"She was the Lady of the Lake," A.J. replied.

"And she trapped Merlin in an eternal forest?"

"She didn't trap him." A.J. belched. "He volunteered to go, for the good of everybody. There wasn't any other way to stop the Kin. That's why they created the eighth day in the first place."

"You're telling me they were real people?"

A.J. sat up and turned to face Jax. "Has Riley told you any of this?"

Jax ignored the question. "Are the legends real or not?"

"Yes. No." A.J. looked confused. "The people were real. The legends are crap."

"Who's this Emrys that you were talking to Riley about?" Jax tried to think back to what he'd heard after they'd tattooed him. "Does this have something to do with the girl next door?"

A.J. frowned. His mouth opened and closed a few times while he crushed the can in his hand. Soda squirted from the top. "Yeah, she's the—"

"Don't answer that, Crandall. Jax, what are you doing?"

Riley stood at the front door. A.J. pointed at Jax, but Riley interrupted him when he tried to explain. "Jax, ask Crandall for the PIN number on his debit card."

A.J. protested, "Hey!"

"Go on," Riley insisted. "Ask him."

Jax's stomach clenched. "What's the PIN number on your debit card, A.J.?"

For three seconds, A.J.'s face grew bright red while he pressed his lips together. Then he burst out "Nine one six oh four," and clapped his hand over his mouth.

Riley laughed. "Well, that was fast."

11

JAX GAPED AT the two of them, afraid to say anything else.

A.J. counted on his fingers. "It's only been five days since we marked him," he said to Riley. "It usually takes at least ten and a couple more visits to Grunsday."

Riley pulled the door closed. "He's older than most newbies. Or maybe it's the nature of his talent."

"He's pretty strong," A.J. said. "Even when I realized, I couldn't stop talking."

"What did I do?" Jax asked, repulsed and fascinated all at once.

"Apparently," said Riley, "you figured out how to use your bloodline magic all on your own."

Jax shook his head. First Grunsday, then a tattoo, and now this? "What's bloodline magic?"

Riley drew his dagger out and balanced it on his left palm. Jax recognized the gesture from the night of the tattoo and started to back away, but Riley ordered, "Sit down and shut up."

Jax's knees folded, and his butt hit the chair before he knew what was happening. His lips clamped shut.

Then he started struggling.

Gripping the chair with both hands, he tried to push himself to his feet. His sneakers scrabbled on the carpet. He clenched his jaw but couldn't force his mouth open.

Riley watched for several seconds. Then he slid the dagger into its sheath. "Okay," he said. "You can talk."

"You jerk!" gasped Jax.

Riley shrugged. "It was the quickest way to demonstrate."

"There's no such thing as magic!" It came out as a wail, a last-ditch effort to hang on to reality as he knew it.

"*Of course* there is. What did you *think* Grunsday was?" Riley threw out his arms. "It was magic that made Grunsday and trapped an entire race of people inside it. And it was magic you were using on Crandall when I came in, forcing him to answer your questions."

"You should've told him before now," A.J. said.

"I was telling him a little at a time, so he wouldn't freak out."

"Good job." A.J. hooked a thumb toward Jax, who was still wriggling in his chair.

"Oops," Riley said. "You can get up, Jax."

Jax shot out of his chair and across the room, as far

from Riley as he could get. He wanted to bolt out the front door and keep running. His heart was pounding and his muscles were coiled, but he fought the urge for flight. If he ran, he'd never get any answers. "Can you make me do anything you want?" he croaked. And in the back of his mind, he wondered, *Can I do the same to you?*

"It has limits, and most of my commands are temporary or wear off in time, so—" Riley broke off his explanation, seeming to realize how scared Jax was. "Jax, I swore an oath to your father I'd protect you. So please. Sit down and let me explain."

Jax flinched but didn't feel compelled to sit.

"You're an inquisitor," Riley said, "and a pretty strong one, developing this much on your own."

"A quality tattoo makes a difference," A.J. pointed out.

"True," Riley said. "Crandall's an artisan. His talent for designing marks probably enhanced your natural skill. Your talent is the same as your father's: forcing other people to give you information. Although, as you can see"—he waved his hand to indicate the distance between the two of them—"when someone *realizes* you've compelled them against their will, there's usually a side effect of making them pretty hostile."

"Oh, crap!" Jax suddenly understood why Giana had answered all his questions and then yelled at him afterward. He slumped into a chair and buried his face in his hands. "Oh, no!"

"Nice going, Pendare. You made him cry." A.J. took his phone out of his pocket. "I'm calling my mom."

Mrs. Crandall smacked Riley upside his head with an oven mitt. "Why didn't you bring him to me in the first place?"

"I thought I had it under control."

Jax glanced around the Crandall home curiously. He'd always pictured A.J. living in a dump one step down from Riley's house, but this was a nice place, clean and decorated with stuff that matched. A.J.'s parents weren't exactly what he'd expected either. His mom was tall and sturdy, with very short hair and arms that might've been more muscular than Riley's. She was wearing an apron, though. That and the oven mitt got Jax's hopes up.

A.J.'s father stuck out his hand and introduced himself gruffly. "Arnold Crandall. Nice to finally meet you, son." Jax extended his own hand cautiously, not sure if he'd be getting it back. Mr. Crandall was bigger and heavier than A.J., but in his case it was all muscle and no fat. With his buzz cut and gravel voice and a handshake that cut off Jax's circulation, he reminded Jax of a drill sergeant. He and his wife *both* looked like drill sergeants.

"I didn't expect him to start interrogating people on his own," Riley was saying. "Melinda's going to meet with him on Grunsday. I thought that was soon enough. Plus, like I told you before, I'm not sure how much to tell him."

"Everything," Jax piped up. "I want to know everything."

"*Everything* covers a lot of territory," Mr. Crandall said. "If you're not sworn on as Riley's vassal, then some things aren't your business to know."

"What do you mean, *vassal*?" Jax stared at the man blankly.

The Crandalls looked at each other, then at Riley. Mrs. Crandall raised her oven mitt again, but Riley sidestepped out of range. "*You* try to explain it!" Riley said.

Mrs. Crandall moved her hands to her hips. "Sit down, Jax. I know this has been a shock, but if it's any comfort, there's dinner afterward. You could probably use a good meal."

"Yes, ma'am," Jax said eagerly. "I could."

Riley flung himself into an armchair, looking chastised.

The Crandalls seated themselves across from Jax, while A.J. leaned against the back of Riley's chair. "All right, Jaxon," said Mr. Crandall. "You studied feudalism in school, didn't you?"

Studied, yes. Learned? Not so much. But Jax nodded.

"Well, Riley is my liege lord, like his father was before him. I'm his sworn vassal, and so are my wife and son."

"You're kidding," Jax said flatly.

"Not in the slightest."

The liege lord slumped in his chair, picking dirt from

beneath his fingernails. "It's just a chain of command."

Chain of command? With *Riley* in charge? Jax scowled. "My father wasn't, was he?"

"Your father was independent," Mr. Crandall said. "No clan, no vassals, no liege lord. Which is why, when he needed help, he came to Riley. And it's why, for your own protection, you really ought to—"

"No." Riley sat up. "His father didn't want him sworn to me. I don't want it. I'm sure Jax doesn't want it. He goes back to his cousins as soon as he's trained."

Mr. Crandall looked like he was sucking on lemons. "Listen to Riley," his wife said softly, and Mr. Crandall grunted and nodded.

Holy cow. He really is the boss of them!

"What about Niviane and Merlin?" Jax asked. "What does an everlasting forest have to do with the eighth day?"

Mr. Crandall ticked off on his fingers. "The real Niviane was a Britannic queen. The real Merlin was a spell caster from a race of sorcerers called the Kin. And what the stories call an everlasting forest is Grunsday—a place cut off from the rest of time. Niviane conceived of the idea; Merlin cast the spell, and—" He glanced at his wife and seemed to edit his words. "And more than a dozen Welsh clan lords contributed their talents and magic to make it happen. We Transitioners are descended from the rulers and clan leaders who helped cast the spell."

"Welsh clan leaders with magic powers?" Jax scratched

his head. It still sounded ridiculous.

"There are people with a talent for magic all over the world," Mrs. Crandall said. "On every continent. Mystics and shamans and fakirs. We aren't the only ones."

"But who are the Kin?" Jax looked at Riley. "Are they the people who live only on Grunsday—like the girl?"

"The Kin are a race of people far more powerful in magic than most," Mr. Crandall explained. "They arrived in the British Isles maybe three thousand years ago. Legends say they came down from the north, but I don't know if anybody really knows for sure."

Jax tried to picture a world map in his head and remember what was above the British Isles. He wasn't any better at geography than history, but he didn't think there was much.

"They coexisted with the native Britannic people for a long time. Kin families allied themselves with Welsh clans and adopted our customs, like taking vassals. But around two thousand years ago, some of the most powerful Kin clans started making war on Normals with their magic. They razed the countryside, enslaved the people, and might have eventually ruled the earth if Niviane hadn't conceived of the Eighth-Day Spell to contain them and give the Welsh clans the advantage of seven days to every one of theirs."

"Merlin was an Emrys, which was one of the more prominent Kin families," Riley added. "But he and a few other Kin clans honored their alliance with our people, fought alongside us, and collaborated on the spell, even though they ended up trapped in the eighth day with the rest of their race. Merlin Emrys sacrificed himself for us. Not *all* the Kin are bad people."

Mrs. Crandall said to Jax, "Melinda can explain more when you meet her."

"Who's Melinda?"

"One of Riley's vassals. You'll like her."

Jax glanced around the room. "Are there any more of you? Vassals to Riley, I mean."

"Just Miller." A.J. cleared his throat.

"You won't be meeting Miller," Riley said. "He's out of town. On business."

From the sudden silence in the room and the stony look on Mr. Crandall's face, Jax guessed that Miller's business was not Jax's business to know.

12

JAX TRIED NOT TO pounce on Mrs. Crandall's dinner like a starving hyena, but A.J. and Riley didn't hold back. Jax figured he'd better grab what he could before it was all gone, and dived for a chicken leg.

"Eat up, Jax. You look undernourished." Mrs. Crandall glared at Riley.

"He eats everything in sight," Riley protested, his own mouth full. "I can't keep groceries in the house!"

Jax looked up, startled. He thought the exact same thing about Riley.

"Nobody can eat like a teenage boy." Mrs. Crandall slung a ladle full of mashed potatoes onto Jax's plate. "The pair of you together are probably like piranhas."

After dinner, Mr. Crandall looked at Riley and jerked his head toward the door. Riley nodded and the two of them left the room. A.J. made a move to follow, but his mother ordered him and Jax to clear the dishes. "I cook.

You clean up," she said. "That's how it works. And scrape the plates before putting them in the dishwasher, Arnold Joseph."

"I do," A.J. protested.

His mother smacked him with a wooden spoon. "Will you ever learn not to lie?"

A.J. looked contrite until Mrs. Crandall left the room; then he waggled his eyebrows at Jax. "It sucks—having a mom with a talent for truth. But she can only detect literal lies. If you lie by omission, she can't tell. Once in a while you have to throw her a bone, though, or she gets suspicious."

"How many kinds of talent are there?" Jax asked.

A.J. disposed of some leftovers by stuffing them into his mouth. "Probably as many as there are families," he mumbled around the food. "Melinda'll teach you about this better than I can."

Jax bundled up the trash and carried it out the back door. He was stuffing the plastic bag into a metal can when he heard Mr. Crandall say, "What're you going to do about the kid, then?"

Jax froze. Mr. Crandall and Riley were around the corner in the backyard.

"I dunno. I really didn't think he'd be a Transitioner, let alone busting out with talent before he was trained."

"He's a little young to swear his loyalty, but he'd be safe with us, and we could use an inquisitor."

"No." Riley's voice was firm. "Do you have any idea what it was like for me to rip him away from his cousins?"

"You didn't have a choice."

"He had family willing to take him in. I'm gonna get him back to them if I can."

There was a long silence. Then Mr. Crandall said, "Son, you always had a family in us. We *wanted* to take you in. If you hadn't been so stubborn . . ."

"I had a bull's-eye on my back," Riley said. "I knew what I was doing."

At school, Giana looked at Jax as if he were dog poop she'd found on her shoe. Jax couldn't get out of sitting across from her in science class, but he stared straight ahead and pretended she wasn't there, even when Billy gave him a blow-by-blow account of her every move.

"Dude, she just gave you the most evil look. What did you *do* to her?"

"Nothing."

He hoped Giana's revulsion for him would wear off. His own aversion for Riley had subsided, but he was still mad. Now that Jax knew what his guardian could do, he realized Riley must've *ordered* the caseworker to think Jax was happy. He probably used his magic to make sure Naomi quit fighting for custody, too. It even explained why the hearing had been canceled.

An eraser bounced off Jax's head, flicked across the aisle by Giana's friend Kacey. Jax clenched his hands, willing himself not to snap. Giana didn't know why she hated him so much; she only dimly understood that Jax had compelled her to talk to him and resented him for it.

He hadn't meant to scare her, and he was sorry he had, but he didn't dare speak to her. Riley had sent him off to school with the warning, "Try not to interrogate anybody until you know what you're doing, okay?" and Jax was half afraid to open his mouth. It kind of burned him up, though, that Giana had no idea the massive coolness she was missing out on.

Busting out with talent. Jax had an extra day of the week and magic of his own. He had a connection with people out of legends, like Merlin and the Lady of the Lake. He even had a mysterious neighbor "haunting" the house next door—a girl who lived one day a week and would be back tomorrow, in fact. A girl nobody wanted to explain to him. A girl Riley had told him to stay away from.

But you didn't order *me, Riley. Your mistake.*

Mrs. Unger waved cash when Jax dropped off a few groceries for her that night. "I have your money. Plus extra."

"You don't have to pay me extra, Mrs. Unger." Jax put the last of her groceries in the refrigerator and pulled one final item from the bag. "I got this for you. Well, for your garden, actually."

"Oh!" Mrs. Unger exclaimed. "Isn't that the cutest thing ever?"

Jax hoped so. He'd finally realized who must be doing all the weeding and tending of Mrs. Unger's garden, and he figured this goofy item might appeal to someone who enjoyed that kind of thing. It was a twelve-inch-high figurine of a smiling garden gnome standing with a bunch of mushrooms, holding a sign that said, *Have a FUN-gi Day!*

To make sure the message was understood, Jax had glued a large index card to the sign that read: GREETINGS FROM YOUR NEXT-DOOR NEIGHBOR JAX.

Mrs. Unger wanted to be able to admire his gift from inside the house. "I don't get out in the yard much," she said. So under her direction, Jax put it on the stoop outside the kitchen door among her potted plants.

Now, what could be friendlier and less threatening than that?

13

EVANGELINE BIT HER LIP and scrutinized the thing on the kitchen stoop, trying to decide if it was supposed to be a kobold or a goblin. Whatever it was, it was surrounded by poisonous toadstools, and the pun on the sign was practically a crime against humor.

She assumed the note added to this strange item was meant for her. Mrs. Unger *knew* who he was. Evangeline put her hands on her hips and wondered what in the world New Boy was thinking, leaving kobolds on her stoop and pushing notes through the mail slot suggesting she "hang out" and "have a soda."

He didn't seem to realize she was a prisoner, living a life-time sentence for a crime committed by others—first by her race in general, then by her father individually.

In spite of this, Evangeline had to admit that Red had treated her decently over the last eight months—or four and a half years, depending on whether one was counting by her viewpoint or his. Sometimes, he was even friendly.

One day the winter before last, she'd awakened to the surprise of new snow. Light flakes had been falling from the sky, so it must have been snowing at the moment of change. There was never any accumulation on an eighth day—only so much snow could fall in a sliver of real time—but Evangeline loved that rare sensation of flakes landing on her face, like cold kisses.

She hadn't left the house while Red was home, shying away from the chance of meeting him, but when she'd heard his motorcycle leave, she'd dug in the closet for Mrs. Unger's galoshes and wool coat. She'd burst out the back door, and that was when she'd seen three snowmen in a row on the property line, facing the Unger house. Each one had a branch sticking straight up from its shoulder, as if waving. *Hello. Hello. Hello.*

Laughing, Evangeline had pulled all the stones and carrot nubs out of their faces. By the time Red had come back, Evangeline had returned to the house. She'd obscured her footsteps in the snow with a broom, and the snowmen were facing the other way, waving at Red's house. *Hello back. Hello back. Hello back.*

That little lark and an occasional basket of cookies was the limit of friendliness she allowed between herself and the boy next door, no matter how lonely she'd gotten in her five years of isolation. He had chosen to treat her honorably, but the history between their two families made things . . . awkward.

After closing the door on New Boy's weird kobold,

Evangeline made herself breakfast and cleaned up as she went along, making sure the only evidence of her meal was the mysterious disappearance of one egg, one slice of bread, and one tea bag. Outside and next door, a voice bellowed, "Jax?" Evangeline peered around the edge of the curtain in the kitchen window. Red stomped down his front steps and into the yard. New Boy's bicycle was gone from its usual spot, and Red turned in a circle, noting its absence. He paced up and down the length of the yard, then turned toward the Unger house and made a shrugging gesture as if to say, *I don't know where the darn boy's gone.*

He couldn't see her, but he assumed she was watching. That was a little conceited of him, but she usually *was* watching. What else did she have to do?

When Evangeline heard the motorcycle depart a little while later, she slipped a weapon into the back pocket of her jeans—just in case—and ventured into Mrs. Unger's backyard. She stretched out her arms, relishing the sunlight and admiring the pink sky. Evangeline knew the sky was *supposed* to be blue—she'd seen pictures. But she didn't know why it *should* be blue. A rosy sky seemed much more natural.

Then she got to work. She hadn't been outside in two days. Instead, she'd watched from her window while New Boy ran amok through the neighborhood, then was tutored in the basics of the eighth day by Red. Entertaining, perhaps, but those two days had equaled two weeks for the weeds in Mrs. Unger's flower beds.

92

While she was pulling up dandelions near the fence at the back of the yard, a flutter of color caught her eye. A butterfly! She couldn't remember the last time she'd seen an eighth-day creature that wasn't vermin. *Brownies*, of course, went everywhere. Her little brother, Elliot, had even kept one as a pet for a few months, until their mother had caught him with it.

Evangeline watched the butterfly fly from one azalea bush to the next, thinking about Elliot's secret pet and about Adelina, who had wanted a pony and never gotten one.

"Um, hi?"

Evangeline shot to her feet and whirled around.

It was New Boy, standing in the middle of the yard, holding his bicycle and staring at her with his mouth hanging open.

Startled that she'd allowed him to come up behind her while she was preoccupied, she bolted for the kitchen door, but he dropped his bike and raced to beat her there. "No, no, no—wait!" He flung himself in front of her and threw out both arms.

Anger flashed through her. How dare he block her path?

Evangeline pulled her weapon out of her back pocket and ran straight for him.

14

SHE CAME AT HIM so fast, Jax didn't have time to react. She tackled him with the ferocity of a small panther, and he went down. The next thing he knew, he was flat on his back, and she had her knee on his chest. She waved an object menacingly in his face.

Pepper spray.

"Don't move," she said, her voice low and hoarse.

"Not going to," he promised.

He did, however, tilt his head, looking around the pepper spray and into the bluest eyes he'd ever seen. They darted restlessly from side to side. Jax realized she didn't know what to do with him now that she'd caught him.

"Show me who you are," she said finally.

"I'm Jax," he said. "Jax Aubrey. Didn't you get my note?"

"Names change. *Show* me who you are." Her eyes flicked toward his left hand. Jax turned it over, so she could see his tattoo.

He didn't know what information she got from his family crest, but she looked even more unhappy. The pepper spray got a little closer to his face. "I'm sorry," he croaked. "I was wrong to get between you and the door. I wanted to say hello"—*and find out who you are*— "but that was a stupid way to do it. If you let me up, I'll get on my bike and leave."

She seemed to mull that over, drawing her bottom lip between her teeth. Then she stood up and backed away. Jax sat up. He expected her to flee, but instead, she watched him, holding the pepper spray in her hand.

"I'm sorry I scared you." He stood up. "I'll leave you alone from now on." That was what Riley had told him to do in the first place, but darn it, he didn't want to. She was too big a mystery, and this was too good an opportunity. "If I could just say one thing first. . . ."

She raised her eyebrows and waited.

"If you had sprayed that when you were kneeling on me, you'd have gotten some in your face, too. You have to hold it at arm's length." He paused, then went on. "Plus, you didn't twist the safety cap open." He demonstrated with his hands. "It won't go off that way, and someone could knock it away and overpower you. *I* wouldn't, but someone more dangerous would."

She twisted the lid and looked at Jax. "Like this?" She extended her arm to point the spray at him.

"Yeahhhh," he said, wondering if he was about to

get a faceful of pepper. But her lips twitched as if she were fighting a smile, and he dared ask a question. "Is it Mrs. Unger's?"

She nodded. "She put it in a drawer and forgot about it, I think." Her voice sounded rusty, like it was rarely used.

Jax picked up his bike and straddled it. "I'm sorry I bothered you. I was just trying to be friendly. Maybe that breaks some kind of rule. I didn't know."

"You don't know much, do you?" She tucked her hair behind one ear nervously, and it rippled down her shoulder like a silvery waterfall.

Jax shook his head. "Not really, no."

"Why hasn't *he* explained things to you?" She nodded toward Riley's house.

"He did tell me not to bug you. But I'm not a good listener."

She smiled, finally. "You don't have to leave," she said. "I haven't talked to anybody in a long time. I'm out of practice." She twisted the pepper spray closed and put the can into her back pocket.

Jax didn't need any more invitation than that. He got off the bike, grabbed one of the rusted folding chairs that had probably been left leaning against the house by the previous owner, and deliberately placed it over the property line, on Mrs. Unger's lawn. Then he unfolded another one opposite, on Riley's lawn, and sat down.

The girl dragged the chair a little farther away and sat

on the edge of it, poised to run. She reminded Jax of a half-tamed deer.

"How long?" he asked. "Since you've talked to someone?"

"*Long*," she said.

Jax wasn't sure what to say next, and while he fumbled for a topic, she filled in the silence. "Maybe five years, for me. Longer, in your world."

"In my world?"

She held up one finger. "I have one day for every seven in the Normal world. Figure it out."

Did she mean what he thought she did? "Are you saying you haven't talked to anyone in *thirty-five years*?"

She plucked at her shirt. "Can't you tell?"

Now that she mentioned it, she was dressed strangely. Her jeans were studded with fake diamonds and crisscrossed with zippers. Her shirt had batlike sleeves and diagonal stripes.

"These clothes belonged to Mrs. Unger's daughters," she said. "I've been wearing them since they were in style."

Jax stared at her, completely floored. This girl looked only a couple years older than he was, but she'd been living in the Unger house since *the eighties*. She met his gaze sadly as he took it in. At that moment, Jax would have happily thrown a brick through the window of any store in the mall and stolen whatever clothes she wanted just to make her smile again. "You don't have access to anything more . . . recent?"

She shrugged. "Magazines. Newspapers. Books."

"Library books," Jax gasped. "I've been getting them for *you* all along."

"Thank you," she said.

He couldn't believe it. Mrs. Unger's ghost was real and not a ghost at all. "Soda," he said, remembering. "I promised you a soda. How about I go get a couple?"

For some reason, that made her bite her lip. It looked like she was trying not to laugh. "Okay."

"Wait here. I'll be right back." Jax dashed into the house, praying they actually had soda. He threw open the refrigerator, found half a six-pack, yanked two cans out of the plastic rings, stuffed a half-empty bag of chips under his arm, and hurried outside.

He was afraid she wouldn't be there, but she was sitting on the edge of her chair and looking nervous, as if she couldn't believe she was still there either. He handed her a soda and set the bag of chips on the ground near her feet. "I'm kinda surprised we have any chips left," he said as he sat down. "Riley can eat a whole bag in one sitting."

Jax popped the top on his soda and looked up to find the girl eyeing him quizzically. "Is that *his* name?" she asked. "Riley?"

"Yeah." Didn't she know? "Riley Pendare."

"Pendare," she said, one corner of her mouth turning up. "Is that what they're calling themselves these days?"

"Who?"

"His family."

"I don't think he's got any family. Neither do I," Jax added mournfully, swigging from his soda. "What about you?"

There was a long silence, and Jax realized her expression, which had been near laughing before, had gone cold. He lowered the can, wondering what he'd said wrong.

"Are you trying to use your inquisition on me?" she asked flatly.

"No, I swear! Or at least, I don't think so," he corrected himself. He hadn't meant to use it on Giana, but he had. "I didn't learn about it until a couple days ago, and I don't really know what I'm doing yet. How did *you* know?"

She tilted her head with a puzzled expression. "Your mark told me."

"You mean the symbols have meaning?"

She put the soda on the ground and picked up the bag of chips. "That's the definition of a symbol. It has meaning."

Jax slapped his hand over his face. "I meant—most people get tattoos with pictures they like. And they don't always know what the pictures mean. Or care."

"If you did that for your mark, it wouldn't work."

He'd never really wondered what the symbols on his family crest meant. He'd just thought they were decorative. His eyes wandered to the girl's left wrist, but the skin there was pale and unmarked.

"My people don't need them," she said, answering his unspoken question. "Or honor blades, either."

That opened up a lot of other questions in his mind about *her people*, but Jax wanted to know something else first. "Will you tell me your name?"

Her eyebrows shot up again.

"You can make one up, if you want," Jax suggested. "You said names change. Just tell me what to call you, instead of *Hey you*." When she didn't answer him, he said, "Okay, never mind. I'll pick something. Like Mildred. Or Lulu."

"Evangeline," she said suddenly.

Had she made that up? He didn't think so. If she was going to invent a name, wouldn't it be something ordinary, like Jessica or Caitlyn? "Nice to meet you, Evangeline," he said. "I'm Jax."

"I know. I got your note." She smiled again. "And your kobold."

My what?

The sound of a motorcycle engine rose over their conversation.

She dropped the bag of chips and was out of the chair before Jax could say a word. By the time he'd stood up, she was gone. The kitchen door of Mrs. Unger's house slammed shut.

"Darn it, Riley." Jax flung himself back into the chair.

Seconds later, Riley coasted into the yard, brought his

motorcycle to a stop, and cut the engine. Jax drank his soda while Riley dismounted and removed his helmet. "What're you doing?" Riley asked.

"Having soda and chips."

"Who with?" Riley looked at the second chair and the second soda. Then he looked up at the Unger house. "No. Way."

Jax shrugged and reached for the abandoned bag of chips. He was having a hard time suppressing his grin. "I can introduce you, if you like," he bragged.

Riley looked back and forth between Jax and the Unger house, his mouth hanging open. Then his gaze settled on Jax. "No." He tossed his helmet at the second lawn chair. It hit the back and tipped the chair over. "She doesn't want to meet me. I'm her jailer."

While Jax choked on a mouthful of chips, Riley turned on his heel and disappeared into the house.

15

JAX FOLLOWED HIM inside, clutching his soda in one hand and the bag of chips in the other. "What do you mean, *jailer*?"

Riley slammed the kitchen cabinet doors open and closed. "Why don't we ever have any food in this house?" he growled.

"Who is she?" Jax asked.

"I told you not to bother her." Riley's eyes dropped to the chips. "Gimme that." He grabbed the bag and dug for a handful.

"I wasn't bothering her. I got home from my bike ride and ran into her outside." Actually, she'd run into him, but Jax would've eaten dirt before admitting she'd knocked him down. "You need to tell me. Even *she* said she didn't know why you left me so clueless."

"She said that?"

"More or less. Who is she? Why is she there?"

"What else did she say?" Riley looked hurt.

"Not a lot. You came back and interrupted us."

Riley answered Jax's second question first. "She's hiding there."

"But you said *jailer*. You're keeping her in Grunsday or keeping her in that house?"

"She can't get out of Grunsday," Riley said, his voice weary. "As for the house, I'm supposed to keep her there, but I doubt she wants to leave anyway."

"How do you know?"

"My father talked to the Kin who put her there. A long time ago. You've figured that out, haven't you? That she's older than she looks? I mean—" Riley corrected himself. "She's barely old enough to drive, but she was born over a century ago."

"Okay." Jax tried to piece everything together. "All of Grunsday is a prison, but Evangeline is a prisoner in her own home, too?"

"Is that her name?" Riley asked in a quiet voice. "Evangeline?"

"How can you guys live next door to one another and not know each other's names?"

"We knew each other's family names," Riley said gruffly. "That was enough."

"Then what's hers?"

Riley paused, and at first Jax thought he wasn't going to answer. But then he said, "Emrys is her family name."

Merlin Emrys. "Holy crap! You mean she's—"

"A direct descendant of Merlin, yes. She's *important*, and a lot of people—Transitioners and Kin—would love to get their hands on her. And not for good reasons, either."

"But I thought we—Transitioners—were the good guys. You know, we made the Eighth-Day Spell to capture the bad guys. . . ." Wasn't that what Mr. Crandall had said?

"No," Riley said forcefully. "I *told* you. These days, most Transitioners use the extra day for their own selfish purposes. It *used to be* that honor and chivalry mattered. But the world changed, Jax. Now it's all about power and greed." Riley crossed his arms over his chest. "Not to me, though. I've got a job to do, and I plan on doing it the way my father would have. It's my business to make sure the Emrys girl stays hidden and safe—the business you were supposed to stay out of. Now, get your honor blade. I'm taking you to Melinda's."

Jax didn't budge. "How long have you lived in this house?"

Riley frowned. "Since I was your age, maybe a little older. Why?"

"Who did you live with?"

"No one."

"A thirteen-year-old can't live in a house with no adults."

"Come on, inquisitor. Figure it out. What d'you think happened to any teacher or neighbor who wanted to know where my parents were?"

Jax clenched his jaw, remembering how Riley had compelled him to get a tattoo, to sleep, to sit down and shut up. "The same thing that happened to anyone who questioned your right to be my guardian?"

"You got it."

"Did you cause Naomi's husband to lose his job?"

Riley flinched. "No! What kind of person do you think I am?"

"But you ordered her not to care what happened to me."

"I did not." Riley dropped his eyes. "But I commanded her to let you come with me. I made her misremember how old I was and made the caseworker believe you were happy and adjusting. I ordered a court clerk to delete that hearing from their schedule." He glanced up at Jax again. "If it's any consolation, Naomi was really stubborn about it. I had to keep calling her to renew my commands." When Jax stared at him, aghast, Riley actually looked ashamed. "I'll fix it. When it's time for you to go back, I promise I'll fix it."

Yeah, by making people do things they don't want to do and think things they don't want to think. "What happened to your family?" Jax tried to conjure the inquisition talent he was supposed to have.

"Your newbie magic won't work on me, squirt."

"Why not? It worked on A.J."

"Because I'm ready for you." Riley took a huge breath. "But I'll answer if you think you can stand to hear it. They were killed. My parents, my sister, my aunts and uncles and cousins. All of 'em."

Jax's stomach turned over. "Like my dad?"

"Yes, they were murdered, just like your dad."

There was a long silence in the kitchen. Riley stood there, pale, but as emotionless as a block of wood. Jax didn't want to show his own weakness, but he had to grab the kitchen counter just to keep himself standing. "By the same people?" he asked finally. "Who? Why?"

"Not the same people. And in either case, the less you know, the safer you are. You want to know who the good guys are? *I am.* Just assume all Transitioners and Kin are dangerous, unless I clear 'em for you." Riley cleared his throat. "Now, go get your blade for the lesson." Then he did something he'd never done before. He took Jax by the shoulder and gave him a solid, brotherly squeeze.

Jax pulled away and ran upstairs, where he barfed up chips and soda in the toilet.

It took ten minutes before he could stand up. He didn't want to meet Melinda. He wanted to hide in his room from Grunsday and the bloodthirsty people who inhabited it. But he had a feeling that skipping this lesson would not be allowed, and the sooner he learned what they wanted him to learn, the sooner he could leave.

When he went downstairs with his father's dagger,

Riley handed him a spare helmet without comment about the long delay.

It was a short ride to the center of town. Riley parked in front of a duplex house and led Jax up the steps to the left-hand door. The porch was littered with toys—tricycles and dump trucks and a pretend stove with plastic food. A woman opened the screen door at their approach.

"Hey, Melinda," Riley said, motioning Jax ahead of him. "This is Jax."

"Nice to meet you." She was tall, perhaps in her early thirties, with dark caramel skin and smiling light-brown eyes. She lifted her left hand in what looked like a wave, but Jax knew she was showing him her mark. "My name's Melinda Farrow, but that's my married name. I'm a Llewelyn by birth and talent. Come in."

She led them through a living room, also cluttered with toys, and into her kitchen. The curtains were pulled back to let in the pink sunlight, and there was a strange cast to the hanging light above her kitchen table. Jax realized there was no electricity in the house, and the bulb was only giving off the afterimage of light.

"I have lunch ready." Melinda waved her hand at a platter of deli meat and cheese. "I figured you'd be hungry. Dig in. I'm not opening the refrigerator to put this back."

Riley didn't hesitate. He took a paper plate and started making himself a sandwich. "Not that I'm complaining, but you know I could get you a generator."

Melinda shook her head. "You'd have to change the outside wiring, and I could never explain it to Scott. I have a hard enough time hiding the radio." She turned to Jax. "My husband doesn't know. Any of it."

"Your kids are getting older," murmured Riley. "You're going to have to tell him sometime."

"We've discussed this before, and it's not your business," Melinda replied in a matching murmur, then turned to Jax. "Speaking of the radio, you gave me a scare last week."

"Melinda is a sensitive," Riley said. "My first line of defense. If anyone with talent comes within a five-mile radius of us, Melinda knows it. Last week, you took your bike out of town on Grunsday morning, didn't you?"

"Yeah. I rode up to the highway and back."

"When you came back into town, Melinda sensed it. She didn't know who you were, and she raised an alarm. I was just heading out to look for intruders when I bumped into you coming in."

"I picture it as a net over the town," Melinda explained. "If talent comes in, I sense it." She looked at Riley. "But I didn't detect him going out. I'm sorry. That's a flaw I've never managed to fix. I wish I were stronger for you. . . ."

Riley shook his head. "Melinda, stop that. You do good work."

Meanwhile, Jax frowned, remembering how he'd crashed into Riley in the doorway last week. "You were in the house the whole time?"

"Sound asleep in bed. Didn't you check?"

No, he hadn't checked. Riley hadn't been in the house the week before. At that point, Jax still thought he was entirely alone on the day between Wednesday and Thursday.

By this time, Riley had made three sandwiches and piled them on top of one another. Now he placed a second paper plate on top and picked up the whole bundle. "I'm gonna take these and go."

Melinda sighed. "On your motorcycle? Let me get you a bag."

Riley turned to Jax. "Melinda'll take good care of you. She finished my training."

Because he lost his parents when he was no older than me.

It suddenly dawned on Jax that he had more in common with Riley than he'd realized. And if Riley had been living on his own since he was orphaned, it explained why he hadn't bothered to cook for Jax or do his laundry or take care of him at all, really. No one had taken care of Riley in a long time. Jax looked at his guardian with new eyes.

"You okay?" Riley asked, scrutinizing him right back.

Jax glanced around the cozy kitchen, at the lunch platter—not quite decimated by Riley's assault—and Melinda. She was the least scary person Jax had met since this all started, up to and including Evangeline and her pepper spray. "Yeah, I'm okay."

16

AFTER JAX HAD EATEN his fill, Melinda cleared the food from the table. "May I see your mark?" she asked, as if it were an honor, and he held out his hand.

She took it in both of hers. "Your mark is placed on your left wrist over the pulse point leading to your heart." Her index finger traced lightly up the inside of his arm. "It names what you are and enhances your potential for magic. This is a tradition so old, we've forgotten its origins."

"Older than Grunsday?" Jax asked.

"Much older. And Grunsday is a silly name Arnie Crandall made up for something we should respect. Making fun of the eighth day is dangerous; it encourages a sloppy disregard for powerful magic."

Jax raised his eyebrows in surprise.

"You're an inquisitor. Riley tells me you've already discovered this. Do you understand what you did?"

He cringed. The term *inquisitor* summoned images of people being stretched to death on the rack. "I asked questions, and people answered. But I don't know why, or how I did it."

Melinda released his arm. "Once you started transitioning to the eighth day, you picked up your potential for magic."

"Riley said I got it from my dad."

"You inherited the ability to cross into the other timeline and the nature of your talent from your dad. But if you had never transitioned, you would never have picked up the magical potential to implement it. You would've been a Normal, like your mother. Even the children of two Transitioners occasionally fail to transition and develop any talent."

Jax nodded cautiously. "So, no eighth day, no talent."

"It's a side effect of our ancestors' casting the Eighth-Day Spell and giving themselves the ability to transition in and out of it. Our magic is bound to the day, so to speak."

"Why did we need to go in and out of it?"

"To monitor the Kin imprisoned there. Can I see your honor blade?"

Jax frowned, unhappy to hear Evangeline called a *prisoner* again, but he opened the ornamental wooden box without comment.

"May I?" He handed her the knife, and she ran her fingers down the length of the blade and over the engraved hilt. "This is not a very old blade," she said. "And it hasn't seen a lot of use."

"Does that make it no good?"

"It's easier than starting with a new one, because your father used it before you." She reached for Jax's arm again, turning his hand over to look at his wrist. "Your mark has a bald eagle, but your father's blade has a falcon."

Jax leaned in to take a closer look at the bird on the hilt of the dagger. "I guess A.J. likes bald eagles better. Does it matter?"

Melinda shook her head and clucked her tongue. "He's been told before not to get creative with something as important as this. But they're both birds of prey, and your talent doesn't seem affected. Do you have a sheath for the dagger?" When Jax shook his head, Melinda returned it and said, "Get one. You can't keep it in a box on a shelf and expect it to work for you. It has to be worn."

That was exactly where his father had kept it—in a box on a shelf. But Jax didn't tell her that for fear she'd think his dad didn't know what he was doing. "I can't wear it to school," he pointed out instead. "They'd expel me!"

"Not to school. But everywhere else—and always on the eighth day. A long time ago, honor blades were used to draw blood to strengthen one's magic, but there's a dark element to that, and honorable people don't do it anymore. The blade is mostly symbolic now."

"Well, that's a relief!" Jax exclaimed.

"Holding the blade while using your magic intensifies the effect because it bears the symbols of your bloodline. It's not absolutely necessary to have your blade in your hand to perform magic, but if you want to be sure your talent is used precisely and effectively, the honor blade will help. Something else that enhances magic is strong emotion. You've heard stories of frightened mothers lifting a car off a child?"

"Adrenaline," said Jax.

"Magic," corrected Melinda. "Adrenaline makes your heart race. Magic lifts the car. Rage is also powerful. Ancient warriors consumed a drug that brought on uncontrollable rage, and in the berserker state their magic protected them. Even loyalty toward one's liege can be powerful."

"Who gets to be a liege lord?"

"Technically, you can swear your allegiance to anyone you're willing to follow, but in practice it tends to be people with powerful talents." Melinda smiled ruefully. "No one's going to follow a sensitive. But as an inquisitor, you might build your own clan someday."

That didn't sound appealing at all—being in charge of a bunch of people. "Why are you sworn to Riley?" Jax blurted out. "Is it rude to ask that?"

"Not at all. My mother was sworn to Riley's father, and *I* was sworn to him, too. When he died, I didn't hesitate to swear to his son. Did it right at Riley's hospital bed, in fact."

"What do you mean? Why was Riley in the hospital?"

Melinda hesitated. "He was hurt pretty badly in the explosion," she said finally. "The one that killed his family. Didn't he tell you?"

Jax shook his head, feeling his mouth go dry. Riley hadn't mentioned he'd been present when his family was murdered—or that he'd almost been killed too.

"It happened at an engagement party for his sister." Melinda's face was grim. "He lost his entire family and most of his family's vassals."

An engagement party. That was . . . beyond sick.

Seeing the expression on his face, Melinda rose from her chair and changed the subject. "Come into the living room and we'll try out your talent."

Jax followed her and sat on the sofa while Melinda lit candles to brighten the room. Jax squirmed. Candles made the whole thing seem more witchy. "Calling on your talent is a matter of intention," Melinda said. "You have to learn how to turn it on and off—otherwise people will spout answers every time you ask a question."

"Like I don't have to obey Riley every time he tells me to do something," Jax said. "Only sometimes."

"Riley's talent is called the voice of command. With practice, you'll be able to tell when he's using it—even if it's directed at someone else. For someone newly transitioned like you, it's more common for your talent to *fail* than to use it accidentally. But Riley says you're an exception, which suggests you're pretty strong." Melinda sat beside him on the couch. "We've got no one else to try this on, so you're going to ask *me* a question, and I'll see what it takes to fight you off." She gave him a lopsided smile. "Feel free to make it a personal question."

Like what? Jax's cheeks burned with embarrassment. To avoid her eyes, he looked at his dagger and ran a thumb over the symbols on the crest: the falcon and the flames, the eye in the center of a scroll. He could ask her why she didn't tell her husband about her magic and the eighth day. But he didn't really want to know that. Instead his mind was connecting dots and groping for what was missing to complete the picture.

The Pendare family had been killed off in a massacre, leaving Riley the sole survivor. His father's remaining vassals had sworn their loyalty to Riley even though he was just a kid, and Jax's father had turned to him for help. Riley deliberately camouflaged his family crest with other tattoos. It didn't seem like he was smart enough to remember the date the gas bill was due, but he quoted stuff from Einstein's theory of relativity and used words like *chivalry*. And when Jax told Evangeline Riley's name, she'd smiled as if he'd said something amusing.

Is that what they're calling themselves these days?

"What's the real name of Riley's family?" Jax asked.

Melinda lurched on the sofa. She clapped one hand over her mouth as if to prevent the answer from popping out, and her eyes widened.

But Jax barely noticed. He stood up without meaning to, almost like he'd been pulled to his feet, and crossed the room to a built-in bookcase beside the fireplace. His hands plucked an old Encyclopedia Britannica off the shelves, selecting one specific volume without any conscious decision on his part. His head buzzed, and his fingers guided him to the page he wanted as if he'd known all along which one it was.

He wasn't as surprised as he thought he should be. He guessed that, in some part of his brain, he'd noticed all along. All this talk about the Lady of the Lake and Merlin—and there was one person nobody had mentioned. It was a glaring omission, now that he thought about it—as if everyone had deliberately avoided saying the name.

Jax looked down at the encyclopedia entry for King Arthur Pendragon.

"Holy crap."

17

MELINDA CONFIRMED IT. *Riley*—the same Riley who left toothpaste all over the bathroom sink—was descended from King Arthur.

"It's been more than a hundred generations." Melinda took the encyclopedia from Jax and looked at the illustration of Arthur accepting a sword from a beautiful woman. "But the Pendragon bloodline is well documented. As is that of the Dulacs. That would be *du lac*, Jax. French for 'of the lake.'"

"You mean Niviane?"

"The Dulac family is very powerful, and very dangerous. We're convinced they're responsible for killing the Pendragons." Melinda closed the encyclopedia and slipped it back on the shelf. "I've never seen an inquisitor get his answer from a book before."

"Why would Dulacs kill Pendragons? Weren't they allies? King Arthur and the Lady of the Lake?"

"Fifteen hundred years ago, yes. But today's Dulacs are little better than crime lords. Their clan leader has her fingers in everything from real estate fraud to government contract fixing, and I don't know how many politicians she's manipulated with her magic. Riley's father thwarted her whenever he could. He always objected when Transitioners used their talents to manipulate Normals for monetary gain, and the Pendragon name held a lot of weight with the Table."

"The Table?" Jax repeated. "You don't mean—"

Melinda's lips twitched with the hint of a smile. "Yes, there still is a sort of Round Table—a council of the highest Transitioner lords. I don't know if it's actually round, and it's probably located in an executive boardroom somewhere."

"These Transitioner lords . . ." Jax still felt the buzz of magic in his head as he pieced it together. "They're the same Welsh lords Mr. Crandall said cast the Eighth-Day Spell? Well, not the *same ones*, obviously, but descendents of those guys?"

"Yes, Jax. And you probably know those 'Welsh lords' better as the Knights of the Round Table."

Jax slapped a hand to his head. How could he *not* have seen that coming?

"Riley could claim a seat at the Table if it were safe for him to come out of hiding. But the Crandalls and I don't think it is. Without Riley's father appealing to their honor these past several years, too many Transitioner clans have ended up in the pockets of Ursula Dulac." Melinda gripped Jax's arm. "Nobody can know one of the Pendragons survived. Ursula would have him killed."

"I won't tell," Jax assured her. *Who would even believe me?* "Maybe he should've changed his name more."

"We told him that, but he was thirteen and stubborn . . . and grieving."

Jax groaned. "I couldn't even learn Washington's generals for history class. Now I've got to keep these clans straight?"

"You want a cheat sheet?" Melinda picked a child's crayon drawing off the floor and turned it over to the blank side. With a colored pencil, she drew a line down the center of the paper and labeled the two columns *Transitioners* and *Kin*. "A lot of people participated in the casting of the Eighth-Day Spell, but there were three who took on the main roles in the ceremony: Niviane of the Lake, who conceived of the spell and brought everyone together; Arthur Pendragon, with his voice of command; and Merlin Emrys, the spell caster." She put the first two names under *Transitioners* and Merlin Emrys under *Kin*, then added stars beside their names. "Riley is descended from Arthur, of course, and the Dulac family from Niviane." She drew arrows connecting the ancient names to their modern counterparts.

"Okay," Jax said, following her so far.

"Arthur's knights were present, as well as a few other prominent leaders of the time. Their participation lent strength to the spell and bound all their descendants as Transitioners, with the ability to move between the timelines. You've met Deidre, right? She's descended from Morgan LeFay. Miller is descended from Sir Owain." Melinda added those names to the chart.

"I haven't met Miller."

"I know," Melinda replied without offering any additional information.

Jax was tempted to try his talent again, but there were other things he wanted to know about more than the mysterious Miller. "What about you—and me? Who am

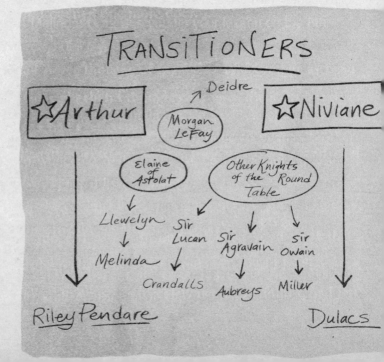

I descended from?" He hoped it was one of the knights.

"That's trickier," Melinda said. "After all this time, family lines get blurred. There are intermarriages, and talents evolve and change under the right circumstances. But there was a noblewoman named Elaine of Astolat present, and she was a sensitive, so it's very likely my family branched off from her line." Melinda drew a line from Elaine, like the branch of a tree, and wrote her family name, Llewelyn. "The Crandalls may have branched off from Sir Lucan, who was an artisan. And you, Jax, probably branched off from Sir Agravain, an inquisitor."

Agravain. He sounded cool. "What about the Kin? Is there only Merlin?"

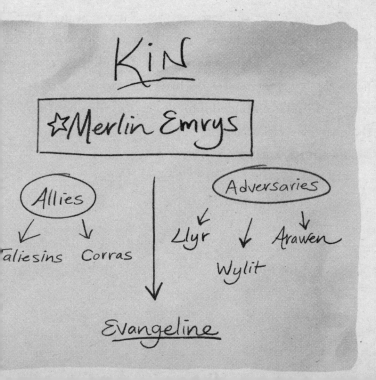

"No. The Kin are a race of people—very fair in complexion and hair, with eyes bluer than any you've ever seen. Merlin was the only Kin present at the spell casting, but there were other Kin families we counted on as allies. Notably the Taliesins and the Corras. I don't know if the Corra family still exists, but the Taliesins do and occasionally still help us." Melinda added those names. "But our main adversaries were these powerful Kin clans, along with all their vassals and branch-off families." Under *Adversaries* she listed: *Llyr, Wylit, Arawen.*

"Do they still exist?" asked Jax.

"Their descendants do, but the very worst of them are detained in a prison, even inside the eighth day."

"The *descendants* of these bad guys," Jax repeated, to make sure he understood. These Kin were imprisoned in the eighth day and then imprisoned *inside* the eighth day—for things their ancestors had done. It didn't sit right with him, and it reminded him of who was missing from the chart. He picked up the pencil, drew an arrow from Merlin Emrys, and added *Evangeline.*

"Is that her first name?" Melinda sighed. "I really didn't need to know that."

"Why not?"

"It makes it personal. I can't afford to feel sorry for her. She's dangerous."

"How can she be?"

"As a member of the Emrys family, she could alter

the Eighth-Day Spell, and if she fell into the hands of the wrong Kin, they'd make her do it. Transitioners have no desire to see the eighth day broken and the Kin released, but there are some, including the Dulacs, who would love to have an Emrys heir under their control. Her timeline runs differently than ours does, so she's probably only ten generations removed from Merlin himself. Her blood could be used for powerful magic."

Jax swallowed uneasily. "You said people didn't use blood in spells anymore."

"I said *honorable* people didn't. Do you understand?"

Jax nodded dumbly. He understood he wanted to complete this training and take off for Naomi's house as soon as school ended. The eighth day was filled with horrible people who blew up entire families during engagement parties, used blood for magic, and imprisoned a teenage girl just because her ten-times-great-grandfather had been a legendary wizard.

18

ON FRIDAY MORNING, Jax found an interesting email in his in-box.

> Hi Jaxattax! My name's Lexi. Terrance said your new & looking to meet others. I know other kids like us & we have a group that meets sometimes & if you dont live too far away maybe you could come. Where do you live? Write me back! Lexi

Lexi's profile picture cleverly revealed parts of a cute girl: one brown eye, one perfect nose, and a hint of a smile. The rest of her face had been cropped out to leave the viewer wanting more. Wouldn't Jax like to meet a cute girl who knew about Grunsday and maybe lived nearby?

Heck, no.

"Crap!" Jax deleted the email with a jerk of the mouse and a stab of his finger.

"Problem?" Riley appeared in the kitchen doorway, drinking the last of the milk out of the carton.

"Nope," Jax said, closing the email window. "Just forgot to save something." Riley returned to the kitchen while Jax quietly panicked.

Lexi wanted to know where he lived. Terrance had asked the same thing. Jax deleted the Between Wednesday and Thursday forum from his browsing history, his heart thumping double time. He'd told them what state he lived in, but otherwise, no harm done. Right? Pennsylvania was a big place.

Just assume all Transitioners and Kin are dangerous, unless I clear 'em for you. But Riley hadn't told him that until after Jax had already made contact with this site. He hadn't known. It wasn't his fault. And besides, they didn't know where he was.

Because they were still asking.

Riley took Jax to a sporting goods store on Saturday to buy a sheath for his dagger as Melinda had suggested. Jax looked at himself in the mirror afterward, a knife at his side and his family crest emblazoned on his wrist. *Naomi will freak when she sees me.*

Feeling tough and adventurous, he Googled his famous ancestor, only to find out Sir Agravain was kind of a jerk—a selfish knight who served his own interests and betrayed his allies. Apparently, even in the time of King Arthur, people on the same side had trouble getting along.

That deflated Jax's enthusiasm and reminded him of what the Dulacs had done to Riley's family. And for what? So they could bribe more politicians without the interference of honorable men? The more he learned about these people, the less he liked them.

His outlook did not improve when Melinda emailed him homework. She wanted him to memorize a few meditative verses before their next lesson on Grunsday, to improve his concentration. *Meditation? Really?* She suggested he practice his talent for information on his textbooks—to pin down exactly what to study for finals.

But if his newfound talent gave him an advantage in school, Jax couldn't see any evidence of it. His grades were as bad as ever. He paid just enough attention to his surroundings to get by—for instance, leaping over Giana's outstretched foot when she tried to trip him in science on Monday. She hadn't gotten over her hostility, and, if anything, she seemed to take pleasure in tormenting him.

To be honest, he spent most of his mental energy planning for next Grunsday. He wanted to talk to Evangeline again—partly because it annoyed the heck out of Riley and partly because her imprisonment was so unfair—but he couldn't figure out how to do it without interference from His Highness, the Freaking Heir to King Arthur. Salvation came on Tuesday night when Riley entered the house, his phone in hand. "Hey, I gotta meet Deidre on Grunsday to see something she's put together. Can I count on you to be here—looking out for things?"

Jax sat up alertly. "Yeah. No problem."

Riley opened his mouth to say something else, and Jax waited for a "Leave the girl alone" command. But Riley didn't say it. Instead, he shoved his phone into his pocket and walked out.

"Can I fight off Riley's commands?" Jax asked Melinda at the start of their next lesson on Grunsday afternoon.

She arched an eyebrow. "If you know a person's talent, you can prepare your mind to reject their magic."

"But A.J. couldn't stop answering my questions even after he realized what I was doing."

"It's easier to block magic than to fight it once it's gotten hold of you. Riley's voice of command is a rare talent and a strong one, but not unstoppable. We'll work on defense once I know you can use your own magic more precisely." Melinda narrowed her eyes. "Although I didn't think you'd need to defend yourself against Riley."

"It was just a question." Jax gave her his most innocent expression. Melinda responded with the piercing gaze of motherly suspicion before returning to the task at hand— teaching Jax to call on his talent when he wanted it and not every time he greeted someone with "What's up?"

Jax pondered what Melinda had said while he biked home, wondering if he could reject Riley's magic. Jax didn't want any commands stopping him from luring Evangeline out of her house this evening. *Nobody* should be as alone as she was.

"That you, Jax?" Riley called from the second floor when Jax got home.

"Yeah," Jax replied warily, taking out his honor blade and holding it in his hand. *I know his talent, and I reject it. He can't make me do anything I don't want to.*

"I need you to disengage the generators at midnight tonight," Riley said as he came downstairs. "Can you do that?"

"Whoa." Jax's jaw dropped.

"What?" Riley snapped, fussing with the collar of his shirt as if uncertain how many buttons he was supposed to fasten and how many it was okay to leave undone.

Jax had to admit Riley Pendare cleaned up good. He was wearing Dockers—pressed and pleated. A button-down shirt. Boots with a shine. His hair was combed back and gelled into place.

"So this is a date," Jax concluded.

"No."

Jax snorted.

"I'm meeting Deidre at her college," Riley said. "She's been putting together old and new technology, trying to make me a motion detector that'll work on Grunsday. She wants to show me her progress, and we'll probably spend all evening in a lab." He looked down at himself. "But she told me to dress nice or don't bother coming."

"Uh-huh," said Jax. "So—you have the voice of command, but the girl with the pistol in her boot is in charge."

"Shut up." Riley stopped fussing with his collar, his eyes wandering to the window facing Mrs. Unger's house. "If you—" He scowled and hesitated, and Jax braced himself.

"If you talk to her again," Riley continued, "tell her you're not part of my clan."

That wasn't what Jax had expected. "Why would she care?"

"Just tell her."

Jax nodded, and Riley threw open the front door without saying anything else. Jax waited inside the house, listening for the sound of the motorcycle. Then he jumped up and scuttled outside to fetch the cooler of food he'd hidden in the cellar.

19

EVANGELINE AWOKE TO A FLUTTER in her stomach. It took her a moment to pin down the reason for it, and when she did, she sat straight up in bed.

Yesterday she'd had her first conversation with another person in years. She'd "hung out" with New Boy and "had a soda."

What had she done? *I cracked the dam, that's what.*

Evangeline's life was not a happy one, but it was tolerable as long as her loneliness remained walled up behind a concrete dam.

Why hadn't she run away when she'd had the chance? She knew Jax had been trying to win her trust when he told her about the lock on the pepper spray, but it had worked anyway. His honesty was so plain on his face.

Talking to Jax had cracked her dam, and she could almost feel water trickling through the leak, making it bigger and more dangerous.

She felt restless.

In the early afternoon, Jax rode off on his bicycle some-where, and Red worked on his motorcycle in the yard. Evangeline crept to the kitchen door and put her hand on the knob. Running away from him yesterday had probably been an overreaction. After all, he'd invited her to speak with him the first day he arrived here. It had been her choice to refuse him and keep her distance thereafter. She was the one who had chosen silence, not him.

What if she walked outside now and introduced herself?

But he already knew who she was: the daughter of a trai-tor who'd sought to break the Eighth-Day Spell. Evangeline's father had consorted and plotted with terrible Kin clans. Worse, he'd worked on a plan to retrieve the most evil Kin of all from the fortress in Wales where they were confined. He'd violated everything their famous ancestor Merlin had believed in and sacrificed for.

Evangeline had been hidden in this house so her father's accomplices couldn't find her and take up his cause. Nobody cared what her own opinion on the matter was.

Outside, she heard the clatter of something metal being thrown into a toolbox. Her hand tightened on the doorknob. There was no need for introductions, but she could ask him what she most wanted to know. *How much longer must I stay here?*

But she already knew the answer to that, too. She would be required to stay here until *his* side needed her for something. Or until the Taliesins thought she was old enough to be married to someone *they* picked for her, like she was the daughter of a nobleman in medieval times. A lot of the Kin behaved like they were still in the Dark Ages instead of the twenty-first century. It didn't make Evangeline eager to rejoin them.

She let go of the door. There was no point talking to the Pendragon boy. He was her prison guard. There was nothing good he could tell her and no common ground they shared.

She stayed away from the windows and kept herself busy in the house, dusting and then alphabetizing the jars in the spice cabinet—because there was no fun in being a ghost if she didn't do inexplicable things. She tried to read the most recent batch of library books, but living through the lives of Normal girls in books didn't satisfy her. *Another crack in the dam,* she thought. Instead she pored over newspapers and magazines and fantasized, not for the first time, about slipping out of this house and losing herself in the world.

In the early evening, she heard the motorcycle leave, and it wasn't long afterward that she smelled smoke.

She jumped up and ran for the kitchen. Fire was one of her greatest fears—as it was for all her people. The Kin were too easily eliminated by fires set on days they weren't present. Nothing was wrong in her kitchen, but Evangeline's eyes were immediately drawn to the window.

Smoke poured out of the house next door.

She barely had time to gasp before she saw Jax pitch

some flaming object out his kitchen window with tongs. He didn't look scared, just annoyed, and he waved the smoke out the open window with a towel. The house wasn't on fire; Jax had just burned his dinner.

That was when Evangeline spotted everything set up on the lawn between their houses. A folding table. Two lawn chairs. Two place settings with plates, napkins, forks, and knives. Candles. Jax was planning a lawn party, and Evangeline felt pretty sure she knew who his guest was supposed to be.

She threw both hands over her face. That silly boy. She wouldn't. She couldn't.

But Jax doesn't despise me. Maybe he doesn't know what my father did.

When she peeked through her fingers, she spotted the other object on the lawn, and something overcame her. Curiosity. Or maybe the leaking of water through the crack of a dam. She was out the kitchen door and walking across the property before she could help herself.

Jax came out the front door carrying a plate with another plate covering it like a lid. He grinned when he saw her. "There you are. I was just going to ring your doorbell."

Of course he was. As if she were a Normal neighbor.

"I hope you like hamburgers." Jax put the covered plate on the table, muttering under his breath, "I hope you *really* like hamburgers, considering how they turned out."

"I can't stay," she said apologetically. She really shouldn't. "I just wanted to see your telescope."

"Do you like it?" Jax glanced toward the telescope, set up on a tripod and aimed at the purpling sky. "Got it for my birthday last year. But you *have* to stay for dinner. I bought all this stuff." He opened up a plastic cooler and lifted items out. "I got buns. Ketchup and mustard. A ready-made salad. And look, there's cheesecake for dessert." He showed her a cream-colored confection in a transparent plastic container. "Girls like cheesecake, right?"

Did they? Evangeline had no idea what other girls liked, but she had never tasted cheesecake. It looked very tempting.

Jax must have seen her resolve wavering, because he grinned with more confidence. "And I made hamburgers from scratch. I know you'd never guess, but it was my first time." He whisked the cover off the plate with a flourish, revealing shriveled meat slabs. They resembled the round plastic disks Mrs. Unger put under the feet of her furniture. One of them was still smoking. Evangeline burst out with a laugh and then looked at Jax guiltily.

But he was laughing too. "I didn't think they'd catch fire so easily. I almost burned the kitchen down."

"I saw," she said.

Jax stabbed a fork into one of the burgers and held it up for her to see. "C'mon, Evangeline. You know you want one."

Suddenly she dissolved into giggles. She hadn't realized how much she missed hearing her name said aloud by someone else. Encouraged by her reaction, Jax hammed it up, poking the burgers and assuring her that even if they were charred, the salad was unharmed. "Unless you *want* the salad burned," he offered. "I can run it back inside and stir-fry it for you."

It wasn't that funny, but she had a sudden memory of her brother, Elliot, clowning around to make her laugh, and when Jax pulled a chair out from the table, she sat down without further objection. He asked what she wanted on her burger, and she had to admit she'd never eaten one.

Jax looked startled but covered it by acting as if this were a good thing. "If I'd known that, I would've pretended they were supposed to turn out like this." He put a blackened disk on a bread roll and squirted ketchup and mustard all over it. "Before we eat," he said, taking a more serious tone, "I have something to tell you. I'm not part of Riley's clan. I don't know why that matters, but I don't want you to think I'm tricking you."

"It's okay. I trust you." Even if Jax didn't owe any loyalty to the Pendragons, Evangeline knew he didn't mean her any harm. And speaking of *Riley*, she might as well ask. "Will he be back soon?" It made her anxious, just thinking he might show up. She didn't know whether he would order her to get away from Jax and go back inside the house—or pull up a chair and join them.

Or which would be worse.

"Not before midnight," Jax said, scraping salad onto her plate. "He's on a date with Deidre. She's—"

"The black-haired girl with all the guns and the flashy car," Evangeline guessed.

"Oh, you've seen her. She—"

"What are you going to look at with your telescope?" Evangeline interrupted. She didn't want to hear any more about where Pendragon was or who he was with. She got up and walked over to peer into the lens. "I don't see anything."

"It's not focused yet. I'm waiting for it to get darker. The sky is a weird color on Grunsday, and last week I thought the moon and stars looked strange."

"What's Grunsday?"

"A stupid name for today." Jax waved at Evangeline's plate. "Ta-da!"

Evangeline returned to the table and sat down for her first meal with another human being in five years. The burger turned out to be crusty on the outside and red and juicy on the inside. She devoured the entire thing and asked for another. Jax gaped at her. "You're kidding."

"It's delicious," Evangeline said with feeling. It was nothing like the leftovers in the back of the refrigerator and the canned goods she scavenged from Mrs. Unger's cabinets. She never dared take much, and none of it was ever satisfying.

The sky darkened while they ate and talked about neutral things. She asked Jax about school, and he told her all about his classes and his dismal grades. She understood some of what he said, but she and her siblings had never been to a school, and as Jax talked, her attention wandered.

Adelina would be about Jax's age now. Evangeline had no idea where the Taliesins had hidden her spitfire little sister, but she knew wherever Addie was, she was probably driving her guardians up the wall. Elliot would be twelve, and Evangeline hoped he was still as sweet and funny as he was when he was seven.

When Jax finished telling her about school, she dared to ask him a favor. "The next time you go to the library for Mrs. Unger . . ."

Jax grinned. "You mean for you."

"Okay, for me. Can you get—" She paused, not wanting to give her thoughts away. "Can you get me books on local history and geography?" Photographs, names of places, a general feel for available means of transportation—that's what she wanted.

She held her breath, thinking her request practically screamed *escape plan*, but Jax didn't seem suspicious. He said, "Whatever you want," and turned in his seat to look at the moon rising over the housetops. "It looks blurry. I know Grunsday is separated from the rest of time, but there *are* physical rules here, right?"

Evangeline shrugged. She knew from the books she read that Normals relied on science to tell them how the universe behaved. She just didn't understand why they failed to notice science didn't make any sense.

"Why are there no animals on Grunsday?" Jax asked.

"There are animals, just not a lot where we live. Insects and vermin, mostly."

"You mean like rats?"

"Some rats—and other pests that go where you don't

137

want them to." It wasn't her place to teach him this, but if no one else had, she couldn't see the harm in it. "The original Eighth-Day Spell included some portion of the animals on the British Isles. They didn't want the Kin to starve, you see. I suppose descendants of those animals still live there, on the eighth day, but very few of them would've come to America by boat, as the Kin did. I wish—"

His eyes searched her face when she stopped talking. "What?"

She didn't know why she wanted to confess something so personal. Maybe because it gave her a thrill to hand over a tiny piece of herself to someone else. "One of the things I've always wanted," she said, "is to pet a cat. Or a dog. I don't care which, although I've heard that cats purr." She watched his mouth turn down and his forehead crumple, and she felt very foolish. "I didn't say that so you'd feel sorry for me."

"I'm not," he answered. "I'm trying to think of a way to get you a cat."

"You can't."

"We'll see." He stood. "Let's set up the telescope."

The telescope required a lot of dial turning and knob twiddling. Evangeline stayed out of his way. She sliced the cheesecake, which was as creamy and sweet as it looked. They ate off paper plates while taking turns viewing the moon through the lens.

"See! I told you," Jax said excitedly. "Everything's blurred. It looks like a picture taken from a moving car."

Evangeline wouldn't know anything about that, but she nodded as if she understood.

The stars didn't satisfy Jax either. "There's something wrong with their light," he said. "They remind me of bulbs left on over Grunsday. Let's try looking at a planet."

Mars was a dot in the sky not very different from the stars, but it greatly agitated Jax. "It's not red," he kept saying. "It should be red. Everything in the sky is wrong."

"So you're saying even the stars aren't as beautiful as they're supposed to be on this day." Evangeline drew back from the lens to find Jax looking at her with pity again and felt embarrassed for complaining. "Thank you for dinner and for letting me look through your telescope," she said, trying to regain a little dignity. "I should go back inside." It was late.

Jax held up a finger. "No, wait. Let me show you what the sky is supposed to look like." He ran into the house and returned with a large book. "This is my science textbook. There are some pictures of galaxies and nebulas in here."

They held the book together, leafing through the pages, and because it was dark, Jax grabbed a candle from the table and held it close. Evangeline was amazed by the brilliant colors of what looked like splashes of paint and fire. "Is this what you usually see in your telescope?"

"Well, not *my* telescope. The Hubble Space Telescope took these."

She looked up from the book. "There are telescopes in space?"

"Yeah, and probes that take pictures—" The candlelight flared.

"Jax!" she yelled. He'd somehow managed to ignite the pages of his book. They jumped apart, and Jax dropped the book. Unfortunately, he also dropped the candle on top of it.

"Oh, crap!" Jax stomped on the fire with one foot. He smothered the flames, but one of the pages smoldered and smoked, so he grabbed a water glass from the table and poured that over the top, which ended the smoldering but further damaged the book. "My teacher's going to kill me!" He looked up at her and laughed, apparently unconcerned about his imminent demise, and Evangeline laughed with him.

Until she felt the world lurch in a familiar way.

There was a fraction of a second for her to register horror and realize she'd done something very stupid and dangerous.

20

SHE MUST THINK *I'm an idiot or a pyromaniac.* Jax looked up from his ruined textbook. "My teacher's going to kill me." At least she was laughing, and Jax was happy that he'd provided entertainment if nothing else.

Then fear flashed across her face.

And she was gone.

Between one blink of the eye and the next, she totally vanished. "Evangeline!" Jax yelled, reaching out as if—as if, what? He could pull her back?

He looked at the sky. Even with his naked eyes he could make out the craters on the moon. Down the street, the pit bull started barking.

It was 12:01 a.m. on Thursday, and Evangeline was stuck outdoors—invisible, unreachable, and vulnerable for an entire week.

Jax circled the spot where she'd been standing. *Oh boy.* This was worse than the time he'd left a window in his dad's car open overnight and it had rained inside. Still, nothing could happen to her, right? Unless a meteor fell from the sky and blasted this spot into a crater, she'd be fine. Jax scanned the skies nervously. *Nah, that's impossible. Or at least unlikely.*

He just needed to meet her here next Wednesday at midnight and make sure she got safely back inside her house.

Jax awoke in the morning feeling guilty for having gone to bed while his new friend was still outside, even if there was nothing he could do about it and she wasn't really there anyway. But he also felt angry. She'd never eaten a hamburger? She'd *heard* that cats purr? That was wrong on so many levels.

And then he felt guilty again, because when he left to go live with Naomi, who was going to talk to her?

He had that on his mind when he went downstairs for breakfast, which was probably why Riley's voice made him jump two inches in the air.

"What'd you do? Set fire to the stove?"

Jax peeked into the living room. Riley lay sprawled across the sofa, wearing the same clothes from last night. Jax wasn't sure if he'd just come in or if he'd been sleeping on the sofa for hours.

"I had an accident cooking some burgers," Jax said. "I'll clean it up."

Riley sat up. "Did you eat alone or did you have company?"

"I had company," Jax admitted.

"What'd you talk about?"

"None of your business."

Riley stood up. "It *is* my business. Her safety is my responsibility."

Somehow Jax doubted that was why he was asking. "We talked about how I burned the food."

"What else?"

"She explained why there aren't many animals on Grunsday. And we looked in my telescope."

"Telescope?" Riley repeated.

"Well, the moon and the stars look different, but she didn't know why."

"Anything else?"

Jax didn't dare tell him he'd kept her out too late and gotten her trapped on the lawn between Grunsdays. "I gave her your message," he said. "Told her I wasn't part of your clan. She said it didn't matter." Then he exhaled in exasperation. "You knew when you left last night I was going to try and talk to her. If you didn't want me to, why didn't you just *order* me not to?"

"That would've been cruel. She's been alone a long time. If she wanted to talk to someone, I wasn't going to deprive her of the chance." Riley frowned. "I guess she thinks you're clueless and harmless."

Jax realized Riley was trying to justify to himself why Evangeline wouldn't talk to *him*. "Maybe she thinks *you're* scary-looking," Jax shot back. Riley snorted and turned around, headed for the stairs. But for just a second, Jax thought he might have actually hurt Riley's feelings.

Over Thursday, Friday, and the weekend, Jax worked on Melinda's concentration assignments more than his schoolwork and once or twice tried his inquisition on A.J. "Cut that out," A.J. growled, flicking through channels on the remote control. "You won't catch me by surprise again."

He even attempted it on Riley once and got laughed at. "Nice try, squirt."

There was no repetition of the time A.J. coughed up his PIN number or Melinda had to cover her mouth to keep from blurting out the Pendragon name. You're stronger when you really want to know, Melinda typed in an email chat when he confessed he was worried about getting weaker. I've noticed that if you don't really care, it's not hard to fend you off.

She cautioned Jax *not* to use his magic at school, but where else was he going to do it? He saw Melinda only on Grunsdays, the day she could meet him without her family present. And trying to force Melinda to tell him her favorite television show was pointless.

The problem was using his magic on his classmates without getting caught. By Tuesday, he thought he'd figured out a way and was ready to give it a try.

So when he passed Giana's seat in science class and she whispered her undertone-but-meant-to-be-heard "Freak," he had no patience for it. He turned and shoved his face into hers.

"Back off. All I ever did was talk to you." Jax dialed back his talent to what he imagined as a trickle and asked, "Do you think you're better than everybody else?"

"Yes," Giana whispered, then recoiled in her seat. Kacey gasped, and other students who heard Giana gave her an offended glare.

"You're not," Jax assured her.

"Dude!" Billy looked impressed as Jax sat down.

Jax crossed his arms. "I was tired of her crap."

While his teacher was reviewing for finals that day, he wrote in his notebook and pushed it toward Billy.

Ask her to narrow down the formulas we need to memorize.

Billy gave him a look that said *She's not going to tell us that.*

"Trust me," Jax murmured.

Billy raised his hand. "Miss Cassidy? Can you narrow down the formulas we need to memorize?"

Miss Cassidy gave Billy the same look Billy had given Jax, but then Jax called out, "Yeah, Miss Cassidy. Which formulas do we really need to know?"

The teacher rattled off three formulas, then frowned and blinked repeatedly. The other students started scribbling in their notebooks. Miss Cassidy glared at both Billy and Jax, uncertain which boy to be annoyed at, and tried to cover her mistake by naming a few more. Billy gaped at Jax, and Jax grinned.

He tried it again in English class and also in math. When he followed up on a question asked by someone else, he got the answer he wanted, and the teachers didn't seem to pinpoint Jax as the reason they were blurting out information. He congratulated himself on his brilliance.

After the last bell, Jax was at his locker when someone shoved him from behind. "Hey!" he yelped.

A hulk from the senior high loomed over him. "You know who I am?"

"No idea," Jax said, but his heart sped up. The guy was accompanied by three others, just as big and just as mean looking, all wearing football jerseys.

"I'm Enzo Leone," the boy snarled. "You been bothering my sister? How'd you like a bloody nose?"

Oh, crap. His revenge on Giana this morning was going to get him beaten up. Enzo snatched up a fistful of Jax's shirt, and Jax grabbed the boy's arm to hold him off. It was like trying to wrap his fingers around a log, but instantly Jax experienced the same buzz of magic he'd felt when his talent had led him to the encyclopedia at Melinda's house.

"What're you afraid of, Enzo?" he asked, the idea popping into his head.

"What?" Enzo let go of Jax's shirt and tried to yank his arm away.

Jax hung on. According to Melinda, touching his victim was another thing that enhanced his magic. "What's your deepest, darkest secret?"

"I wet the bed till I was eleven." Enzo's eyes goggled.

Jax almost gasped in surprise—not at Enzo's secret, but at the realization that he could use his talent for defense. "How often did you wet the bed, Enzo?"

"Almost every night." Enzo gripped his own throat with his hand as if trying to throttle himself. He wrenched away from Jax, stumbling against his buddies, who all burst out laughing.

"Do you want me to keep asking questions?" Jax whispered.

A spasm of fear crossed Enzo's face. He broke and hightailed it down the hall, shoving middle schoolers out of the way. Jax grinned triumphantly—and then he spotted the Donovan twins watching him from across the hall, their matching green eyes narrow with suspicion. Tegan whispered to her brother, who clenched his fists and stepped forward.

Jax braced himself. *You want some too? Bring it on, Thomas.*

Suddenly, Billy Ramirez stepped between them. "What did you just do?" he asked Jax, oblivious to Thomas behind him. "*How* did you do it?"

"I don't know what you're talking about," Jax said gruffly.

"Miss Cassidy and Giana's brother. What'd you *do* to them?"

"Nothing." Jax elbowed past Billy and looked up and down the hall. The Donovans had vanished.

Billy dogged his heels. "Don't tell me *nothing*. I know what I saw."

Jax turned back to Billy. If there was anyone who'd believe the real story, it was this guy. His friend would think Grunsday was the most awesome thing since *Doctor Who*.

"You can tell me," Billy said.

"No," Jax whispered. "I really can't."

21

LUCKILY, BILLY STAYED after school for robotics club, and Jax didn't have to fend off more of his questions on the ride home. The bus disgorged Jax at the end of his block, and he spotted A.J.'s truck and Deidre's T-bird parked in the street. He quickened his pace when he saw Deidre passing rifles from the back of her car to Mr. Crandall and A.J., who piled them into a foot locker in the bed of the truck.

"What's going on?" Jax demanded.

"Talk to Riley," Mr. Crandall said curtly.

"Where'd the guns come from?" Jax stared at Deidre. Now she held a rifle that was almost as big as she was. Deidre might've been tiny, but she handled the gun like she knew what to do with it.

"My family's in the business," she said with a smile.

Jax gulped. "What kind of business? Mercenary army?"

"Private security." Then she winked.

What was that supposed to mean? That he was right the first time?

Jax ran into the house and upstairs, where he found Riley packing a duffel bag in his bedroom. "Are we under attack?" Jax asked breathlessly.

Riley looked up. "Nothing like that. I have to take a trip. I'll be gone through Thursday. Maybe Friday."

Straight through Grunsday. "Where? And why are you taking guns?"

"Better you don't know," said Riley. "Less for you to worry about."

"But—" Just telling him that gave him plenty to worry about.

"I don't expect any trouble *here*, but Melinda is on security, and if you need help, call A.J.'s mom. I just need you to hold down the fort."

"What—"

Riley zipped the duffel bag closed and tossed it at Jax. "Put that by the front door. I'll be down in a second."

Jax carried the bag downstairs, frowning, and as he passed through the living room, he spied Riley's cell phone on the coffee table. A second later, he'd dropped Riley's luggage on the floor and was thumbing through phone menus. Riley had made calls to Mr. Crandall and Melinda that afternoon, but prior to that, he'd received a text from Miller—the vassal no one wanted to talk about. Hearing Riley's footsteps overhead, Jax quickly scanned the messages.

Miller: wylits vassals headed for taliesins.
arrival certain by grunsday night.
Riley: not good
Miller: i can get there 1st
Riley: dont blow yr cover. ill go
Miller: u sure? could get ugly
Miller: 1st kill is hardest
Miller: dont think u can do it. ill go
Riley: ill do what i have to

By the time Riley came downstairs, the phone was on the table, the duffel bag was by the door, and Jax was casually clicking through channels on the TV. "Probably nothing will happen," Riley said. He put the phone in his pocket and slung the duffel bag over his shoulder. "But keep your phone on you. And the radio on Grunsday."

"Okay."

Riley left, and Jax darted to a window to watch the truck and the T-Bird pull away. He tried to think of a way he might have misinterpreted those texts, but he couldn't.

Riley was off to kill somebody.

Melinda chatted with Jax that evening.

Melinda: You ok?
Jaxattax: yeah but where did they go?

Melinda: To check out a security problem. Don't worry

Jaxattax: they took guns

Melinda: Just a precaution

Jax didn't buy it. Melinda had told him herself that somebody had wiped out Riley's family and nearly killed him as well. Jax swallowed hard. *When did I start worrying about Riley?*

Melinda: You don't have to stay there. Riley lived alone so many years, he forgets it's not normal for a boy your age. You can stay with Mrs. Crandall.

Jaxattax: no im ok—supposed to hold down the fort

Melinda: LOL. See you for your lesson on the 8th day. Call if you need me.

Jax barely slept that night. He skipped school the next day because he regretted what he'd done to Giana's brother and wondered if the brute would pound him into dust today. He also knew Billy would hound him with questions he couldn't answer, and sure enough, texts started rolling in minutes after the school day ended.

Billy: where r u? cmon jax. tell me whats going on. i can help.

Jax didn't answer any of them, and when the doorbell rang around eight o'clock that evening, he groaned. It had to be Billy, come to ask his questions in person. Jax ground his teeth together. His guardian was off on some James Bond mission, he had to meet Evangeline on the lawn at midnight, and he didn't need one more thing to deal with!

But when Jax opened the door, he found a strange man on the stoop. "Jax? I'm Mrs. Unger's nephew." The man stuck out his hand, and Jax shook it automatically. "I hear you run errands for her. Thanks for looking out for my aunt."

Jax shrugged. "It's not a big deal."

"It *is* a big deal. Not many kids take the time to look after an old lady." The fellow looked about fifty years old, with a shock of white hair and a solid build. "I'm dropping off a rug for my aunt's bedroom. She said maybe you'd help me carry it in." He pointed his thumb at a conversion van parked outside Mrs. Unger's house. The back passenger door was open, and rock music pounded from the stereo.

When Jax hesitated, the man added, "My aunt said she's got cash."

Jax groaned. "She doesn't have to pay me."

The man grinned. "You know how she is."

"Yeah, I do." Jax closed the front door and followed him to the van, where a rolled-up carpet lay wedged between the front- and second-row seats.

Mrs. Unger's nephew climbed into the vehicle, saying, "I'll get in and push. You pull from the outside."

Jax glanced back at Mrs. Unger's house, expecting to see her standing on the stoop waving her wallet, but the front door was closed, the curtains drawn, with no lights on in the front room. "Um, where is—?"

"I think the plastic's caught on the bottom of that seat," the man shouted over the music. "Can you get it?"

"Sure." Jax leaned into the van and felt around.

Pain shot through every nerve in his body.

He screamed, his limbs failing him. He went down face-first, his nose slamming into the floor of the van. Every part of his body was on fire, twitching and flopping. He couldn't even lift his face to breathe.

As suddenly as it had started, it stopped. The echo of pain racked his body, but he lifted his head and gasped for air. The bass in the music vibrated the vehicle in time with his pain, as if the whole world throbbed. There was a weight on his back, and when Jax struggled, a hand shoved his head down.

"Yeah, I know. Getting Tasered is no fun. Lie still if you don't want it again."

His arms were pulled behind his back, and something cold closed around his wrists with a ratcheting sound. "Help!" he yelled.

"Shut your mouth, Jaxattax," the voice spoke in his ear. "Or I'll Taser you again. Nobody can hear you anyway."

The weight disappeared from his back, but before Jax could react, the door of the van slammed shut. Feet stepped over his head. Then he felt the van shiver with the closing of the driver's door, and the vehicle jerked into motion, rocking to the Killers' latest song.

22

SO STUPID.

Jax's body convulsed in pain and fear. How could he have fallen for something every child had been warned against? He should have slammed the front door in the man's face. He should have grabbed his dagger.

His dagger.

Melinda had told him to wear it whenever he wasn't in school, and Riley had told him to keep his phone or his radio on him. But he hadn't. The sheath was uncomfortable to wear when he was sitting around the house. He'd left it on the coffee table with the radio, and the phone was charging. He kept them all *handy*, but not on him.

Jax moaned. He'd been asked to *hold the fort*, to watch over Evangeline, and within hours he'd gotten himself kidnapped.

Evangeline. Would they come for her next?

Jax heaved his body upright. His hands were cuffed

behind his back. His nose throbbed, and his tongue stung as if he'd bitten it while convulsing.

The man in the driver's seat extended one arm in Jax's direction, his hand clasping a black, blunt-nosed weapon. "You can sit up," he called out, "but stay *real still*. If I have to pull this van over, you're going to regret it."

"You're Terrance from that stupid website," Jax guessed.

"I'm Lexi too." The driver laughed. "As for *stupid*— stupid is giving me the same username and password you use for your email account. Didn't they teach you any better at school?"

Jax groaned. Of course, he'd been taught not to use the same username and password for everything. He'd ignored the advice. Everybody did.

Terrance held the Taser in his right hand, but Jax was more interested in his left hand. When the van made a turn to the right, Terrance's left hand arced upward, and Jax got a look at his wrist.

He had no tattoo. He was a Normal.

Jax hung his head and tried to think. Had he been snatched by a nut job who knew nothing about Grunsday? No, there was too much stuff on that website that matched what he'd been told. This guy knew *something*. What Jax wouldn't have given for Riley's voice of command right now! But of course, Jax had his own talent. He started muttering one of Melinda's chants.

Terrance swung the Taser toward him again, and the van lurched sideways. "No spells, Jax."

He knew what Jax was doing. That couldn't be good. "I'm praying," Jax snarled. "Praying you drive into a ditch, because I'd rather die in a car accident than be chopped into pieces by a psycho killer!"

"I'm not going to chop you into pieces," Terrance shot back. "You're my golden ticket, kid. Do what you're told, and you won't get hurt. But if you ask me a question—any question at all—I'll Taser you till you pass out."

Jax sagged against the rolled-up carpet. Terrance knew his talent.

"Cheer up, Jax. You didn't like living there anyway, did you?" Terrance's voice rose an octave. *"Naomi, I don't like it here. Riley is mean, and the only person who's nice to me is Mrs. Unger."* He dropped into his normal register. "Only Naomi didn't come, did she? She dropped you like a hot potato."

So Terrance had read his email and chats. Crap, even Riley's address had been in an old email Jax sent to Naomi back when he first moved there. And this guy knew about magic, even if he didn't have his own. But he was also giving Jax information, practically volunteering it. Was Jax's talent working for him even when he didn't ask a direct question? Melinda said he was stronger when he really needed to know.

Jax prodded him but made sure not to phrase it as a question. "You don't know anything about me."

"I know you were left alone this week." Terrance smirked in the mirror. "Nobody's going to miss you for days."

Melinda would miss him. She was expecting him for his lesson tomorrow, and when he didn't show up, she'd contact Mrs. Crandall, and they'd . . . do what? A Normal wouldn't have activated Melinda's security net, and he already knew that she wouldn't detect Jax's leaving. She'd have no idea what had happened.

Sitting for hours with hands cuffed behind his back was a torture that started small and grew steadily unbearable. Jax squirmed, trying to ease the pressure on his arms. He also managed to survey the vehicle. Besides the rolled rug Terrance had used to lure him in, there was a large toolbox in the back of the van and what appeared to be garbage bags.

The bags worried him. Bodies were disposed of in garbage bags.

Jax watched the clock face on the outdated dashboard. When midnight came, Terrance would vanish. But Jax was worried about what would happen to the van. He remembered the car he'd seen frozen on the highway because it had been moving with velocity on Wednesday at midnight. Would that happen in this case? Would Jax be trapped inside the van, unable to get out? Or would Jax's presence in the vehicle be enough to send it hurtling seventy miles per hour into Grunsday—minus the driver?

At eleven thirty p.m., Terrance left the interstate and headed into a town over the border of Ohio. Rain pattered against the windshield, and Terrance flicked on the windshield wipers. He drove quickly and, as near as Jax could tell from the mirror, kept his eye on the clock. Finally, with less than ten minutes to spare, Terrance drove the vehicle into a strip shopping mall. He cut the engine and exited through the driver's door. He walked around the van, opened the passenger door, and thrust the Taser into Jax's face. "Get out. Slowly."

Slowly was the only way Jax could move. He had no arms to help him. He fell trying to step out of the vehicle, and the pavement smacked his knees. Then Terrance planted a hand on the back of Jax's head and shoved. "Get your head down."

This was it. Terrance was going to kill him. Jax filled his lungs with breath to yell and plead . . . when suddenly his left hand fell forward. A second later, pain tore through the tortured muscles of his arm.

"Get up," Terrance ordered, jerking on his other arm. Those muscles screamed, too. And then Jax realized his right hand was cuffed to Terrance's left one.

"What the—"

Terrance laughed. He held up their connected hands and shook the cuffs. His other hand still held the Taser.

"It's a piggy-back ride," he explained. "In a couple minutes, either you're going to drag me into the other world, or . . ." He grinned. "Or one of us is going to get a hand cut off."

Jax looked at the metal rings joining their hands. If he transitioned to Grunsday with everything on his body—and meanwhile, Terrance went to Thursday with everything on *his* body—they couldn't both take the cuffs with them. It took Jax about one second to picture the possible result. Then he started screaming. He grabbed the handcuff and yanked on it, trying to wriggle his hand loose. Terrance let him do it. In fact, he threw back his head and laughed.

At the instant Jax had planned to meet Evangeline, he transitioned into Grunsday handcuffed to a madman.

When Terrance was tired of laughing, he grabbed Jax and shook him into silence. "That's enough, kid."

Terrance led Jax away from the van to a shopping-cart return. He didn't seem to care that the rain had turned to mist, hanging in the air. He didn't look at the sports car frozen in transit on the street. Jax realized Terrance had been to Grunsday before and already knew the handcuff trick would work.

He'd frightened Jax for fun.

Terrance removed the key from his shirt pocket and

unlocked his own cuff and closed it around a railing in the shopping cart return. "Wait here, kid."

When Terrance climbed into the van and drove across the parking lot, Jax thought it was over. Terrance was going to leave him now that he'd gotten what he wanted. Then Jax saw the reverse lights come on, and the van hurtled backward, tires squealing on the wet pavement—straight into the glass windows of one of the stores.

"Holy crap!"

Jax looked up at the building front. It wasn't a store. It was a bank. Terrance was a freaking bank robber.

Terrance drove the van out of the broken glass and off the sidewalk, then emerged from the driver's seat whistling happily. He went around to the back of the vehicle and opened the rear door. Jax couldn't see what he did next but assumed he was unloading the toolbox and the garbage bags.

When Terrance vanished inside the bank, Jax turned his attention to the shopping-cart return. It was rusted and, with any luck, flimsily made. He grabbed the railing with both hands, braced his feet, and whaled on it. The handcuffs clanged against the steel, and the shopping carts rattled, and Jax never heard footsteps behind him until Terrance pressed the Taser into his back.

Jax flinched. "Trying to leave me, kid?" Terrance asked pleasantly.

"Let me go," Jax begged. "You got what you wanted.

Go rob your bank and let me go. It's not like I can call the police."

"Our partnership's not over yet. Take the key and unlock that other cuff. I don't have to tell you not to run, do I?"

He didn't.

Inside the bank, emergency lights dimly illuminated the main room, and glass crunched underfoot. "Do you know what I do for a living?" Terrance asked. "I build vault locks. Do you know what I think about while I build 'em? How to break into them."

He nudged Jax with the Taser, steering him toward the teller windows. Jax understood what Terrance wanted and fastened the open cuff to the steel security grate.

"Nobody knows how to beat a lock better than a lock maker. The only problem is the alarms and the sensors and the pesky police." Terrance nodded toward the ceiling. "And the cameras."

Jax looked at the security cameras on the ceiling. He could see dim red lights, but he knew they weren't working.

Terrance dismantled the lock on the steel door beyond the teller windows and, cackling with self-satisfaction, disappeared, presumably to crack the vault. As soon as he was out of sight, Jax grabbed the security grate and shook it in frustration, ashamed of himself for being so afraid of the Taser that he cuffed himself wherever he was told to.

He was painfully aware that Evangeline would've reappeared a few minutes ago. Was she okay? Terrance didn't seem to know anything about her. That was the only good thing in this situation at all. Terrance had wanted a way into Grunsday; he didn't know he'd blundered into the business of Riley Pendare and his vassals. Jax forgot for the moment that he wasn't one of those vassals and imagined Riley and the gang coming for him. He wished Terrance and his Taser could come face-to-face with Mr. Crandall and Deidre's really big gun. *That would wipe the grin off Terrance's face.*

Jax spent a few seconds picturing that scene, unlikely as it was, and when he saw movement outside the broken glass front of the building, his heart leaped with hope. Somehow, they'd tracked him here. They were going to bust in here, just like in the movies, and rescue him.

A figure slipped through the broken window. It was too small to be Riley or any of the Crandalls, and when the person pulled down the hood of his sweatshirt, Jax gasped out loud.

Thomas Donovan put a finger to his lips. *Shhhh.*

23

JAX'S KNEES WOBBLED. His perception of the world as he knew it had taken another blow. Thomas Donovan. Here. On a Grunsday. Which meant . . .

From the back of the bank, Terrance cackled loudly, and then Jax heard the sound of a drill. Thomas pointed toward the open doorway and made a gun with his hand—sticking his forefinger straight out and his thumb up. He raised his eyebrows questioningly.

Jax wondered how to answer that. He copied the gesture and shook his head. Then he curled two joints of his forefinger to make a snub-nosed weapon, touched his own chest with it, and mimed a convulsion.

Thomas nodded and darted outside.

"Wait," Jax whispered desperately. Had Thomas just stopped by to take a survey of bank robbers' weapons?

Finally, to Jax's relief, he reappeared. He entered the building and crept around the edge of the room. Terrance's drill stopped, and Thomas hastened his steps. When he reached the corner of the room closest to the steel door, he sank down beneath an ornamental potted tree and disappeared from sight.

Movement in the bank entrance caught Jax's attention, and somebody else walked in. This time it was a grown man with the same carroty shade of hair as Thomas. The man nodded a greeting at Jax, swung a baseball bat onto his shoulder, then looked back at the entrance and made a "come here" gesture.

Tegan darted in through the broken window. She spared Jax only a brief glance before pulling the hood of her sweatshirt over her head and taking position behind the man, who must've been her father.

The senior Donovan faced the open steel door. He positioned the bat like a baseball player—even took a couple of practice swings—then called out loudly, "Terrance Hodd, are you havin' a bank party without your good friend Michael?"

At the word *friend*, Jax's heart sank. The Donovans knew Terrance. They were probably his accomplices.

Terrance's voice from the back room confirmed it. "How'd you find me, Michael?"

"Smelled you out. I figured you were planning to strike out on your own, but you forgot—I *know* which banks carry your locks. It was just a matter of findin' the one that reeks of you casing it." Donovan looked at Jax. "Looks like you got yourself another way in and out of the eighth day. Were you thinkin' of cuttin' me out of my share?"

"Your share?" Terrance appeared. He looked at Jax, then at Donovan and Tegan standing beside him—as if marking everyone's position—and held up a gun. Not a Taser. A small black revolver with a nasty, oversized hole in the barrel.

Jax's mouth went dry. Terrance had a real gun after all.

"You never earned your share, Michael," said Terrance. "I'm the one who knows how to break into vaults. All you and your kid ever did was get me in and out of this crazy world—"

"Not to mention teachin' you about it in the first place," Donovan murmured.

"—and as you can see, I've got somebody else to do that now."

"Terry." Donovan shook his head. "As a father, I don't approve of kidnappin' kids to rob banks. It's one thing when they're born to it." He glanced at Tegan, who grinned and shrugged.

"Michael." Terrance flashed his crazy grin, the one that made Jax shiver. "As a father, you should've known better than to bring your kid into this. Now I'm going to have to take him out, too."

"But I never told you everything, Terry." Donovan's smile didn't waver. "And you're so dense, you never realized my kid . . . *is twins*."

Thomas hurtled out of hiding and plowed into Terrance's back. Terrance went down, firing the revolver as he fell. Jax ducked instinctively. The discharge echoed loudly, accompanied by breaking glass. The shot had gone wide.

Donovan swung the bat down on Terrance's hand. The bank robber howled, and his handgun spun across the floor. Thomas fished the Taser out of Terrance's back pocket, jumped up, and fired it. Terrance convulsed.

Tegan hollered at Jax, "Where's the key?"

"In his shirt pocket!"

Donovan put his foot on Terrance's neck, pinning him to the floor, the bat hovering just off his head. "Should've brought a seven-iron," Donovan remarked cheerfully. Thomas found the handcuff key and tossed it to Tegan. Then he and his father hauled Terrance to his knees and dragged him into the back of the bank.

The moment Tegan unlocked the cuff, Jax grabbed her left arm and shoved her sleeve up. He got a glimpse of a tattooed crest with what looked like hunting dogs standing on their back legs before she yanked her arm away and glared at him. "You knew about me," he hissed. "And never said anything."

"You were an idiot," she sneered. "Showing people your mark and using your magic openly. Tommy wanted to pound you." She might have said more, but shouting from the back of the bank caught their attention. "C'mon," she said, grabbing him by the arm. "They might need help."

A short corridor led to the vault. Jax and Tegan arrived in time to see Terrance struggle to his knees, only to be brought down by another hit from the Taser. Jax felt sick, watching him flop around on the floor. "Gimme the cuffs," said Thomas. His sister darted forward.

The elder Donovan knelt in front of the vault with a finger inserted into one of the drill holes. His face was pressed against the vault door, his eyes cast upward with a look of concentration. "I think . . . Ah, there we go." He jumped to his feet and swung the vault door open triumphantly. "And you thought I wasn't payin' attention, Terry."

Terrance responded with a string of curse words. The twins had managed to cuff his hands behind his back, but he was still struggling. "Are you totally useless?" Thomas yelled at Jax. "Grab some electrical tape from his box and give us a hand!" Jax blinked stupidly for a moment, then fetched the tape and wrapped it around Terrance's ankles while Tegan sat on his legs.

Donovan examined the door. "It'll still lock when we're done. That's a bit of luck."

"I'll kill you," Terrance growled.

"Hush up, Terry, or Tommy'll zap you again." Donovan handed a garbage bag to Tegan. "Since we're here . . ."

"Yeah, Dad." Tegan darted into the vault and started filling the bag with bundles of cash from the bins and drawers.

Donovan picked up a fat wad of hundreds and slapped it against Jax's chest. "Here you go, kid. Your share."

"No thanks!" Jax exclaimed.

"Suit yourself."

"You want Terrance in the vault?" asked Thomas.

"You can't!" hollered Terrance. "I need one of you to get me out of this place!" Jax understood he didn't mean the bank.

"True." Donovan and Thomas dragged Terrance into the vault. "You'll be stuck here till somebody rescues you. Course, nobody opens this vault on the eighth day. They'll be here on Thursday, but *you* won't be. They'll repair it and lock it. I don't expect anybody'll be lookin' in here on any day *you'll* be present . . . although eventually they're gonna wonder why the place stinks so bad. . . ."

Terrance started cursing foully. Even after Donovan swung the vault door closed, they could hear him faintly through the drill holes.

24

THE TWINS PUSHED Jax down the hall toward the front of the bank. "You can't leave him there," Jax protested, feeling nauseous. "To starve to death slowly."

"What do you care?" Thomas said. "That gun was for you."

"No worries." Michael Donovan grinned. "Terrance doesn't belong in the eighth day. He'll pop back into his own time, easy enough. The eighth day will spit out any Normal at midnight, whether he's handcuffed to one of us or not."

"He doesn't know anything about the eighth day except what we told him. And we lied a lot." Tegan grinned proudly.

"Couldn't have him shooting us in the back, thinking he didn't need us," her father explained. "Likewise, he never saw Tommy and Tegan together."

Meanwhile, Jax had stumbled over his own feet. "What do you mean, *that gun was for me*?"

Tegan shrugged. "It would've been a lot of trouble to keep you prisoner till he wanted another piggy-back ride."

The entire world pounded in time with Jax's heart. If the Donovans hadn't shown up tonight, his life expectancy would have been no more than the duration of Grunsday.

"He'll transition back to his normal time at midnight," Donovan said. "And minutes later, the police'll be haulin' him out of there."

"Aren't you afraid he'll turn you in?" Jax asked.

Donovan laughed. "He don't even know our real last name, and we don't stay in one place for very long anyway. C'mon, let's take you home. Terrance left us a ride, keys in the ignition."

Show these people where the last remaining Pendragon lived? That seemed like a very bad idea. "I'm okay," Jax said. "I'll call someone to come get me on Thursday."

The twins exchanged glances, and their father gave Jax a speculative look. "We're driving your way," he said. "Why would we leave you here?"

There didn't seem to be a way to ditch them, especially after they'd saved his life. So he followed them out to the parking lot and named a town on the opposite side of the school district from where he really lived.

A dumpy-looking Toyota Tercel was parked beside Terrance's van. Michael Donovan tossed a set of keys onto the hood before opening the van and waving everyone inside. Jax wondered why the Donovans were abandoning their car. Then it hit him. The car was stolen.

Donovan drove Terrance's van into the street. "Steers like a dump truck," he told Thomas, who was riding shotgun. "The A-Team meets Scooby-Doo."

"Did you know Terrance had me?" Jax asked.

"We knew he must've found *somebody* to get him into the eighth day," Donovan said. "He stood us up for a job last week and disappeared. We had to track him down."

"You didn't join one of his stupid websites, did you?" asked Tegan. "He's been phishing for months and months online, but no Transitioner with an ounce of brains would fall for something that obvious."

Jax sank down in his seat, feeling his cheeks burn. Tegan and Thomas exchanged grins, as if they knew he'd done exactly that and it was no more than they would've expected from him.

The mist continued through the night, beading up on the windshield. Donovan stopped for fuel, but not at a gas station. He siphoned gas out of cars at a bus depot. Then he stopped for "the other kind of fuel," by which he meant ransacking a convenience store. The twins stuffed the pockets of their sweatshirts with candy and bags of chips. Donovan took a shopping basket and filled it with sodas, whistling happily. There didn't seem to be any method to their looting, as if they weren't thinking more than a few hours ahead. As far as Jax could tell, they treated the eighth-day world like it was their personal shopping mall—here solely for their own gain—just as Riley had warned him most Transitioners did. In spite of his disapproval, Jax was so parched from his ordeal that he beat down his conscience and helped himself to a single bottle of water. As he was walking out, he passed a display of pet food and paused.

I've heard that cats purr, Evangeline had said.

"Hey, Thomas," Jax called. "Is there such a thing as a Grunsday cat?"

"What's Grunsday?" Thomas asked.

"That's what I call the eighth day."

"You want a cat for the eighth day?"

"I want to know if there *is* such a thing," Jax said.

"An eighth-day cat or dog is a rare commodity." Michael Donovan eyed him with interest over the shelves. "Expensive to acquire, but I'll bet I could find one."

"Bound to be the pet of some Kin." Tegan added her two cents around a mouthful of cheese doodles. "They get nasty when you steal from 'em."

"I didn't ask you to steal one. I only asked—" Jax grunted in exasperation. "I'll wait in the car."

The best way to avoid talking to the Donovans was to pretend to fall asleep, and to Jax's surprise, he really did doze off. Thomas had to shake him awake when they neared their destination.

"Which way, Jax?" Michael Donovan asked.

"Straight ahead." Jax kept an eye out for likely-looking housing communities. In the seat next to him, Tegan was sound asleep, her head lolling on her shoulder and her hair fallen across her face. "Left at the next light," he said.

In the rearview mirror, he saw Donovan frown. "You sure?"

"Yes."

Thomas and his father exchanged glances, but Donovan made the turn. Jax continued to direct them, solely by the quality of the houses, and finally said, "Stop here."

"Which house?" Donovan brought the van to a gentle stop and looked over his shoulder with a smile that was way too innocent for Jax's liking.

"I'd rather you stop here." Jax made a show of looking ashamed. "I live with someone who'd kill me if he knew I was dumb enough to get myself kidnapped by a bank robber."

"I can understand that." Donovan's smile widened into a grin.

Jax opened the door. "I'm grateful, sir. You saved my life. Uh, see you at school, Thomas."

Thomas eyed him over the back of his seat with a smile that eerily echoed his father's. "Bye, Jax."

Jax glanced across the van at Tegan. She was still asleep. He hopped out of the vehicle and walked down the street.

When he realized Donovan wasn't going to pull away, he looked back and waved, then sauntered between two of the houses. As soon as he was out of sight, he crouched and waited. After a few seconds, he heard the van reverse and turn around, and when the sound of its engine could no longer be heard, he sank to the ground in relief.

First thing he did was find a bike to steal.

He tried not to compare himself to Terrance or the Donovans. Instead, he remembered what Riley had told him: *I'm not a thief, but I have stolen when I needed to.* When he finally found a house with an unlocked garage door and a bike inside, Jax wondered when Riley Pendare had suddenly become a model of acceptable morality.

He was only eight or nine miles from home, and with any luck he could make it back before his scheduled lesson with Melinda. No one would ever know he'd been gone.

Except Evangeline.

Mounting the stolen bike, Jax tried to figure out what he was going to tell her.

25

EVANGELINE LOOKED AROUND IN HORROR.

She was standing under the nighttime sky in a wet mist, alone and vulnerable. How could she have been so careless? The first thing her parents had taught her, even before she'd been able to speak in complete sentences, was the dire importance of being in a secure location at midnight.

Evangeline bolted for the house, only to find the back door locked. For a second she panicked and looked for a rock to break the glass. Before she found one, however, reason caught up with her. Breaking the window would frighten Mrs. Unger. There was another way in. Years ago, she had stolen and hidden a key to the front door for just such an emergency.

It took her a couple of minutes to remember the right window and even longer to tease the key out of the crack between the stucco wall of the house and the underside of the windowsill. Her fingers had been smaller then. While she worked at it, she cast angry glances next door, where Jax's bike was locked up in its usual spot. Jax had left her outside and hadn't come back for her.

Once she'd retrieved the key and let herself in, she slammed the door and locked it. *I should be angry at myself,* she thought. *Jax has no idea what it's like. I let another person distract me from the time—and that was stupid.*

My life is ruled by time.

She didn't sleep well that night, too irritated at herself, disappointed in Jax, and engulfed in overwhelming longing for her own family.

If I had given the Taliesins a different answer five years ago, would they have let the three of us stay together?

After whisking Evangeline and her siblings through the woods and to a safe location, the Taliesin brothers had separated the children and questioned Evangeline—she being the eldest and most likely to understand the situation. "Do you know why we rescued you?" the one with the hawk-shaped nose had asked.

At that point, she still thought they must be allies of her father's. They were Kin, after all, and she'd been told that all Kin wanted the same thing. "To end the exile of the Kin and dissolve the Eighth-Day Spell," she promptly said.

When he hit her, she felt surprise before she felt pain. The blow was hard enough to send her sprawling across the floor.

"I told you she was too old," he said to his brother. "We should have left this one behind. The younger two children might be re-educated."

"I'm not certain about that," the other mumbled, rubbing his leg. Addie had kicked him in the shins.

Evangeline, meanwhile, thrashed on the floor, trying to make her limbs obey her. Too old? She was *eleven*. She didn't understand why they were angry. She didn't know what they wanted from her. *I didn't mean it,* she wanted to say. *Tell me what answer you want me to give, and I will.* But her jaws and her teeth throbbed.

"Every misguided attempt to interfere with the Eighth-Day Spell has ended in catastrophe," the hawk-nosed man said, scowling down at her. "We have records—disaster after disaster, throughout the centuries, caused by fools like your father."

The second man started to help her up, but the cruel one swooped in and grabbed her by the throat, hauling her to her feet. "You are nothing but a vessel, girl. A vessel for the bloodline that maintains the eighth day."

She clawed at his fingers, but he tightened his grip, and spots floated in her eyes.

"We'll put you somewhere safe," he said. "But if I think, even for a second, that you've taken up your father's cause, I'll kill you myself. Do you understand?"

The room grew dim around her. Her head spun, and her hands fell to her side.

"If we cannot keep you hidden, we must prevent your being used as a weapon." The other man spoke urgently, as if he knew she was close to passing out. "Understand that, child.

No one is going to save you for your own sake."

Evangeline had often wished her eleven-year-old self had been clever enough to renounce her father and declare that the eighth day must be upheld at any cost. But the fact was, they probably wouldn't have believed her, and no answer would have changed the truth of what they said.

Nobody would ever care enough to save her for her own sake.

She gave up trying to sleep at dawn and went downstairs, where she discovered the books she'd requested on the kitchen counter—local history and geography. Jax had been thoughtful enough to get them, which made his failure to check on her last night even stranger.

When she looked outside, his house appeared the same as it had at midnight, but Evangeline shivered uneasily. The house gave off a feeling of emptiness. She couldn't put her finger on why, but she felt very strongly that no one was home—and that no one had been home last night when she'd reappeared. *Something's wrong. Jax would have been here if he could have been.*

She slipped outside and crossed the property line to crack open the door of their shed and peek inside. The motorcycle was there, and that caused her a stab of alarm. Both boys seemed to be absent from home without their usual means of transportation.

But they weren't expected to report their travel plans to Evangeline. Fat Friend had a truck, and Black-Haired Girl had a car. The boys could have left with either one of them.

Walking up to the front door was harder than opening the shed. Despite her growing certainty that they weren't home, it took all her bravery to mount the front steps. The door was unlocked and swung open, giving Evangeline her first glimpse inside.

Squalid was the word that came to mind.

The house was much smaller than Mrs. Unger's and looked as if it had been decorated by an old woman and then fallen into the hands of unsupervised boys—boys who didn't know how to use a vacuum and weren't in a hurry to clean up dirty dishes. Inside-out sweatshirts lay draped over chairs, and balled-up socks littered the floor. On a low table in the living room, Evangeline spotted a sheath with Jax's dagger in it and a walkie-talkie.

Where had Jax gone without his honor blade? Where had they *both* gone, leaving the front door unlocked?

She could scry for them. All she needed was a small, personal piece of each of them.

Now she grew bold, running upstairs. The absolute silence of the house assured her that she was alone, but this was still a violation of every rule she'd made for herself. She pushed open the door of the first bedroom and knew from the telescope leaning against a wall that it was Jax's. She got what she wanted from a hairbrush on his bedside table, pulling out a few strands of brown hair and carefully tucking them into the back pocket of her jeans.

Now for the other one.

She ventured across the hall to the second bedroom. She had no right to snoop in his personal belongings, but she headed for his dresser anyway, where, amid scattered change, crumpled receipts, and gum wrappers, she found a comb with a few strands of auburn hair. She reached for them, but then her eyes fell on a photograph tucked into the corner of his mirror.

A girl—and not the black-haired one. How many girl-friends did Riley Pendragon have?

Evangeline felt foolish. She had no business doing this, and he wouldn't thank her for spying on him. She turned away, but a sudden thought made her stop and look at the photo again.

The girl had auburn hair and a familiar smile. This wasn't a girlfriend; this was *family.* Jax said Riley had no living rela-tives, but this girl was someone he'd been close to, someone he still missed, someone whose picture he cherished. A sister, most likely. Evangeline wished she had a picture of *her* sister.

With sudden resolve, she plucked the hair from his comb, pushed it into a different pocket, and left the house.

Back in Mrs. Unger's kitchen, she filled a metal baking pan with water, carried it to the table, and cast Jax's hair into it. While she waited for the water to grow still, she located saffron and put a few silky strands on her tongue to dissolve.

She closed her eyes and recited the words of the incantation in the old language.

At first, when she opened her eyes, all she could see on the surface of the water was a reflection of the ceiling light above. Whispering the words of the spell, she leaned closer. The reflection wavered, and an image of Jax appeared. He was riding a bicycle—not his regular bike, but a very fancy one. Evangeline's relief was quickly replaced by annoyance. She'd been worried about him, and he was fine. He hadn't returned last night because in the seven days between her existence, he'd found something better to do.

Evangeline blinked to clear the image, and the pan of water returned to its normal state. Jax was perfectly safe, and Riley probably was, too. There was no reason to scry for him.

If she was smart, she'd stop now.

Biting her lip, Evangeline plucked Jax's hairs out of the water and put the other ones in their place. She shook a few more threads of saffron out of the spice jar, laid them on her tongue, and repeated the incantation for the spell. It wasn't very long before another image appeared in the water.

Riley was leaning against the side of Black-Haired Girl's car. She had the roof up to protect the vehicle from the weather, but neither of them seemed to mind standing in the rain themselves. They were talking intently, and Riley slicked back his wet hair, looking worried. Black-Haired Girl smiled up at him, nudging him with an elbow. He relaxed a bit and grinned at her.

Evangeline splashed the water with her fingers, obliterating the image.

Riley was on a date, and Jax had gotten a new bike. How nice that they enjoyed such Normal lives.

She picked up the pan of water and threw it across the room into the sink. Water flew everywhere, and the pan hit the sink so hard that plates rattled in the cabinets.

When the doorbell rang a couple of hours later, Evangeline knew who it was. Only one person had the nerve to march up the front steps and press the button like that, over and over. When she didn't answer, he started pounding. "Evangeline? Are you in there? I know you're mad at me, but you've got to let me know you're okay." More pounding. "Evangeline?"

Finally she gave up and opened the door.

Jax exhaled with relief. "Look, you have every right to be angry, but I didn't mean to leave you alone last night." He rubbed his hand against his face, wiping off the misty rain. "Can I come in and explain?"

"No."

"Will you come out?"

"No."

"I'm sorry," he began again.

"Jax." She gripped the doorknob tightly, steeling herself. "I want you to leave me alone. No more messages or gifts. No lawn parties, no electricity. Just stop."

He wilted. Evangeline bit her lip. It wasn't his fault, and she owed him an explanation. "Your life goes by so fast for me," she said. "I only catch glimpses of it, and I can't participate."

"Oka-a-ay," he said, his brow furrowed. "But I don't understand why we can't be friends."

"Because it *hurts*, Jax."

She saw his eyes widen in understanding. His hands floundered, as if he were trying to come up with a response. Instead, he took a step backward and down, off the front stoop.

Evangeline closed the door.

26

BY FRIDAY AFTERNOON, Jax had taken to stabbing his math book with the tip of his father's dagger. That would make *two* ruined textbooks he had to turn in, but he had bigger things to worry about than the disapproval of his science and math teachers.

The Donovans hadn't been in school on Thursday or Friday. Jax should have been relieved. *They're probably on the lam, and they'll never be back.* But their absence made him nervous, as if losing track of them were dangerous.

Billy, on the other hand, was in his face every day. "You're skeeving me out," Jax complained.

"That's what everybody says about you," Billy retorted.

Across the aisle in science class, Giana hunched in her seat. She hadn't hissed any insults or tried to trip him since their last encounter. Jax ignored her. He couldn't believe he used to want to talk to her. She was mean and a bully and a coward. *Giana* wouldn't have had the guts to stand up to an armed bank robber.

Which made the seat behind Jax seem even emptier.

Billy lowered his voice. "Enzo's telling everyone you put a spell on him."

"Yeah. I'm a witch," Jax whispered. "You got me."

"Wish it was true, dude. 'Cause that would be cool."

Alone at home with Riley still gone, Jax considered getting a pair of handcuffs and inviting Billy to spend the night next Wednesday. Then he stabbed the algebra book again. What if he handcuffed himself to Evangeline? Could he pull her into Thursday? Or would she yank him forward seven days and into the next Grunsday?

It was worth a shot. But she'd told him to leave her alone. This time Jax stabbed the cover of the math book so hard, the dagger stood upright, quivering.

The front door burst open, and Riley and the Crandalls spilled into the living room, laughing and carting in rifles as if they'd just returned from a hunting trip. Thinking about Terrance's gun, Jax's stomach turned over.

That gun was for you, Thomas had said.

They seemed oblivious to Jax, who watched for a moment before calling out, "Was it a successful mission?"

"Yeah," Riley answered. "Everything okay here?"

"Never better," Jax grunted. Terrance, he'd discovered from online news, was behind bars. Authorities were "puzzled" by the circumstances of the robbery but didn't plan on letting their suspect go anytime soon.

Jax wondered what made his guardian any different from Terrance. "Did you make your first kill?" he asked.

Riley stared at him. "What?"

A.J. and his father exchanged glances.

"Did you make your first kill?" Jax repeated. "Miller didn't think you'd do it."

Miller didn't think you'd do it. Jax saw Riley mouth the words silently. Then he whipped his phone out of his back pocket. "You little sneak," Riley said, thumbing keys on the phone to find his text messages.

Mr. Crandall clapped Riley on the shoulder. "Told you! Having an inquisitor in the house is going to give you some trouble."

Riley stabbed at the buttons on his phone, probably deleting messages.

"Nobody got killed," Mr. Crandall assured Jax.

"Where's Deidre?" Jax demanded. "Why did you need all the guns? Why does she even have so many?"

"Deidre's back at college," Riley said. "And the rest is none of your business."

"Tell him, son," Mr. Crandall said to Riley. "This would go a lot easier if you'd accept that the boy belongs with us." Pushing A.J. toward the door, Mr. Crandall called to Jax, "Keep at it. I know talent when I see it."

Jax and Riley looked at each other warily. Then Riley grabbed his duffel bag, brushed past Jax, and headed upstairs.

Jax wrestled his father's honor blade out of the math

book. *His* honor blade. If Melinda was right, he needed to think of it as *his* to make it work for him.

"So, what does *she* have to say this week?"

Riley, coming back down the stairs, asked the question with a casual air, as if he didn't care, but Jax wasn't fooled. "Nothing," Jax said. "She wants me to leave her alone. She says making friends *hurts*."

Riley stiffened. "I warned you."

"Why does she have to live like that?" Jax demanded. When Riley didn't answer, he added, "Do you want me to keeping snooping on my own?"

"She's an Emrys." Riley sat on the edge of Jax's desk. "Merlin Emrys cast the spell that created Grunsday. He collaborated with Niviane and Arthur, betraying his own people and going willingly into imprisonment with them. But fifteen hundred years is a long time for a spell to last, unless it's carried by a bloodline. The Emrys family keeps the spell active, and if they die out, the alternate time-line will pop out of existence." Riley snapped his fingers. "Along with all the people trapped inside."

Jax flinched, imagining the eighth day popping like a soap bubble.

Riley pointed next door. "This girl's father plotted to break the spell. He joined up with some very bad Kin clans, but he was stopped before he could act."

"Stopped?" Jax asked suspiciously. "You mean he was killed."

Riley nodded. "Even without him, his allies kept trying. Twenty years ago, a Kin lord attempted to alter the Grunsday spell, and the magical backwash from his failure devastated a Midwestern town. An entire housing community was blown apart between Wednesday and Thursday—dozens killed. It was blamed on a freak midnight tornado. After that, my father volunteered to help keep the remaining Emrys heirs under protective custody."

"So Evangeline isn't the only one left?"

"There's at least one more. It's not my business to know who or where. But remember how I was gone your first Grunsday? I was tracking down a Kin man who'd been offering to sell information about a hidden Emrys heir. Turns out he was a scam artist. He knew nothing."

"You're not really Evangeline's jailer," Jax said. "You're her *guardian* too."

Riley shrugged. "From her perspective, it probably looks like the same thing. My family's been watching over her since before I was born, but from a distance. I'm the one who decided to move next door."

"Why?" Jax asked.

"Because when you're the only person left to guard something important, you don't want it let out of your sight." Riley met Jax's eyes. "When your dad showed up here, I was worried, but it turned out he only wanted to help."

"My dad . . . ?"

"He was hired to find her and decided *not* to complete

his end of the bargain. His employer was a Kin lord named Wylit—the same one who blew up that town. Wylit's vassals have been hunting for Evangeline for years, thinking she'll help them break the spell. Your father knew *my* father, from long ago, and tracked *me* down using the same talent you have. He was trying to do the right thing."

Jax swallowed hard. Every time Riley told him something about his father, a little piece of his old life was hacked away. This time Jax felt like he'd gotten a chunk back. His father had chosen the side *protecting* Evangeline.

"Would it be such a bad thing?" Jax asked. "For the spell to be broken? To let Evangeline and her people live in all the days of the week?"

"Yes," Riley said grimly. "You wouldn't want to turn Wylit and some of these other Kin loose on the world. As for Evangeline, I'm sure you don't have any idea how strong she really is, or *could* be, if trained by the right people. Or by the *wrong* people."

Jax shook his head, not believing it. He'd never seen her show any magical talent. She'd attacked him with *pepper spray*. With the safety lock on.

But Riley continued. "Your dad knew it was dangerous to cross Wylit. I think he planned to move across the country, maybe change your family name like I did. Asking me to look out for you was a backup plan. I wouldn't have refused him in any case, but he did me a big favor."

"What did he do?"

"Wylit's a slippery one, Jax. *My* father failed to catch him, and so did the Morgans, the Dulacs, and every other clan that tried. But your dad hooked up with them some-how—worked for Wylit's vassals and then helped me plant a spy among them. That's what *I* got out of the deal, and *I swear*, I've been trying to do right by you ever since."

"Then tell me where you went this week," Jax said.

Riley sighed. "To convince a pair of Kin men to move from the place where they've been hiding for the past forty years. I had warning their location had been discov-ered and Wylit's vassals were coming for them. But you read that on my phone, didn't you?"

"The weapons were in case the other guys got there first?"

"Mostly. But these Kin of the Taliesin clan are the ones who hid Evangeline and probably know where the rest of her family is. They've sort of been allies with our side all along, but they've never been what you'd call *friendly*. If they weren't willing to cooperate, or if they were able to resist my commands, things could've gotten . . . rough."

"You didn't—"

"No, we didn't," Riley said. "Deidre suggested moving them to her college campus, where she could guarantee there were no Kin and no Transitioners other than herself present. They agreed."

Jax frowned. "Is Evangeline safe now?"

Riley ran a hand through his hair. "I'm not satisfied.

I want to look for another hiding place. Then I'll have to convince her to move. And you realize, Jax—I'll move, too. I go where she goes."

"What about me?"

"Nothing's changed. I want to put you back with your relatives."

Jax hurled his dagger into his textbook again. Riley jumped off the desk, startled. "You're wrong," Jax said. "*I've* changed."

On Saturday morning, Jax took a long bike ride. He used his own bike. He'd left the stolen one at the local police station on Grunsday evening with the address of the owner attached. *Sorry*, he'd written on the note.

Riley had no idea Jax had been kidnapped. Jax had made it to his lesson with Melinda on time, and no one except Evangeline knew he'd been gone at all. And she clearly wouldn't be telling anyone.

Pedaling aimlessly through town, Jax tried to figure out what he wanted to do now. Mostly, he kept thinking of the things he didn't want to do.

He no longer wanted to live with Naomi. Living among Normals no longer seemed as safe as it used to. When Terrance had abducted Jax, it had been Riley and the Crandalls he'd hoped would save him, and the Donovans who actually had.

He didn't want to swear loyalty to Riley, either. Jax had grown to like him better and admitted there might even be things to admire in him. However, Jax didn't want to be part of Riley's "chain of command."

Finally, he didn't want to give up on Evangeline. He'd never met anyone who needed a friend more than she did, whether it hurt or not. If Riley was going to move her, Jax wanted to go too. If she had to be imprisoned for her own safety, then darn it, Jax wanted to make sure she had at least one other person to talk to. The question was whether Riley would let him come, if Jax wasn't one of his vassals. He apparently confided in Deidre, and she wasn't a vassal. But she had other talents Riley valued.

Jax grinned, leaned back on his seat, and let the bike coast.

Jax had a talent too.

That afternoon, he made a list of the requirements for a "safe house" for Evangeline and had a very good idea. What if they hid her in a boarding school? She liked books. Well, she could have a whole library for herself. And if she hated her eighties clothing, she could "borrow" more modern ones from other girls. Missing food would be blamed on the students, and what school wouldn't love to have a resident ghost? From the little Jax knew about Evangeline, he couldn't think of any circumstances for hiding her she'd find more tolerable.

Well, besides coming out of hiding altogether, of course.

He sat down in front of the computer, laid his dagger beside the keyboard, and whispered one of Melinda's meditation chants to harness his talent. By the time Riley came home from work, Jax hoped to have a list of schools and a well-thought-out argument to counter any objections.

He was only beginning his search when the front door opened and Michael Donovan walked in.

27

JAX STOOD UP so fast, he knocked the chair over. "What're you doing here?"

"Is that any way to greet a friend?" Donovan asked cheerfully, setting a pet carrier on the coffee table.

"How'd you find me?"

"Smelled you out, boy!" Donovan grinned. "I knew you didn't live where we left you. We just sniffed around the neighboring towns till we found you. How else was I going to deliver your eighth-day cat?"

Sniffed? Like dogs? Jax stared at the man, aghast, then bent down and peered inside the cat carrier.

It was empty.

"Well, it's not there *now*," said Donovan. "Won't be back till the eighth day."

Just as Jax opened his mouth to ask how dumb Donovan thought he was, his phone rang. *Oh, no!* Jax knew who it was before he picked up the phone. "Yeah?"

"Melinda called," said Riley. "We've got Transitioners in town. I'm on my way, and so is A.J.'s mom." Jax stared across the room at Donovan, and Riley demanded, "Jax, do you hear me?"

"Yeah" was all Jax could say.

"It's probably nothing—people passing through who don't know we're here. But if you see anybody, you run. You hear me?" The sound of the motorcycle drowned out Riley's voice.

Jax thumbed the phone off. "You have to get out of here."

Donovan's grin never wavered. "But we haven't discussed a price for the cat."

Jax picked up the carrier and tossed it at him. "I mean it! People are coming, and they won't be happy to see you." If Riley found this man in the house, he might make his first kill after all. And it would probably be *Jax*.

"Smells like somebody important lives here, Dad. No relation of his, though."

Jax gasped to see Thomas walk down the stairs from the second floor. "How'd you get in here? What were you doing upstairs?" Then, with greater alarm: "Where's Tegan?"

"Takin' a look outside." Thomas sauntered into the kitchen and opened the refrigerator door. "Got anything to eat?"

Jax chased after him and, spotting the kitty jar on

the kitchen counter, had an inspiration. "Here's cash." He pulled out a wad of crumpled bills and shoved it at Thomas. "Take your 'cat' and get out of this house! Get out of this town!"

"Not a nice welcome for people who saved your life," Donovan commented.

"I'm trying to save *your* lives now!" Jax sprinted through the house and out the front door to see what Tegan was up to.

He found her standing in the yard, sniffing the air. "Tegan!" He grabbed her by the arm. "You guys set off a security shield, and people are coming. You have to leave *quickly*!"

Her eyes narrowed. "A security shield?"

The squeal of tires a block away made them both turn around. Michael and Thomas were just leaving the house, Thomas counting the cash and Michael holding the cat carrier under his arm. "Scatter," Tegan said.

Jax had been shouting at them for the last minute and a half, but Tegan's one word sent them running. Thomas scrambled over the fence at the back of the property, while his father made a sharp left turn, crossed the street, and walked between two neighbors' houses. When Jax turned around, Tegan was gone.

Mrs. Crandall's car jumped the curb pulling up in front of Riley's house. The driver's door flew open, and Mrs. Crandall climbed out. She stalked toward Jax, looking left and right. Mr. Blum, who was fertilizing his lawn, eyed her curiously.

"See anybody, Jax?" Mrs. Crandall called out.

Jax remembered her talent. "No strangers." That was the literal truth. She gave him a sharp look, but the approach of Riley's motorcycle distracted her. She lifted an arm and drew a circle in the air with her finger. Riley acknowledged by raising a hand, then turned off to circle the block. Mrs. Crandall turned off the ignition in her car. "Wait inside, Jax."

Jax returned to the house and released his breath in a gush. Was the Donovan talent *smelling* people out? That was disgusting! And what had Thomas been doing upstairs? Jax took the stairs two at a time. At the back of the second floor, he found a window open, and when he stuck his head out, he saw the shed directly below. *Well, that's how he got in.* Jax shoved the window closed and locked it.

He took a look around Riley's room, but there was no way for Jax to tell if anything was missing. On his way out, he glanced at the photograph of the girl tucked into Riley's mirror. *Is that his dead sister?* With that reminder of what was at stake, Jax went downstairs to wait.

Later, Jax looked Riley straight in the eye and said, "I went out to look around and didn't see anybody who didn't belong here. Then Mrs. Crandall drove up, and she told me to stay inside."

He braced for Riley's command: *I order you to tell me the truth.* But it didn't come. "Melinda says these people have passed through her net before. She thinks they might be loners who live not far from here and occasionally shop at the Walmart or get off the highway for gas."

Jax barely kept his mouth from dropping open. *Of course* Melinda had detected the Donovans before. They probably lived only ten miles away. Jax could have mentioned them at any time after discovering he had classmates who were Transitioners, and Riley wouldn't have been surprised. He wouldn't have had to say a word about being kidnapped.

But he *hadn't* mentioned them to Riley, and now he'd told an outright lie. If he changed his story and confessed, Riley would lose all trust in him. And if Riley didn't trust him, he wouldn't take Jax with him when he moved Evangeline. Jax would end up back at Naomi's, living every Grunsday by himself.

He was going to have to stick with his lie and hope he'd seen the last of the Donovans. He'd given them money, which was all they cared about. There was no reason for them to come back to this house. Jax had nothing more to offer.

"So we're good?" he asked in what he hoped was an innocent voice.

"I guess so," Riley said, as if trying to convince himself, but he still looked worried. "Doesn't hurt to be cautious, though."

Riley called in sick to work on Monday to keep a watch on the house next door and almost lost his job for taking another day off. He didn't exactly command his boss not to fire him, but Jax heard him say over the phone, "Have a little sympathy." Jax shivered. As Melinda had predicted, he was getting a feel for when Riley was using his talent.

Jax went to school for his final exams. To his relief, the Donovans didn't turn up.

"Maybe they moved," one of the kids said.

"I hope they enjoy repeating seventh grade in their new school," Miss Cassidy grumbled. But when she picked the blank test off Tegan's desk, Jax heard her add, "It's a shame. *She* had potential."

That evening the doorbell rang, and Jax froze, picturing the Donovan trio and possibly their cat carrier. When Riley opened the door to Mr. and Mrs. Crandall instead, Jax felt light-headed with relief. Riley, however, looked grim.

Mr. Crandall cleared his throat. "We request a formal audience."

"Yeah, I was expecting this." Riley held the door open wide.

Rather stiffly, the Crandalls each produced their honor blades and laid them on the coffee table before sitting on the sofa. For a moment, Jax thought they were withdrawing their allegiance, but when Riley laid his knife beside theirs, Jax decided it was some weird ritual. Okay, he could play along. He laid his dagger on the table as well. Mrs. Crandall gave him a nod of approval.

Mr. Crandall cleared his throat. "Saturday," he began.

"Was a false alarm," Riley finished.

"We were unprepared and undermanned."

"It was a false alarm," Riley repeated. "Just some random Transitioners. And I spoke to Miller. He's heard nothing."

"Miller may not know everything," Mrs. Crandall said. "And Arnie's right. We didn't have enough people to cover this house."

"I was here within three minutes of Melinda's call."

"A lot can happen in three minutes," Mr. Crandall said. "And you always assume *she'll* be the target, but it could just as easily be you."

"It's not your fault, Riley," Mrs. Crandall assured him. "You have to go to work. We all have to work and pay the bills. The problem is there's too few of us."

"You're not just our liege lord. You're like a son to us. Which is why we want to ask you if you've considered the Morgans' offer. They've shielded you from the Dulacs all these years, never letting on that you were still alive, and you know it's because they always expected you and Deidre to end up together."

"But they're wrong," Riley said quietly. "I have no interest in getting engaged to Deidre."

Jax sucked in his breath. Riley—get engaged to marry the heavily armed Deidre? The first time Riley forgot to bring home groceries, she'd shoot him!

"A family connection wouldn't be enough to satisfy Deidre's mother anyway," Riley went on. "Sheila Morgan's going to expect me to swear my loyalty to her. I'd have to turn over my vassals. Is that what you want, Arnie, to serve the Morgans?"

"You know I don't," Mr. Crandall said stiffly, "but I also don't want to see you killed trying to protect the Emrys girl. The Morgans have the organization, the weaponry, and the manpower to do this job right. And they could protect *you*. You could come out of hiding."

"I don't want their protection."

"Riley—"

"Deidre and I have been friends since we were kids. Our families have been allies since *the beginning*. If that's not good enough for the Morgans, I'll make do without their help." Riley picked up his honor blade and stabbed it directly into the coffee table. The Crandalls fell silent. "We stick to the plan: find a safe house for Evangeline Emrys and move her there. That's it."

28

ON GRUNSDAY, Jax awoke knowing Evangeline was present next door and he was supposed to leave her alone. "Should we hook up her generator anyway?" he asked Riley, handing him the information on boarding schools he'd compiled.

"No." Riley scanned the pages. Surprisingly, he'd liked Jax's idea. "She's fine. We're going to have to uproot her next Grunsday. Let's not make her mad at us today."

Jax nodded reluctantly. He hated knowing she was alone over there, but he was anxious to see her moved. The Donovans were probably long gone, especially if Terrance had given the police their descriptions. Jax didn't expect them to come back, but the sooner he, Riley, and Evangeline were out of here, the better.

That afternoon at Jax's weekly lesson, Melinda wanted to work on his mental defenses. "Defend against my talent," she instructed him.

"But you can't—" Jax paused, not wanting to insult her. Melinda was a *sensitive*. She couldn't *do* anything to him.

"You're feeling guilty," Melinda said. "Over something you did wrong and lied about."

Jax realized she was reading his emotions as easily as looking through a book. Instinctively, he slammed the book closed on her.

Melinda smiled. "That's more like it. Let's try that again."

Defending his mind against this gentle woman was harder than he could have guessed, but Jax rose to the challenge. He was afraid of what she might see in him.

"You're strong for someone so recently turned," Melinda said when he flopped over on her couch, feeling wrung out like an old sponge. She rumpled his hair fondly. "Your father would've been proud of you."

Really? It was still hard to reconcile his dad with all of this. "So, he could do what I do?" Jax asked.

"Talent is inherited just like eye and hair color. That said, talents usually run stronger in one gender than another. Female sensitives are more talented than males, and the reverse is true for inquisitors. But you can get your talent from either parent."

Jax looked at his wrist. "You need the right mark for it to work, though."

"We don't mark our children until they demonstrate a

hint of talent. Or we take them to a sensitive who can *read* talent. In your case, you only had one Transitioner parent. Riley and A.J. knew how to mark you."

"So your kids will all be sensitives," Jax concluded. "Like you."

"If they transition at all." She sighed. "There's a burden in this life that will rob them of their innocence. Riley grew up alone, trying to guard that girl and worrying about his vassals, even though *we* were the adults. He refused to live in the same house with the Crandalls because he was afraid of getting them killed. And we all uprooted our lives to move here after his family was assassinated—to help hide him *and* the girl—away from other Transitioner clans and everyone we used to know. To be honest, I hope my children take after their father and never need to learn about magic *or* the eighth day."

Jax wondered if his father had felt the same way. He turned his honor blade over and over in his hands, thinking about it. "If it's so important to carry your blade," he asked suddenly, "why didn't I ever see my father wearing this one?"

"A lot of Transitioners prefer to conceal them. It alarms Normals, seeing somebody walk around with a dagger. You've never noticed mine, have you?" Melinda ran her hand down the leg of her jeans, revealing the outline of a sheath beneath the denim.

But Jax shook his head. "Riley said Dad knew he was

in danger. So if your dagger can make your magic stronger, why didn't he have it with him when he . . . ?"

"Didn't he?" Melinda looked startled. "I just assumed the blade was recovered from—" *His body.* She cut herself off and didn't say it.

Jax shook his head miserably.

"Maybe I misread this." Melinda took the dagger from his hands and examined it again. "I did think it strange that he'd used it so little, but maybe this wasn't his primary blade. Maybe this was one he had made a few years ago and used just enough to get it ready."

"Ready for what?"

"Ready for you, Jax." She handed it back, and her eyes were filled with tears. "He probably meant to give this blade to *you* when—if—you transitioned."

She insisted on feeding him dinner, and Jax didn't argue. While they ate, he asked her to explain the system of liege lords and vassals. He already understood the *vassal* part. But he wanted to know what responsibilities the liege lord had. "I once heard A.J. say Riley wasn't allowed to let him starve."

"There doesn't seem to be much danger of that! But a liege lord is obligated to defend his vassals and provide for them in times of adversity. For instance, if the Crandalls lost their jobs or their house, Riley is supposed to take care of them."

"He can't afford to do that." Riley could barely take care of himself.

"No," Melinda agreed. "Riley is not in a good position to fulfill his obligations. I don't think either the Crandalls or I would expect Riley to provide us with a new home or job, but those are the old rules—and a lot of Transitioners still follow them."

"And if Riley swore his loyalty to someone else . . ."

Melinda nodded solemnly. "You've heard about the Morgans, I guess. Yes, if Riley swore allegiance to Sheila Morgan, he wouldn't be permitted to keep his own vassals. We'd be turned over to her. The Morgans would be obligated to protect Riley from his enemies, which is not a bad thing. To some extent, I trust the Morgans. They helped us cover the fact that Riley survived the bombing when it first happened, and they've kept the secret all these years." Melinda looked Jax in the eye. "But I wouldn't be happy with Sheila Morgan as my liege. She's a mercenary, and her actions are usually self-serving. If she wants Riley to marry her daughter, it's for the prestige of his name and because his talent is handy in combat. She'd like to have grandchildren with the voice of command."

Jax felt a new sympathy for Riley when he got home that evening and found him repairing strings on a guitar. Jax watched for a moment and then commented, "Never saw you with that before."

"It belonged to my sister, Alanna." Riley picked up the guitar and strummed the beginning chords of "Stairway to Heaven." Or tried to.

"You suck, dude," said Jax.

"Yeah, I know."

It was a long evening—no television, no computer, and almost no conversation. Jax went through his school papers and notebooks. Riley fooled around with the guitar, playing melancholy tunes badly. Jax would've gone to bed early to escape Riley's poor excuse for music, but he was waiting for midnight. It looked like Riley was, too, and probably for the same reason. While *she* was present next door, they kept vigil.

The explosion at eleven thirty jolted them to their feet.

Riley ran outside with Jax on his heels. Over the rooftops of neighboring houses, the sky glowed red.

The radio clipped to Riley's belt squealed. "Emergency! Emergency!"

He fumbled it free, nearly dropping it. "Is that you, Melinda? Over."

Melinda didn't wait for Riley's "over" signal. Her cries overlapped his and were partly cut off by his transmission. "The whole back half of the house's on fire!" she screamed. "My family's in here!"

Jax's flesh broke out in goose bumps. Melinda's house was on fire, and she couldn't get her husband and kids out because *they weren't there on Grunsday.*

"I'm coming!" Riley shouted into the radio, even though Melinda was screaming and couldn't hear him. He turned to Jax. "Get Evangeline out of that house."

"This is a trap," Jax said hoarsely. *And I'm to blame. Oh crap, oh crap, I'm to blame.*

"I have to go anyway," Riley replied.

Jax shuddered and nodded.

"Take her somewhere safe before midnight. And give her this." Riley unbuckled the knife sheath from around his waist and handed it to Jax, belt and all.

His honor blade? "Are you sure?"

"It's all I have to give her. Now, go!" Riley threw open the shed and disappeared inside. A second later, the motorcycle roared to life, and Riley peeled out—without a helmet, without any help, to fight a fire and try to save children he couldn't carry out of the house.

Jax took only a second to wallow in fear for Melinda and her kids, and then he pelted across the yard to warn Evangeline.

29

EVANGELINE HAD SPENT her entire day poring over the local geography books and taking notes. Trains, she concluded, were not a good idea. She'd have to find one that was stopped and taking on passengers at midnight on Wednesday for her to get on during the eighth day—and unless it was stopped somewhere else at the same time the following week, she'd probably end up stuck aboard it.

A stolen car would be better—except she didn't know how to drive, and even Jax would guess what she was planning if she asked him for a driver's manual.

Then she remembered. She wasn't talking to Jax anymore.

She paused and glanced at the living-room window that faced the neighboring house. If she ran away from here, Riley Pendragon would probably come looking for her. *How worried should I be?* Her spell-casting talent gave her a wide range of magical options for eluding him and defending herself, while his voice of command would work only if he caught her.

She didn't know where she wanted to go, or how to begin looking for Addie and Elliot. She only knew she needed to get out of this house before she went mad.

The dam is broken, she thought. *And there's no stopping the water now.*

An explosion rattled all the windows of the house. For a brief second, she wondered if she'd inadvertently cast a spell while thinking about dams bursting. Then she jumped to her feet and threw open the living-room curtains. There—emanating from somewhere near the center of town—an unnatural redness lit the sky.

Evangeline whipped around and ran into the hall. She opened the front door in time to see Riley take off on his motorcycle, while Jax sprinted up the front steps of her house. She waved him inside, and his face showed relief that she wasn't going to insist he leave her alone *now.* "What's happening?"

"House fire," Jax gasped. "But I think it's a distraction, to get Riley out of the way. It was one of his vassals—and her kids are in danger. He had to go—"

"Of course he did," she said. A vassal came first.

"He said to give you this and for me to get you out of here." Jax thrust a leather sheath into her hands, the belt still attached.

Her heart thudded when she realized she was holding Riley's honor blade. Things must be serious for him to send her this. "All right, let's go."

"I know it's close to midnight," Jax said, "but my friend Billy's house is on the next block. You'll be safe there."

They made it as far as the sidewalk when Evangeline saw the vehicles converging on them from two different directions, driving with their lights off. Jax spotted them too. He grabbed her hand, yanked her around the corner of the house, and stopped dead. Dark shapes swarmed over the fence behind the houses.

"Back in the house," Evangeline said. "It's protected."

"Protected how?" But he let her pull him up the front steps. The vehicles screeched to a stop outside the house. Evangeline slammed the door shut and darted into the hallway next to the stairs, where she could see the front and back doors simultaneously. Jax pressed himself against the wall beside her.

The back door was the first one they tried. Evangeline heard the roar of pain as someone burned his hand on the doorknob. The windows proved a similar barrier. Dark shapes appeared outside the glass frames, one by one, then backed off.

"What's doing that?" Jax asked.

"My spell," she said. "No harm shall enter that way." Nevertheless, her heart pounded. The intruders couldn't come in, but they could force her out.

They knew it too. The assault on windows and doors stopped, but through the front door sidelight, Evangeline saw someone walk up the steps. She heard the ominous sound of a metal can hitting the concrete stoop outside.

"Daughter of the Kin!" a man's voice boomed. "We have not come to harm you."

A lie. Otherwise her spell would not have repelled them.

"We require you to come out and identify yourself. If you are who I believe you are, we have a great honor to bestow on you. If we are mistaken, we shall leave you in peace."

But they weren't mistaken.

"Refusing is not an option." Evangeline heard the rattle of the metal can again and the sloshing of liquid as the man picked it up and shook it. She didn't need a glimpse of it through the sidelight to know it was a container of gasoline.

No harm could enter through the windows or doors, but flames could consume the house, burning Jax alive along with Mrs. Unger, who'd reappear in her bed a few minutes from now. And Evangeline might not be around long enough to feel the flames, but she'd end up dead just the same.

"You have one minute to come out," the man called.

Jax stared at Evangeline. "What'll we do?"

She searched his face. He was as scared as she was. She could feel him shaking. But his eyes were flinty and his mouth set with anger.

"We're going to cooperate until we see a chance to get away from them," she said. "Turn around." When he just blinked at her, she made a twirly motion with her finger, and he turned. Then she pulled her arms out of the sleeves of her blouse. Throwing the belt for Riley's sheath over her right

214

shoulder and under her left arm, she buckled it into place. It was uncomfortable, but the dagger lay near her heart, and she could reach down the neck of her blouse to grab it. Then she put her arms into her sleeves again and surveyed her reflection in the hall mirror. Finally, a useful purpose for her nineteen-eighties clothes! The blouse was loose and boxy, with sleeves that draped from wrist to shoulder. Its diagonal stripes hid any bulges.

"Girl, show yourself!" the voice bellowed from outside.

Any second now, they'd torch the house. Evangeline looked at Jax and realized they'd kill him as soon as they had her in their grasp. He was superfluous. Her heart lurched. Her brother and sister had been depending on her, and she'd failed them long ago. She'd allowed them to be taken from her.

That wasn't going to happen to Jax.

She grabbed his arm. "Swear to me. If you're my vassal, they'll honor my right to protect you."

His eyebrows knit together, but he didn't argue. "Tell me how."

"On your knees with your dagger. Swear on your bloodline. The words don't matter. Just *mean* them."

Jax pulled out his blade and dropped to his knees. He held the dagger up like he was ordering a cavalry charge, but there was no time to correct him on his form. "I swear, on the Aubrey bloodline, my loyalty and service to you, Evangeline Emrys."

"I accept you," she said. Grabbing his face in both her

hands, she kissed his forehead, then strode down the hall to open the front door. The man outside towered over her by a foot and was three of her in width. He wore a dark suit, and his sand-colored hair was cropped very close to his scalp.

Evangeline recognized him, even though he'd been no older than twenty when she'd met him thirty-five years ago. His eyes lit in recognition, too. She had aged only five years.

John Balin.

Balin was a Transitioner, vassal to the Kin lord Myrddin Wylit. Evangeline's father had distrusted all Transitioners and had protested strongly over including Balin in their plans. But Wylit had insisted, and apparently he'd been too important an ally to cross.

At the age of eleven, Evangeline had dimly understood that. But she'd also recognized insanity when she saw it. Every time Wylit came to the house with his Transitioner vassal, she'd taken Addie and Elliot and gotten out of his way. Quickly.

"Lady Emrys," Balin said, "Lord Wylit will be very pleased we've found you at last."

"Call off your men and back away," she said, trying to summon the arrogance of a high-ranking Kin lady. *Because that's what I am.* "I'm coming out, but if you touch me or my vassal, your lord will hear of it."

He honored tradition and her right to defend a vassal, just as she'd hoped he would. "I give you my word. You and your vassal have safe passage."

Evangeline kept her head high and opened the screen

door. Three vehicles were parked in the street. One of them was strangely long and boxy. Six or seven men waited on the sidewalk, all dressed in dark clothes.

Jax left the house behind her, his hands held up in a gesture of surrender. But that didn't stop someone from leaping off the roof overhanging Mrs. Unger's stoop to knock him down. They tumbled off the steps together on the side that had no railing, and before Evangeline could protest, Jax was in the hands of a man with carroty hair and a boy of similar coloring. They thrust him to his knees when he tried to stand, twisting his arms behind his back. A second boy—no, a girl— darted forward, snatched a phone from Jax's back pocket, and tossed it aside.

"Get off me!" Jax shouted.

"Now, Jax," said the man cheerfully. "We're gettin' you out of harm's way."

Evangeline clenched her fists. She was outnumbered and bluffing, but she turned a gaze of fury on Balin. "I see your word is worthless."

"He won't be harmed," Balin assured her. "I'll bring him with us."

"We weren't paid for Jax," the girl said, and the carroty-haired man called out, "That wasn't part of the deal. He stays here."

"Don't do me any favors," snarled Jax.

"Lady Emrys, come." Balin motioned her forward, ignoring the outraged exchanges between Jax and the people holding him. Then Evangeline saw the object being lifted out of the back of the long vehicle.

Her heart flopped over. "No."

"This is how it's done," he said. "For you, it will last no more than a minute."

Every pretense of calm and coolness deserted her. "No!" She fumbled at the neck of her blouse for the dagger.

Two men came at her from either side, catching her hands and feet and lifting her off the ground. She shrieked and thrashed, but their hands were like iron.

Behind her, Jax yelled, "What're you doing? No! Don't put her in there!"

A man standing at the back of the hearse opened the lid of the casket. "Jax!" Evangeline screamed, knowing he couldn't help her and calling for him anyway. Her captors swung her over the yawning coffin and let go. She hit the silk-lined interior hard enough to knock the breath out of her.

Then the coffin lid dropped closed.

30

JAX DIDN'T KNOW what was worse: hearing Evangeline scream his name as they dumped her into the coffin or knowing he was failing his oath within seconds of making it. "Let her out of there!" he shouted.

"They aren't hurtin' her." Donovan leaned down to say this in his ear, and Jax pushed off his knees with all his strength. The top of his head smashed Donovan in the nose. Jax hurled his body sideways, knocking Thomas off balance, and broke away.

He knew he was going to be in trouble once he got to the brutes who'd thrown Evangeline into the casket, although that didn't stop him from hurtling toward them. At the last second, the man with the gasoline can whistled sharply, and the men stepped out of Jax's path.

He thudded against the side of the casket and heaved the lid up.

The coffin was empty.

The pit bull started barking.

"Hey!" The dog's owner shoved his screen door open and started down his front steps wearing only a T-shirt and boxer shorts. "What's going on? Did something happen to Mrs. Unger?"

A hand grabbed Jax by the scruff of the neck and hauled him around the side of the hearse. Any thought of calling for help was squelched by the muzzle of a gun pressed against his ear and the cold, dark gaze of Gasoline Guy. Jax swallowed hard and stood very still.

One of the men left the casket to cross the street and distract the neighbor. "No need for alarm, sir. We have the wrong address. But what do you think *that* is?" He pointed at the red glow in the sky, and as if on cue, the fire station siren wailed across town.

Meanwhile, the coffin was lifted into the rear compartment of the hearse. Understanding hit Jax like a smack across the face. The coffin was a means to transport Evangeline. These people were using it the way Donovan had used the pet carrier—except Jax was sure there'd never been a cat in that carrier and Evangeline was definitely in the coffin. He could *feel* her there, as if the oath he'd made not two minutes ago bound them like a thread. She was in that casket, but there was no way to get her out until next Grunsday.

Somebody loomed on Jax's left side. "You want me to take this boy out back, John?" *Out back* sounded like a bad place to be, perhaps the last place he'd ever be.

"No. I gave my word I'd bring her vassal along. And look who he is." The first man grabbed Jax's left wrist and yanked it into the air.

"Aubrey. Now that's interesting."

"Get his blade."

Jax didn't fight as they unbuckled his sheath and pushed him into the passenger section of the hearse. If he wanted to stay close to Evangeline, he had to cooperate. And with every fiber of his being, he wanted—*needed*—to go where that casket went.

"We're taking the other kids as well," Gasoline Guy said to the other one.

"You sure you want them?"

"They found the Emrys heir when no one else could. I want them." While the sirens roared and neighbors gathered across the street to look at the glow in the sky, the leader of these thugs walked away from the hearse and approached Michael Donovan.

"Well, Balin, are you satisfied?" Michael asked. He had the same amused lilt in his voice as when he'd called out Terrance at the bank. "You said there'd be a bonus if the Kin girl was the one you were looking for."

"Yes, I did." The man picked up his gasoline can again. "Your family has a valuable talent, Donovan. I'll be recruiting your children for the service of my lord." Then he bashed Michael in the head with the can. Michael went down like a felled tree, and the twins bolted. Thomas shot toward the rear of the house, and Tegan made a dash for Mrs. Unger's open front door.

One of the men reached through the bars of Mrs. Unger's railing and caught Tegan's ankle. She fell face-first across the threshold. He dragged her backward and scooped her under his arm like a football. With a hand over her mouth, he carried her to the hearse and chucked her in through the open door at Jax's feet.

Two others cornered Thomas and herded him toward the hearse. The boy held his arms out to either side in apparent submission. But when he got to the door, Thomas grabbed the frame, thrust himself upward, and scrambled over the top of the vehicle. Gasoline Guy—Balin—reached for him and missed. Jax heard Thomas's footsteps pound across the roof and saw him leap off the other side.

"Go, Tommy, go," shouted Tegan.

The man Balin waved a hand at the driver. "Go—before we have to shoot the bystanders." He slammed the door shut and stalked toward one of the black Land Rovers parked behind the hearse.

As the vehicles pulled away, Jax saw Billy Ramirez running down the street from his house in bare feet, wearing *Lord of the Rings* pajamas. He was looking at the glow in the sky until he spotted the crumpled form in front of Mrs. Unger's, then he diverted to cross the street, cutting in front of the hearse. The driver cursed, turning the wheel and barely missing him.

"Billy, look out," Jax yelled, pressing his face against the window.

Billy saw him and shouted, "Jax, what are you doing in there? Jax!"

The hearse passed him and picked up speed.

"Where are you taking us?" Jax growled at the two men in front, summoning his talent and reaching over the seats to put his hand on one of them.

The guy beside the driver grabbed his wrist and turned around. Jax found himself facing the man who'd offered to take him *out back*. "Your magic won't work on me, inquisitor." His fingers tightened on Jax's arm. "My brother may have promised your liege lady he'd bring you along, but no one said you had to arrive with all your teeth." This guy was younger than the man with the gasoline can, but his eyes were the same cold, dark color, and he had a vicious smile. He shoved Jax backward and cranked up a glass partition between the passenger compartment and the front seats.

Jax stumbled into Tegan, who pushed him away. He pushed her back. "You sold me out!" he yelled. "You sold out my friends! Why? What did I ever do to you?"

"We sold some Kin girl to one of her own kind," Tegan yelled back. "It's got nothing to do with you. It wasn't supposed to hurt anybody."

"Oh, yeah?" Jax dragged her to the window of the hearse. "Do you see that glow in the sky? That's my friend's house on fire. Her kids are trapped inside, and my guardian's trying to get them out." He shook Tegan. "You did that, didn't you? How else did they know to pick her house?"

Tegan wrenched herself loose. "You said there was a security shield in town. I found it. I didn't know they were going to set her house on fire." Her face was flushed. "We're not killers."

"Really? Your dad showed Terrance how to get into Grunsday so he could kidnap kids and kill them when he was done with them. And you sicced these maniacs on Melinda so they could kill her family."

"Shut up!" Tegan hissed.

"But you messed up, didn't you? You did such a good job, they want to keep you."

"Dad and Tommy'll come for me." Tegan retreated across the hearse from Jax and huddled in the opposite corner of the U-shaped bench seat.

"What'd you do it for?" Jax asked bitterly.

"Money."

"A garbage bag full of cash wasn't enough?"

"Dad lost that at the horse races," Tegan said. "And he owed more."

Jax's heart sank into his stomach. He should have known when they took the cash from his household kitty that the

Donovans couldn't hang on to money. They were always going to be scavenging for more. *I led them to Evangeline.*

Tegan confirmed it. "Tommy thought you had the scent of someone powerful on you, so we came to check it out, and I smelled Kin next door. High-ranking Kin. Dad knew about these people who were searching for a high-ranking Kin girl and—" Suddenly, Tegan broke off and glared at him. "Stop it," she said through clenched teeth.

Jax hadn't even realized he was using his talent on her. But he wasn't going to let her go now that he had her. "Who are these people?" They had to be the ones Riley had mentioned, the people his dad had briefly worked for and then betrayed.

The ones searching for an Emrys heir to break the Eighth-Day Spell.

Tegan shook her head furiously, fighting his interrogation, but couldn't stop herself from answering. "Dad knew a guy who knew a guy who knew about 'em. They're vassals to some Kin liege." She looked him up and down with disgust. "Like you are. What'd ya do something so stupid for? I can *smell* the oath on you. Transitioners aren't supposed to swear to Kin! We've got eight days to their one. Why would you put yourself *under* one of them?"

"You'd have to care about somebody other than yourself to understand," Jax retorted.

"This wasn't supposed to happen," Tegan said.

No. Jax had seen the surprised look on Donovan's face

when he fell. None of it was supposed to happen, and it was Jax's fault it had. He'd been too cowardly to tell Riley about the Donovans, and now Evangeline had fallen into the hands of enemies, and Melinda . . .

Remembering how quickly the sirens had sounded, Jax tried to convince himself that Riley or one of the Crandalls had called 911 in the first possible instant. But any neighbor might have made that call after midnight on Thursday. For all Jax knew, Riley and Melinda were dead, along with her family. Jax had not only been irresponsible, he'd been a liability to everyone. He was painfully aware that Evangeline had taken him as a vassal to protect *him*, not because she believed he could protect *her*.

He twisted around to look at the casket.

"She doesn't feel it, you know."

Jax turned a resentful glare on Tegan, who added, "It'll be like a second or two before they let her out. She won't feel the time passing."

"You don't know what she feels," Jax said. "So just shut up." Maybe it would be only a second of terror for Evangeline inside that coffin, but it was a second that would last for *seven days*. She was living it now—and would still be living it an hour from now, and a day from now, and a week from now.

Jax couldn't save her from that endless moment or end it any quicker for her.

* * *

They drove all night and into the next morning, crossing into Ohio. It was past noon when the hearse and the following Land Rovers pulled up in front of an isolated farmhouse. They were met by a wiry woman with a face like a mean little terrier, who opened the door of the hearse. "Hands behind your heads," she said. "Keep your mouths shut and walk single file to the door."

Jax climbed out behind Tegan. He put his hands on his head, but instead of following instructions, he headed for the back of the hearse, where men were unloading the casket. The terrier-faced woman grabbed his wrist and twisted it behind his back, trying to dislocate his arm or possibly rip it off. He gasped in pain and struggled to get free.

A sharp whistle preceded a shout. "Let him go."

Jax staggered as the woman released him and received an unexpected hand of assistance from the older Balin. "Take it easy, Aubrey," he said. "We're not going to harm your liege."

"Harm her?" Jax repeated. He watched as the casket was carried into the house. "You threatened to burn her alive. You threw her into a coffin!"

"No one will harm her now that she's in our custody," Balin amended.

"What do you want with her?" Jax threw as much talent as he knew how to muster into that question. He had no honor blade, and there was no time for meditation, but he was seething with anger and that might help.

It was like hurling magic at a blank wall. Balin didn't even twitch. He answered Jax's question with one of his own. "Where does your loyalty lie? With your liege or with the person you were living with?"

"With *her*." If Jax had to choose between Evangeline and Riley, he would choose Evangeline. Riley would *want* him to choose Evangeline.

"Who is he?" Balin asked. "What's his name?"

It took two beats of the heart for Jax to find an answer. "He had an arrangement with my liege. If she wants to tell you his name, she will. But I can't answer without instruction."

"*Can't* or won't?"

Balin was asking whether Jax was magically compelled to silence or just being a loyal vassal. He almost lied, but instinct—maybe talent—took over his tongue. "Won't."

Apparently, that was the right answer, because the man almost smiled. "Very well, Aubrey." His gaze didn't leave Jax's face even though he addressed the terrier-faced woman. "Take this boy into the house. If he wants to stay with his liege, he'll make no trouble."

Jax stared into Balin's eyes and gave one brief nod of agreement.

31

THEY LEFT JAX locked in a room for the entire day, with nothing to do but think about his own mistakes and imagine horrible endings to the fire at Melinda's house. They fed him and let him out to use the bathroom, but they told him nothing. His talent bounced off most of them uselessly, and he might have thought it had failed him altogether if he hadn't managed to get one guy to tell him the name of the town they were in. Before he could follow up with a more significant question, the terrier-faced woman smacked Jax across the mouth and sent the guy who'd answered his question away.

Jax glimpsed the mark on her wrist, right before she fattened his lip with the palm of her hand, and it was the same as the one on the two Balin men. Most of these thugs were part of the same family, Jax realized. It wasn't that his talent wasn't working. It just didn't work on Balins.

On Friday morning, they escorted him out of the house

but wouldn't let him get into the hearse. "You're riding in the car, Aubrey," the senior Balin told him. "You're not traveling to the same place she is."

Jax broke out in a sweat. His whole body itched as he watched men load Evangeline's casket into the hearse. "You swore we'd stay together."

"No," Balin said calmly. "I gave my word you'd get safe passage."

"But—"

"You'll be taken to one of my lord's vassals for examination. He'll determine whether or not it's safe to take you anywhere near my lord."

"Bring Evangeline with us, then," Jax pleaded.

"That's not safe for *her.*" Balin put his hands on his hips. "I hope I've not misjudged you. I don't want to break my word, but I can. It's not the same as a bloodline oath."

"Is this a test? To see what I do? Because you're making it impossible for me to fulfill *my* oath!" In a corner of his mind, a small, timid Jax wished the mouthy Jax would shut up.

"If you want to serve your liege," Balin said quietly, "get in the car, pass our security test, and you'll be there when we open that casket in six days."

Six days before he'd see Evangeline again.

The hearse pulled away from the farmhouse. Jax ran both hands through his hair and looked up at Balin. *He wants me to pass,* Jax realized. *He likes me. This man is a killer, and he* likes *me.* Jax took a long, shuddering breath, then walked obediently toward the Land Rover. His heart hurt, as if the vehicle that had driven Evangeline away had torn off a chunk of him when it left. *Is this the way the Crandalls feel about Riley? Or is it only when you're* failing *your oath that you feel this bad?*

Tegan scampered out of the house. The last time Jax had seen her, she'd been wearing her usual sweatshirt and jeans. This morning she wore shorts and a flared tank top with shiny silver sequins. She climbed into the car, over Jax, and slid out of sight just as the terrier-faced woman ran out of the farmhouse. "That little thief!" the woman hollered. "Where is she? She stole . . ."

"What?" demanded Balin. "She stole what?"

The woman stopped, glancing at the older Balin in his dark suit and his younger brother dressed the same. "Nothing," she snapped. Jax guessed flashy tops and shorts weren't standard issue for their brute squad.

Jax turned to his fellow prisoner. "Steal anything *useful?*" Tegan wiggled a hand inside a pocket of the shorts and pulled out a wad of cash. She unfolded it, checking the denominations: two fives, a ten, a few ones, and some colored bills. Mexican pesos. "Well, that's a big help," Jax said.

Tegan raised an eyebrow. "What'd *you* get?"

Jax glared. He hadn't stolen anything. "You have a plan?"

"Escape. You?"

"I have to stay with them. They have Evangeline."

"Then you're an idiot." Tegan looked like she wanted to say more, but the Balin brothers got into the car, and she clammed up.

It was a silent ride. The Balins didn't engage in conversation, and Jax had nothing to say to Tegan. They were deep in Kentucky by evening, when the Land Rover stopped at an abandoned industrial complex behind a tall barbed-wire fence. The older Balin got out and briskly walked in first. His brother waved Jax and Tegan out of the car and in the front door. They were taken to a large, empty warehouse, where they found John Balin engaged in heated conversation with another man.

He was in his mid-twenties and wasn't dressed like the rest of the Balin clan. He wore a baggy, untucked concert T-shirt over cargo pants. His hair was shaggy, uncombed, and jet black except for a white patch on the side of his head.

"I didn't know anything about this!" The young man pushed a pair of wire-rimmed glasses up his nose. "Isn't it my job to prevent you wasting time on information from a dubious source?"

"We found her, Owens. Which *you* failed to do."

"I should have been there."

"Your job is to follow orders. You keep forgetting

that." Balin's voice was deadly cold. He'd spoken more warmly to Jax.

The guy called Owens didn't seem to care. "Whose orders?" he demanded. "I swore my allegiance to Lord Wylit, not you."

"Lord Wylit speaks through me."

"Yes, well, I only have your word for that, don't I?" Owens walked toward Jax and Tegan, his sneakers squeaking on the floor. "And who are these two? Is this really the time to recruit vassals out of middle school?"

"I brought them here for you to evaluate," said Balin, crossing his arms. "Do it."

Evaluate? What kind of evaluation? Jax doubted it was going to be an oral quiz. He braced himself for some sort of magical attack.

Tegan had apparently reached the same conclusion. She recoiled from the man's approach, but Owens caught her by the back of her neck with his right hand and yanked her forward. He put his left hand on top of her head. Tegan screamed and fell to her knees.

"Hey!" Jax yelled. "Get your hands off her!"

Just as suddenly as he'd grabbed her, Owens let go. Tegan sagged to the floor. "Scent sensitive," Owens proclaimed, looking at John Balin. "But you already knew that. Totally undisciplined, though. Worthless."

"We supply the discipline," Balin said dryly.

"She's not susceptible to discipline," Owens replied.

"You'll never make anything out of her. In fact"—he groped around in a pocket of his cargo pants, came up with a fist-sized pistol, and released the safety lock—"the best thing would be to just shoot her."

Jax hauled Tegan to her feet and pushed her behind him. Owens eyed Jax curiously.

"Put the gun away, Owens," Balin said evenly.

"Ask my opinion and do the opposite," Owens muttered, thumbing the safety of his gun on. "Who could've predicted that?"

"I'll worry about the girl. What do you see in the boy?" Balin prompted.

Jax held up an arm defensively when Owens turned to him, but the young man batted it aside impatiently. He did nothing but place a hand on the top of Jax's head, but it felt like the hand reached right into Jax's brain.

Jax pushed against it, the way Melinda had taught him. Then a blinding, debilitating pain shot through his head. He yelled and staggered backward into Tegan. Clenching his teeth together, he concentrated on not passing out.

The hand was back now, rummaging through Jax's head as if his brain were a drawer full of disorganized photographs. Invisible fingers teased out exactly what they were looking for, and the memory of being Tasered by Terrance surged upward. Then Jax was handcuffed to the grill in the bank, and Thomas signaled him from the doorway. Jax was forced to remember the day the Donovans had invaded his house, and finally he saw Mrs. Unger's hallway where he'd sworn himself to Evangeline.

Owens removed his hand. The pain and the forced memories vanished.

"The boy's newly turned," Owens said to Balin, "and barely trained. Easily molded at this point. The strongest thing in his mind is his oath to the Emrys girl."

"Who was he living with?" Balin asked.

Owens hesitated. "A Transitioner using a false name. The boy wasn't taught to read marks and doesn't know who he is."

It took all Jax's strength of will not to show his relief. At least he'd hidden Riley's identity. Or had he? Owens hadn't looked for any memories of Riley, only the ones that explained how Jax had gotten himself into this predicament.

"The boy is as devoted to his oath as you are to yours," Owens said to Balin.

Balin turned to his brother. "Angus, take the recruits to separate rooms. We'll move in the morning."

"Where?" Owens asked. "Where are we moving?"

John Balin walked out of the room without answering.

Jax was locked into an office on the second floor—a room with a metal desk, a swivel chair, and two steel filing cabinets. He sank into the chair, still trembling.

A man who could rip memories from his head was not a good person to have as an enemy. If Owens came back, Jax would have to fight harder. Melinda had told him it was possible to fight off any kind of attack, if the person was ready for it. In fact, Jax *had* pushed Owens out for a second. Owens had inserted the pain because of that push. Was it a *memory* of pain? Was that the key to Owens's talent, then—disabling his victims before looking through their heads? If Jax could ignore the pain, maybe Owens wouldn't be able to treat Jax's brain like one of these filing cabinets.

A light tapping made Jax whirl to face the sole window in the room. When he saw who was there, crouched on the ledge outside, he crossed the room and fumbled the lock open. The window frame was stuck from years of grime, but Jax heaved at it.

As soon as the opening was wide enough, Tegan slipped her legs in. The rest of her followed like a limbo dancer. "Are you crazy?" Jax demanded. Then, because he already knew the answer to that, he asked, "Are you escaping?"

"Can't. They've got men with rifles on the fence," Tegan said.

"Then what are you doing climbing around out there?"

Tegan stared Jax in the eye. "You got between me and the gun."

"Yeah, well, it was just—"

She lunged at him. Jax put up his hands to fend off an assault, but she threw both arms around his neck and hugged him.

Someone cleared his throat loudly, and they both turned to see Owens standing in the doorway. Jax swept Tegan behind him with a wave of his arm. *This is getting to be a terrible habit.*

Owens shoved the door closed, his eyes darting from Jax to Tegan to the open window. "You." He pointed a finger at Tegan and then at the window. "Get back to your own cell, or I really will shoot you."

Tegan darted to the window and squeezed herself out, reversing the motion that had gotten her in.

"You." Owens turned his finger on Jax.

Jax braced himself. This time he'd concentrate, no matter the pain. *It's not real. It's a memory. I can take it.*

Owens lowered his hand. "I *could* say something about your taste in friends, but there isn't time. I have a message for you." He crossed the room in two strides and stuck the object in his other hand into Jax's face.

Jax flinched, expecting a gun, but it was a phone. It took him a moment to focus on the message in the texting box.

Riley: jax you idiot

32

JAX GRABBED THE PHONE and keyed in his most important question.

```
Miller: melindas kids ok?
```

He barely had time to register the name preceding the message before Riley answered.

```
Riley: evry1 ok
```

Jax glanced nervously at Owens and quickly thumbed in:

```
Miller: this is millers phone but guy w/me
is owens
Riley: miller owens right
```

Jax groaned at his own stupidity. Riley's vassal

Miller—descended from Sir Owain. Melinda had *told* him that!

Miller Owens waved his hand at Jax in a hurry-it-up gesture and glanced toward the door. "Keep it short."

```
Riley: where is E
Miller: hiding her somewhere. not with me
Miller: i swore 2 her
Riley: quick thinking on her part. kept u
alive.
```

Jax licked his dry lips and ignored the temptation to resort to excuses and explanations.

```
Miller: what do I do?
Riley: trust miller. im coming
```

"That's enough." Miller took the phone from Jax's hands, turned it off, and shoved it in a pocket. "I don't want them catching me with this phone."

"You're Riley's vassal?" Jax couldn't believe it. This guy had offered to shoot Tegan. He'd rummaged around in Jax's head, torturing him while he did it.

"Yeah," said Miller.

"But I heard you say you were Wylit's vassal."

"I am. Want me to swear to you, too? No, wait. This'll prove it faster." Miller opened one of the filing cabinets and threw a manila file on the desk. He took out his blade and balanced the dagger on his palm. "I swear the loyalty of the Owens bloodline to these papers. I will protect them from harm with the last breath of my body." Then, with a wild grin at Jax, he flipped the blade into its sheath, located a lighter in one of his many pockets, and lit the folder on fire.

He laughed while he did it.

Jax might've been new to the world of magic, but he still felt sick—like he'd seen something unnatural. His oath to Evangeline was the only one he'd ever made, but he knew instinctively that it was impossible for him to betray it. "How—?"

Miller beat the flames out against the desk, his eyes pale gray and dilated behind his wire-rimmed glasses. "An unexpected side effect of a fractured skull. Oaths don't work on me anymore."

Jax's eyes jumped to the patch of colorless hair on the side of Miller's head. "Does Riley know?"

"Riley was there when this happened to me. He knows I'm free to betray him, and he trusts me anyway. But let me tell you what this means for *you*, Jax." Miller gave him a small shove. "I'm not compelled to protect you like he is. If you get in the way of my main objective, I'll let you sink or swim on your own."

Jax gulped. "What is your main objective?"

"Preventing the end of the world." Miller grinned so

wildly, Jax didn't know whether to take him seriously or not. "Specifically, I need to keep Emrys away from Wylit."

"What does he want from her?"

"He wants her to alter the Eighth-Day Spell."

"You mean release all the people inside it?" Jax still wasn't convinced that was a bad thing.

"No, he wants to push Grunsday into the space filled by the other seven days."

"Reverse it? Seven Grunsdays and one for everybody else?"

"Only Grunsday," Miller corrected. "With the rest of time snipped out of reality."

Jax felt a cold trickle down his spine. "Can that be done?"

"It's been done before. There're a lot of vanished civilizations in history—the Khmers, the Minoans, a long list of ancient American cultures . . . The Native Americans were *really* into magic."

Some of this was familiar to Jax from that stupid show Riley liked. *Is this why he was always watching it?*

"Besides," Miller went on, "a failure's almost as bad as a success. Wylit tried this once before, and it backfired spectacularly. I don't know how he got out alive, but the younger brother of your Emrys was killed in the attempt. Wylit's spent the last couple decades looking for another member of her family so he can try again."

"Her brother was killed?" Riley hadn't told Jax that

part. "Does *she* know?"

"Do you want to tell her? Riley couldn't bring himself to do it, and it's not my job. *My* job is to keep her out of Wylit's hands. Or better yet, eliminate Wylit altogether."

"Why didn't you do it when you swore your fake oath to him?" Jax glared at Miller. Any guy who would encourage Riley to make a "first kill" and point a gun at Tegan shouldn't have any trouble assassinating his new liege lord.

"I was under orders to let him live at that point," Miller said, taking no offense at being presumed a killer. "He's not the only bad Kin guy out there, and we were hoping he'd lead us to others. Now that things have taken a turn for the worse, I don't know where he is. John Balin's paranoid about security—keeps us other vassals in the dark about details. He won't tell me where he's stashed Emrys or where the spell-casting ceremony's supposed to take place. He doles out information on a need-to-know basis, and he's never liked me because *your* father introduced us and later betrayed him."

Jax flinched at that. *These people killed my dad. I can't forget that.* "What should I do?" Jax asked.

"Try to stay alive."

"Can you get my dagger back?"

Miller shook his head. "You'll have to convince Balin to give it back yourself." Before Jax could ask *how*, Miller said, "Let me tell you about the Balins. They're hereditary vassals." When Jax shook his head, Miller explained impatiently, "They're *born* vassals, because some idiot Balin in the Middle Ages swore to the Wylit bloodline and bound all his descendants to the oath. They're *insanely* loyal, but they like to pick up recruits with useful talents, because the only Balin talent is having a head like a rock."

"A what?"

"I can't get into their heads. You can't get in. Riley wouldn't be able to make any of them wiggle a finger. They're impervious to outside magical influence, and they take this hereditary oath very seriously." Miller poked Jax in the middle of his chest. "Convince John Balin you're devoted to Emrys, and you'll win him over."

"I *am* devoted to her," Jax said angrily. "And her name is Evangeline."

"I don't want to know her name. I have a mission to complete." Miller held up one finger. "Option one: Kill Wylit." A second finger. "Option two: Rescue Emrys." Then he threw out both hands, as if in surrender. "Final option: Kill Emrys before Wylit can use her."

"No," said Jax. "No." He clenched his fists. "*You can't.* Riley said if she dies, it might extinguish Grunsday and all the people in it."

Miller walked toward the door. "We think there's another hidden Emrys to hold the spell, but even if there isn't, it can't be helped. We Transitioners will survive it either way, but if it's a question of sacrificing a few thousand Kin versus seven billion Normals, then I'll do what

I've got to do." He glanced over his shoulder as he opened the door. "I might not like it, but I don't have a choice."

Miller closed the door behind him. Jax dropped into the swivel chair and looked at the smoking papers on the desk. For a few precious minutes, Jax had thought somebody braver and smarter than he was going to rescue both him and Evangeline.

Now his hopes were a smoldering mess, just like that folder.

"Did that guy hurt you?" Tegan asked in the morning. She was waiting for Jax beside the Land Rover.

"No."

"What'd he want?"

Jax couldn't trust her with the truth. "To question me."

"He smelled sick," Tegan said. "Not diseased. Sick like—*broken*. That's what I told John Balin."

"You told him *what*?"

"Balin wanted to know what Owens smelled like. He said that's why he brought me here—to tell him what I thought of Owens."

Jax blinked rapidly. Balin had said he wanted Miller's assessment of Jax and Tegan. Had it been the other way round? Did Balin suspect Miller was a traitor? Jax looked around. Balin was giving orders to his brother, Angus. Miller was nowhere in sight. Jax turned back to Tegan.

"You shouldn't tell Balin *anything*!"

Tegan narrowed her green eyes. "You mean I should just suck up to him like you do? *My lady this, my lady that* . . . all that vassal crap he likes so much."

"Look." Jax grabbed her arm. "He's trying to recruit you. Don't use your talent for him."

She pulled away. "I do what keeps me alive and loose and ready to run. I know how to survive in this world better than you do. I don't *need* you jumping between me and guns."

"Well, I promise never to do it again!" Jax snapped, looking over her shoulder. John Balin was walking toward them.

"Donovan." He took her by the arm, steering her away from Jax. "You're coming with me."

Meanwhile, Angus threw open the rear passenger door of the Land Rover. "In," he ordered Jax.

They were being separated. First Evangeline. Now Tegan. And Miller—Jax scanned the area again. There was no way to warn Miller that Tegan had been used against him. He looked at Angus. "Where are you taking me?"

Angus folded his arms, stone-faced. "Get in the car, Aubrey."

Jax looked up into this man's cold eyes and imagined him behind the wheel of a car on a dark night, swerving viciously into the side of another vehicle. Then he did as he was told.

* * *

On Monday night, Jax was driven across the border into Mexico.

He didn't hold out much hope they'd be stopped at Immigration, and they weren't. An official stamped a passport with a picture bearing no resemblance to Jax and handed it back without question. He had followed Angus Balin to the car, angry that he hadn't realized the significance of the pesos mixed in with the money Tegan had stolen from the farmhouse. *Where was that talent for information I'm supposed to have?* Jax could've told Miller, maybe given him an idea where they were headed—but instead he'd been too much of an idiot to recognize a clue when he saw one.

Miller was Jax's best hope of rescue, but that gave him little comfort. *The final option.* Did Riley agree? That killing Evangeline might become their only choice?

But he didn't know if Miller would catch up with them anyway. He'd seen no one but Ugly Angus since Friday, and he only had John Balin's word that Jax would be present when they let Evangeline out of that casket on Grunsday. He had long since given up asking Angus questions—where they were going or what had happened to Tegan. He didn't dare ask about Miller.

On Wednesday, they skirted around Mexico City and headed into the countryside, toward a mountain range. Each individual mountain peak was conical, like a volcano.

Oh God. They aren't planning to throw her into a volcano, are they?

Then Jax spotted a road sign suspended over the highway:

↑ PIRÁMIDES

"No way," Jax whispered.

Thanks to that television show Riley liked to watch, Jax knew exactly what spot had been chosen to conduct the end of the world.

33

THE WORLD LURCHED, and Evangeline's scream died in her throat. Seven days had just passed without her, and the silk-lined prison rocked with the rhythm of footsteps.

She screamed again, furiously pummeling the sides of the coffin. They might have flown her halfway around the world by now. Jax—for whom she was responsible—might have been left behind or seven days dead for all she knew.

The only certain thing was that she was still among enemies. Her hand went to the Pendragon dagger lying next to her heart. Riley would come to retrieve it. That promise had been implied in the gift. But he hadn't reached her yet, or he would've had the coffin open already.

Perhaps he'd been killed trying.

She stifled panic at the thought. Whatever had happened in the last seven days, Riley had sent her this blade so she could draw magic from it. It had been a generous gift and a sign of trust. Evangeline took control of her breathing. For his sake, and for Jax's, she would go down fighting.

She slipped her right hand inside her shirt. When she ran her fingertips over the engraved crest on the dagger's hilt, she experienced a jolt of power. Emrys magic on a Pendragon blade. She wondered if such a thing had ever been done before. Perhaps not since Merlin and Arthur and the Eighth-Day Spell.

Evangeline murmured the incantation for the only spell she knew that required no symbolic objects to invoke it, just the energy of her own body. She clenched her hands into fists. Magic tingled on her flesh, dancing along her forearms with startling intensity. Holding both fists tight against her sides, she rocked back and forth with the movement of the casket and planned for the moment they set this thing down and opened it.

The motion of the casket stopped, and Evangeline clenched her hands experimentally. The magical charge stung her flesh like she was holding fistfuls of lightning. The casket thumped onto the floor, and her heart pounded, adding fuel to her prepared spell. When the lid opened, Evangeline elbowed herself upright, stood, and scanned the room.

John Balin faced her in a room that contained a bed, a chair, and a television bolted to the wall. A skinny woman with a pinched face stood beside him, armed.

"She has a spell prepared," a voice piped up. Evangeline's eyes snapped back to Balin. A girl with carrot-colored hair stood behind him.

Balin and the woman drew their guns. "She's built up a big charge," the girl said. She was obviously a sensitive with an acute awareness of magic, and Evangeline recognized her as one of the people who'd subdued Jax—only a few minutes ago by Evangeline's timeline.

"Lady Emrys," Balin said. "Disperse your spell—and gently."

Evangeline shook her head. "You didn't go to all this trouble just to shoot me."

He smiled grimly and raised his voice. "Bring in the boy." A man who looked like a younger version of Balin dragged Jax into the room and shoved him to his knees. Balin pressed his pistol to the back of Jax's head. "If you begin hostilities, all bargains are dissolved between us."

"Don't—" Jax started, but the two men together forced his head down further.

Brave Jax. Evangeline was absolutely certain he'd been going to say *"Don't worry about me"* and not *"Don't shoot."*

John Balin spoke evenly. "Don't make me kill this boy for no reason. Even if you get out of this room, the hotel is full of my men and you are very far from home."

Evangeline was outnumbered and outmatched, and Jax would die if she made the wrong move. Reluctantly, she uncurled her fingers and pressed her palms into the lining of the coffin lid. A loud *poof* preceded the combustion, and the fabric burst into blue flames. She stepped out of the coffin and slammed the lid closed to smother the fire.

Balin didn't take his gun away from Jax's head. "Donovan."

The girl inched forward, sniffing inquisitively. Her eyebrows shot up, and her eyes went straight to Evangeline's chest.

Evangeline's heart sank. This girl was very talented; the ones with scent sensitivity often were. Even over the stink of magic fire in the coffin, she'd pinpointed the hidden honor blade. But then the girl stared Evangeline in the eyes and said, "She's clear."

Only then did Balin holster his gun, although the pinch-faced woman kept hers handy. The man who'd brought Jax in hauled him to his feet. Jax tried to walk toward Evangeline but was pushed to the door instead.

"Leave him here," Evangeline exclaimed.

"If my lord gives permission, you'll have your vassal back. Until then, he stays under guard."

"Then bring Wylit to me at once." Evangeline snapped her fingers as if she were the person in charge, but her voice cracked.

Balin smiled coldly at her attempt to take control. "My lord has not yet arrived, but when he does, you will be summoned." He looked her over from head to toe, and a spasm of distaste crossed his face. "In the meantime, you'll change into something appropriate for the occasion." The woman held up a dress of frothy white fabric. Evangeline snatched it, but when she started toward the bathroom, Balin ordered, "Donovan, go with her."

They weren't even going to let her into the bathroom alone. The girl, Donovan, didn't look happy about it, but she slipped into the room with Evangeline and shut the door behind her.

The sole window was narrow and high up the wall. No escaping that way, even if she overpowered the girl. With an angry twist of her wrist, Evangeline turned on the faucet full blast and faced Donovan.

The girl eyed her sourly. "Let's see it."

Evangeline pulled the blouse over her head, revealing the dagger strapped across her chest. "Why didn't you tell them?"

"So you'd owe me."

"Why'd you tell them about my spell, then?"

The girl shrugged. "So *they'd* owe me."

Evangeline drenched a washcloth in water and wiped her face and neck. She stank of fear and panic. No wonder she'd been sent in here to clean up. "You're not a vassal?"

"I'm no one's vassal."

"Are you another prisoner?" The girl didn't answer. Evangeline threw the wet cloth into the sink in frustration. "Can you at least tell me where I am?"

"Mexico."

Evangeline shook out the dress they'd given her. It was a full-length white dress with a train, like a bride might wear. Or a human sacrifice in a magic ritual. There were only thin straps instead of sleeves, and it was backless.

Donovan snorted. "You're going to have to hide that dagger somewhere else."

★ ★ ★

Late that morning, Evangeline was escorted to a dining room in the hotel. The ceiling was crisscrossed by dark beams, and a mural covered one of the walls. A tall Kin man with long white hair stood in front of the mural, examining it with interest.

His vassals were lined up on either side of him. Balin stood at the head of one line, with the Donovan girl beside him. On the other side, Balin's younger lookalike held Jax by the shoulder. Evangeline lifted her chin and straightened her back, bracing herself to face a man who'd made even her father nervous.

Then Lord Myrddin Wylit turned around, and she couldn't contain a gasp of shock.

He was horribly burned—and not by fire. There was no mistaking the signs of magical backlash: the bluish tinge to his ruined skin, which hung from his face in peeling shreds. Some very powerful spell had gone terribly wrong.

"Evangeline Emrys," he said, drawing out her name between thin white lips. "I am very pleased to have freed you from your captivity."

"I was not a captive," she said, hoping her cold expression covered the tremor in her voice. "I was exactly where I wanted to be."

"In hiding?" Wylit scoffed lightly. "With your one fledgling vassal?"

"Don't presume to know the extent of my connections," she said.

Wylit indicated his chief vassal. "Balin informs me that he

253

found you a prisoner of Transitioners, cut off from the Kin, and that you only took the boy as your vassal at the last second. You may keep him, by the way. My gift to you."

Jax looked startled when the younger Balin handed back his honor blade. Evangeline motioned him over with a subtle curve of her fingers. Jax took the hint, strapping his dagger around his waist and crossing the room to her side.

"It's very kind of you to give me something I already had," Evangeline said. "If you would like to win my trust with a more significant gift, you could grant me safe passage home."

"I'm sure you understand that's not possible. I brought you here for a purpose."

"I don't even know where *here* is."

Wylit raised a hand toward the mural and stepped to one side.

Now that she gave it her attention, she saw it was a map titled *Zona Arqueológica de Teotihuacán*. Three pyramids were connected by a long road lined with smaller temples.

"Teotihuacán," Wylit said. "City of the Gods. When the Aztecs rose to power in the thirteenth century, this city had already been in ruins for seven hundred years. The Aztecs had no knowledge of the people who built this place—only legends of their greatness. Do you know why?"

"Because the people who lived here were wiped from existence," Evangeline guessed. "Their timeline destroyed."

Wylit gazed at the mural. "Imagine a city with a population in the hundreds of thousands at a time when London was a Roman village—obliterated in the span of a few seconds by a handful of Indian shamans." Wylit turned to Evangeline. "The perfect location to right an ancient wrong."

"You want to bring them back?"

He laughed. "Hardly."

"Then you're still following my father's plan to undo the Eighth-Day Spell."

Wylit's voice hardened. "Your father's plan was flawed."

Evangeline said nothing. She knew her father had been misguided. Even when she was a little girl, his passionate speeches on the matter had made her uneasy, especially when she saw what kind of allies rallied to his cause and how her mother had grown more and more reluctant to participate. But she listened silently to Wylit's reasoning.

"The Kin are scattered across the earth, hidden among Normals. We've had no more than ten generations to their hundreds and are outnumbered by billions. The Wylit line has been lucky, served for centuries by the Balin family, but most Kin were weakened by this imprisonment. What would Normals do if an unexplained race suddenly appeared among them? Mistake us for aliens? How long before they decided to kill us all?"

"Then what do you have in mind?" *Spit it out,* she wanted to say.

"To push the seven-day timeline off this world," Wylit said. His Kin blue eyes gleamed. "To even the odds against our Transitioner enemies by giving us the same number of days they have—and to eliminate Normals entirely."

"Leaving a world full of empty cities," she whispered. It was a terrible, chilling image. Evangeline might not have known, at age eleven, the correct answer to give when the Taliesin men rescued her from the attack on her father's home. But in the five years of isolation since then, she'd learned about the Normal world as best she could from her position as an outsider. She knew what her ancestor Merlin had been trying to save—and on which side of the conflict she stood.

"It can't be done," she said loudly to Wylit, hoping that was true.

"I've *seen* it done," Wylit replied. "In my mind, I've seen this world emptied for our use."

Prophecy was the Wylit talent. In ancient times, people took great stock in the visions of a Wylit clan leader. But Evangeline had learned from her mother that prophecies had a way of unraveling. "Be wary of those who claim to know the future," her mother had said. "Constant, multiple, contradictory visions will drive people insane and cloud what they see." Evangeline's mother knew that very well. Prophetic visions had been her family's talent too, as well as their curse.

"Forgive me, Lord Wylit," Evangeline said cautiously, "but your injuries suggest you've already attempted this and did not succeed."

"My previous attempt was premature," he admitted. "I failed to procure everything necessary—including a spell caster as strong and spirited as *you.*" He smiled at her as if she were a pleasant surprise. "Additionally, we need representation of the three main bloodlines who led the casting of the spell. You, of course, are an Emrys. But we need to account for the Dulac and Pendragon bloodlines as well. It took a great deal of trouble to locate appropriate artifacts, but I have finally done so." Wylit beckoned her to approach him. "Come, Evangeline Emrys. Meet one of your greatest enemies."

Evangeline glanced at Jax in puzzlement, and they trailed behind Wylit to a table at the back of the room that held a large wooden crate. "Taken from a barrow in the Celtic foot-hills," Wylit explained, "a long-lost, once-famous queen, hidden in obscurity for over a millennium."

After one peek inside, Jax recoiled, covering his nose and mouth. Evangeline had more restraint. Her life, Jax's life, the lives of billions of people depended on Wylit's being *wrong*. She needed to know what she was looking at. "It's a well-preserved body," she said at last. "Probably a Celtic queen or princess. But there's no way of telling who she was."

"She's a Dulac," the Donovan girl called out. "I can smell her from here."

Silently, Evangeline cursed the girl. She could identify specific families? That was unfortunate—and probably the reason Evangeline's hiding place had been discovered. It would have taken stronger wards than she could make to defend against *that* talent.

Wylit, meanwhile, looked pleased. "This is the recruit you spoke of, Balin? Quite a gift she has. Come, child. Tell me what you think."

The girl's eyes darted guiltily toward Jax, who shook his head at her. But she crossed the room anyway, gripped the wooden slats, and leaned over to sniff deeply, as if the crate were filled with roses instead of a mummified corpse. "This was a high-ranking Dulac," Donovan said. "A queen, I think. I can't say for sure she was Niviane of the Lake—but who else would be buried with *that*?"

"Spotted it, did you?" Wylit looked at the girl as if she were a dog with a clever trick.

"Can't miss it. Reeks to high heaven."

Wylit reached into the crate. "Who else, indeed?" he said. "She's the one who gave it to him, and after his death, Sir Bedivere returned it to her."

He pulled something free from the mummified remains and held it up in the air. "Behold, the blade of King Arthur Pendragon—Excalibur."

34

IT WAS A DAGGER.

Jax was shocked. Excalibur was supposed to be a sword. But a moment later, he realized it made perfect sense. *Of course* Excalibur was the honor blade King Arthur used to enhance his voice of command in battle. The iron weapon was black with corrosion, but in better shape than the mummy it came off. Jax could still make out part of the engraved coat of arms on the hilt.

"Today we rest," Wylit said to Evangeline. "My vassals have preparations to make at the site, and I'm awaiting arrivals not expected until this evening. We will commence after sundown. In my condition, I cannot tolerate natural light . . ."

"Of course not. Nature abhors botched magic," Evangeline said matter-of-factly.

Jax sucked in his breath. He couldn't believe how brave she was, standing up to this shredded-faced freak who looked like a cross between Emperor Palpatine and Freddy Krueger. The crack about *botched magic* seemed like it went too far, but Evangeline turned away from the creep and flared out the long skirt on her dress as if she didn't care whether she offended him or not. "I require that you return me to my room now."

Wylit signaled his men. Evangeline and Jax were escorted to the room where they'd held her last night. As soon as the door closed, Evangeline threw her arms around Jax. "Are you all right?" she asked.

He felt her trembling and hugged her back, realizing how much of an act she'd been putting on in front of Wylit. "I'm okay. I was worried about *you*."

"Jax, I'm so sorry you were dragged into this."

"I led the Donovans to your hiding place," Jax said, swallowing hard. "They found you because of me."

She smiled sadly. "People have been after me since before you were born. It's not your fault."

"Riley's coming for us."

Evangeline sank down on a corner of the bed. "But?"

"But I don't know what kind of plan he has or even if he knows where we are." Jax hated to squelch her hope of rescue, but she needed to know. He sat down beside her and explained how Riley had planted a man among Wylit's vassals who could be sworn to more than one liege. "Riley said to trust him. But Miller told me that if he couldn't rescue you, he'd have to . . ."

"Kill me." She didn't look surprised. "If it comes to it"—Evangeline lifted her chin—"you let him do what he has to do. Billions of people are a lot more important than I am."

Jax shook his head but didn't argue with her. It didn't matter. Miller wasn't here; Riley probably wasn't going to get here in time; Jax and Evangeline were on their own.

"If you see any opportunity to escape by yourself," Evangeline said, "I want you to take it. Don't stick around for me."

"No way."

"You're the only friend I've ever had. I want you to be safe. I can order you to go."

He thought that over and tested it against what little he knew of magic—and his new vassalhood. "You don't have Riley's voice of command. You can't compel me to leave if my place is with you."

"Jax, I'm only pretending that Wylit owes me any courtesy or respect, and he's only pretending to give it. When I refuse to do what he wants, it'll get ugly."

Jax thought of her brother and knew that now was not the time to tell her what had happened to him. "Then let's do more than refuse." He stood up. "Let's mess up his ritual. If everything isn't exactly perfect, it won't work, right?"

Evangeline stared at him. "A small thing could throw a massive spell like this off, but it's also dangerous and unpredictable." She paused to think. "Wylit's not going to let me cast a spell in the middle of his ceremony, and if I set something up in advance, that Donovan girl will know. Whose side is she on?"

"Her own."

"Everyone's going to be watching me, but they might not keep as close an eye on *you*."

Yeah, what am I going to do? Ask a bunch of questions? Jax doubted that revealing someone's bedwetting issues was going to get them out of this kind of trouble. "The Balins aren't affected by my magic," he said. "They don't think I'm much of a threat."

"If I give *you* a spell to hold, maybe your friend won't tell."

"She's not my friend," Jax said. Then her words sank in. "Can you actually *give* me a spell? Like what you had last night?" He didn't understand the difference between a spell and a talent, but she'd set a coffin on fire with her bare hands, and if he could do that . . .

"That spell's too hard to hold for more than a couple minutes," she said. "It would have to be something else. Do you think you can remember a brief incantation in Welsh?"

"I'll be freakin' Harry Potter if you need me to be."

"If I send you out to tell them I demand food or something, can you steal a candle and matches? If natural light hurts him, I can work with that."

He nodded. "There's candles on the tables in the courtyard outside this room."

"They might kill us if we do this," she warned him.

"So what else is new?"

35

AFTER SUNDOWN, Jax and Evangeline were moved from the hotel into one of the Land Rovers and driven down a cobblestone road to the Avenue of the Dead. Information on Teotihuacán swam up from Jax's memory, although he would've sworn he'd never paid any attention to *Extraterrestrial Evidence*. There were three famous structures in this ancient city: the Pyramid of the Moon at the end of the avenue; the Feathered Serpent Pyramid, hidden behind hills almost a mile away; and the Pyramid of the Sun—the third largest pyramid in the world.

It was going to be one heck of a climb to the top.

Wylit couldn't do it. His men had brought a sedan chair to carry their lord like a king. Heavy and wooden, with carvings on the legs and back, it was cushioned in red velvet and topped by a canopy. Two poles were bolted to the arms so that four men could carry it. When Jax saw Wylit emerge from one of the Land Rovers, he didn't know whether to laugh or throw up.

The Kin lord had dressed himself like an Aztec king. He was bare chested, which exposed more of his flaky, peeling fish skin, and bare legged beneath a short skirt. To top it all off, he wore a headdress of feathers fitted around the carved wooden face of a serpent.

"This is bad," Evangeline murmured. "He's invoking the shamans of this place."

"Aren't they all dead?" Jax whispered.

"Encapsulated in an alternate timeline and snipped off from reality, but still here . . . in a manner of speaking."

Jax shuddered, remembering how Evangeline had been in the coffin and not in the coffin at the same time. The people of this city had vanished waiting for a "next day" that never came. In a way, they were *still* waiting.

Up and down the avenue, men with guns were deploying on the tops of other structures. A pickup truck bumped along the concrete road on its way to the Pyramid of the Moon with a double-barreled machine gun in the bed. "What's that?" Jax asked.

The nearest of Wylit's vassals who wasn't a Balin promptly responded, "Twin M2 Browning. By the orders of my lord."

Jax had to smother a smile even though there wasn't much to smile about. He hadn't needed to chant a verse or even direct his question at that man. Evangeline's magic buzzed at the back of his head, and he felt empowered.

They were ordered to start climbing, just behind the men carrying Wylit and ahead of the two Balin brothers. Jax glanced around discreetly, but there were enough armed vassals on site to block any escape attempt. Their path up the pyramid was illuminated by floodlights set up on the landings and powered by generators. After the first section, Evangeline struggled to mount the steep steps, and Jax carried the train of her gown. When he looked up to see how much farther they had to go, he spotted Tegan on the second terrace.

"A little help?" he called.

Tegan didn't budge. "I've been up and down *three* pyramids today, sniffing out security. She can do *one*."

Evangeline staggered onto the level surface and said, "You didn't have to drag a wedding train behind." She'd braided her hair to get it out of the way, but loose strands were plastered to her face and neck with sweat.

Jax hauled the white fabric up the steps and dropped it in a heap. "Have you sworn on with your new masters?" he snapped at Tegan.

"No," she replied, looking Jax up and down with a sniff. "I'm not as stupid as you are."

She smelled Evangeline's spell on him. Jax watched her, not sure what to expect from her after five days as Balin's pet bloodhound. But he'd never known what to expect from Tegan.

"My mom's a Normal, you know," she said.

Like, he hadn't expected that. "No, I didn't know."

"She ran out on us years ago." Tegan dropped her voice. "Doesn't mean I want her snuffed out like a candle." Then she gave Jax a strange, distant smile. "Did you know there's a tunnel under this pyramid? Runs all the way to that smaller one on the other side of the ruins."

Jax blinked. "Actually, yes," he said, surprising himself. That TV show again.

"*They* don't," Tegan murmured, glancing at Wylit's vassals. "Very interesting smells, those tunnels . . ."

"Donovan," barked John Balin, coming up behind Jax. He motioned with his hand for Tegan to continue up the pyramid, and Jax was gratified to see the climb had left even Wylit's chief vassal breathless.

Tegan ran up the next set of steps, and Jax turned to Evangeline. She stared back at him. What had Tegan been trying to tell them? Could they possibly hope . . . ?

"Keep moving," Balin growled.

Jax gathered up Evangeline's train, and they ascended the towering staircase. When they reached the fifth terrace, there was still one more level to climb, a rounded hill of large stones sunk into cement leading to a level cobblestone surface on the summit.

Wylit's men must have been busy all day. A table of dark wood and iron filigree had been set up like an altar. It had probably been stolen from the hotel, along with another table to hold the crate with the mummy. The locals were going to wake up on Thursday to some really puzzling paranormal activity on the pyramid.

Then Jax remembered. There wasn't supposed to be a Thursday.

"My lord." John Balin offered his arm to Wylit when the sedan chair was set down. "Take care where you step." The Kin lord swayed as Balin guided him to the altar. *I should take a running start and push him over the edge,* Jax thought. He tightened his muscles and pictured himself throwing an old man off the top of a two-hundred-foot pyramid.

First kill's the hardest. Miller had texted that to Riley.

But there were four men plus Balin between Jax and Wylit, and the pyramid didn't drop off abruptly anyway. A good push would send the old man tumbling down the hill, where he'd roll a few yards and end up on the fifth level terrace, ticked off but still alive.

One of the men who'd carried Wylit to the summit directed Evangeline to the altar, while another one warned Jax to stay where he was with an outstretched hand.

Wylit surveyed the ruined city below. "Almost two thousand years ago, a mighty civilization vanished from this place," he said. "A century after that, on the opposite side of the world, another civilization was confined to a prison made of time." He turned on Evangeline. "Your ancestor betrayed us to our enemies. Why do you think he did it?"

She glared back at him. "The Llyrs and the Arawens were abusing their power, and too much blood had already been spilled trying to stop them."

"I'm sure there was a great deal of blood spilled in the casting of this spell," Wylit said, his lip rising in a sneer. The skin of his face crumpled like wet tissue paper. "Sacrifices were made."

"No, I don't think so." Evangeline frowned.

"You believe Merlin, Niviane, and Arthur were too virtuous to cut a few throats? You are naive, child." There was a mocking tone to Wylit's voice Jax didn't like at all. "And what constitutes a sacrifice? It's not a *sacrifice* if the offering isn't worth something to us, is it?"

Evangeline was looking really worried now, and Jax didn't like the way the conversation was going. *Time to use this spell.* He edged his way around the men to get a good view of Wylit, fighting a reluctance he couldn't explain. *This has to be the moment,* he thought. But for some reason, he seemed to have two left feet. He stumbled and lost his balance. Balin turned and gave him an annoyed look.

"*I've* brought a sacrifice," Wylit said. "Something lovely and valuable and full of life, given to me by my most trusted vassal."

Tegan shrieked as two men grabbed her under the arms and carried her forward. Jax was thrust out of the way by an elbow to his temple that sent him staggering backward, his head spinning. "Dad!" Tegan screamed at the top of her lungs. "Dad, help me!"

Holy crap, they were going to sacrifice Tegan! Jax staggered upright, shaking his head and trying to make his lips form the words of Evangeline's spell. But one of Wylit's men wrapped an arm around his throat and held him tightly.

Tegan fought while her captors tied her hands. Finally one of the men clocked her so hard, she fell over on the stony surface of the pyramid and lay still.

"You can't do this!" Evangeline shouted at Wylit. "She's just a girl!"

"She is just a girl," Wylit agreed. "Not enough of a sacrifice for this ritual. You must give up something, too. Perhaps a boy to go with my girl?"

Jax was dragged forward and forced to his knees beside Tegan. "Sorry, boy," Balin said from across the summit. Jax heard Evangeline scream at Wylit to let him go, but all he could think as they wound the twine around his wrists was how he'd blown his chance. Evangeline had given him one weapon to use, planted it in his head like an itch he couldn't scratch. It would take only a few words and a hand gesture to release it, and now his hands were tied behind his back.

The Balin brothers, meanwhile, had taken hold of Evangeline. "Did you think I didn't know your plans?" Wylit snarled at her. "I see the future. All possible futures, and in every single one, you are a traitor to your race."

The older Balin wrapped Evangeline's right wrist in twine, binding it to the iron filigree of the table, while the younger one held her other hand for the same treatment.

"You're insane!" Evangeline screamed. "You deserve to be imprisoned here." She started to shout something Jax didn't understand, something in another language, but John Balin stuffed a cloth into her mouth and secured it with a long strip torn from a hotel bedsheet.

"You'll cast the spells I want you to cast and no others," Wylit warned her. "I know what you planned, and who you planned it with." He hauled up the skirt of Evangeline's dress, uncovering Riley's dagger sheathed against her leg. "Another Pendragon blade!" he crowed, drawing it out. He laid the dagger on the altar beside Excalibur and turned to Evangeline. "Do you think that's enough to invoke the Pendragon bloodline for this spell? You'd think so, wouldn't you? But there's more on the way."

A car horn rose above Wylit's voice. Jax turned his head to look over the side of the pyramid.

A black Land Rover with its high beams on careened down the Avenue of the Dead and screeched to a halt. The driver's door flew open, and a man with black hair except for one white patch on the side of his head leaped out.

"I've seen this already in my dreams," Wylit said, staring at the sky and not bothering to look. "A devastating betrayal by a broken and bitter man—and a gift for me."

Miller Owens threw open the back door of the car and immediately had to duck. A pair of legs kicked at him viciously. Miller warded off the blows and backed away. Some of Wylit's men on the ground ran to assist, grabbing the occupant of the backseat by his feet and hauling him out so roughly, his head hit the bottom of the car and then the road.

Even at this great distance, Jax had no problem seeing it was Riley, bound and gagged and delivered to his enemies by his friend.

36

JAX PRAYED it was a ruse, but when they finally dragged Riley to the top of the pyramid, his hopes faded. Riley was bound with his hands behind his back and a cloth rag in his mouth. He was bleeding from the nose and a cut over one eye.

Miller mounted the summit behind him, looking winded and sweaty in a different concert T-shirt and the same cargo pants. Wylit's men took their hands off the prisoner for just a second, and Riley launched himself at Miller with a growl. They sprawled across the cobblestones, but Miller threw him off and climbed to his feet. "Not such a hotshot without your voice, are you?" Miller snarled, kicking Riley in the gut.

"That's enough, Owens." John Balin checked the prisoner's bindings to make sure he was secure. Miller's kick had knocked the wind out of Riley, and Balin didn't have any trouble hauling him over beside Jax. "Go keep an eye out below," Balin snapped at his brother. He looked nervous to have so many men jammed on the platform.

Angus and several others retreated to the lower level, leaving Balin and one other man, plus Miller, who bowed to Wylit. "My lord," he said. "I bring you the last of the Pendragons."

Wylit gripped Evangeline's chin and forced her to look at Riley. "An even more fitting sacrifice than your vassal, don't you think?"

"We can spare the boy, then." Balin lifted Jax to his feet and pulled him backward. Jax felt dizzied by this sudden reversal. An ally had delivered Riley to be slaughtered, and an enemy was trying to save Jax's life.

Seeing Jax get a reprieve, Tegan tried to stand up. Miller glanced at Jax, then grabbed Tegan by her tied hands and the top of her head and shoved her down beside Riley. "You stay where you are. Sacrificing a pretty girl is traditional." Tegan shuddered at his touch and sank into a heap. Jax glared at Miller, hating him more than ever.

"We have assembled in this place of desolation," Wylit shouted, raising his arms to the sky, "to defy the eighth-day prison! Hear the words of Myrddin Wylit and heed my will!" He drew Excalibur across the palm of his hand. "My blood comes from an ancient line of sorcerers."

Without warning, he slashed Evangeline's left arm. Jax's hands clenched, and Riley jerked in reaction, but Evangeline didn't flinch. She stared at Wylit with fury.

Wylit smeared his hand across her wound, then raised it to the sky. "This is the blood of a direct descendant of the spell caster who wrought this prison. The power of our blood will push the walls of this time outward until it is a prison no more. At our command, the eighth day will swell until it consumes all the time on earth. The eighth day will be the *only* day."

Evangeline shook her head. Although her mouth was gagged and her wrists were tied, she made a rude gesture with both hands. Jax almost laughed. It wasn't something he would've expected from Evangeline. But Wylit whirled around and swung Excalibur down so quickly, she barely got her fingers out of the way. "Interfere with my spell," Wylit hissed, "and I'll chop off the bits of you I don't need."

She wasn't just being defiant, Jax realized. Melinda had told him that intentions and symbols were important in magic, and Evangeline had said something similar in the hotel when she lit a candle in front of a mirror to work her spell. Evangeline's gesture was meant to oppose Wylit's statements. She was working against him in every small way she could.

Wylit held the iron blade aloft. "I also bear the blade of King Arthur Pendragon, named Excalibur, on which he bound this spell fifteen hundred years ago."

Riley's head jerked up. Behind his gag he mumbled something Jax thought was *You gotta be kidding me.* Nearby,

Miller shuffled his feet and scanned the sky.

"Furthermore, I have the body of Niviane of the Lake, who conceived this spell and helped Merlin Emrys and Arthur Pendragon cast it. I invoke the presence of all three villains and take control of their magic with the blood of my vassals and a valuable sacrifice." Wylit pointed Excalibur at Riley. "The last of his line, a descendant of the king who imprisoned us." Wylit's lips peeled back to show his rotting teeth. "I will cut out his heart on this altar for the right to win this world."

Light flashed above them, and a bolt crossed the purple sky. It wasn't lightning. Lightning didn't shoot across the sky and *stay there*. It looked like a crack in a plaster wall.

Or a crack in whatever barrier held Grunsday separate from the rest of time.

John Balin reached into his suit jacket, removed his gun, and fired it straight into the air. "Loyal vassals, your blood!" he shouted. The man next to Balin unsheathed his honor blade, cut his palm, and raised his hand to the sky. This was the original purpose of the honor blades, Jax remembered from Melinda's lesson. The offering of blood enhanced the spell. Balin holstered his pistol, then used his own dagger to slice through the twine on Jax's wrists. Jax gasped in surprise as his hands fell free.

"Now, boy," Balin said. "Join us or die." He yanked Jax's own blade out of its sheath and slapped it into Jax's right hand. "Add your blood to the spell."

Jax looked at Evangeline with absolute certainty. She nodded, then turned toward Riley and squeezed her eyes shut. Jax couldn't tell if Riley took the hint. Gripping his dagger tightly, he flung his left hand out at Wylit, closed his eyes, and shouted out the phrase he'd memorized.

The spell Evangeline had planted in his head poured out of him like ejecta from a volcano. Even through his eyelids, he saw the explosion of light. It wasn't a fireball—just natural light, the flame of a candle multiplied ten thousandfold in a mirror. Balin and the other man cried out in surprise, blinded by the flare, but Wylit howled in agony.

As the flare faded, Jax opened his eyes and saw two things he hadn't expected. Tegan was off the ground, her hands free, sawing at Riley's bindings with a penknife. And Miller pulled a walkie-talkie out of his pocket, yelling, "Now, *now!*" Then: "Jax, duck!"

37

JAX DUCKED.

Miller whipped out his gun and fired point-blank at the man standing behind Jax.

Down on the Avenue of the Dead, a series of explosions shattered the silence of the abandoned city.

Miller spun on his heel, firing at Wylit. Balin pushed the old man behind the crate and returned fire with such vigor that Miller had to retreat down the side of the pyramid, skidding and losing the walkie-talkie on the way.

Tegan finally broke through Riley's bonds. He pulled the gag out of his mouth with one hand and pushed Tegan out of the line of fire with the other. "Drop your gun and hit the ground!" he shouted.

His command didn't affect Balin at all. With Miller gone, Balin turned his gun on this new threat, and Riley, who'd started in Evangeline's direction, was forced to turn and dive behind Wylit's sedan chair for shelter. "Get over the side, Jax!" Riley yelled.

Jax scooped up Miller's walkie-talkie, scrambled to the edge of the summit, and rolled down the incline. The stones bruised and pummeled him as he dropped to the terrace below. Behind him, he heard more shots fired, and his heart thudded with fear for both his friends on the summit.

But a moment later, Riley slid down beside him, unharmed. "Throw your clansmen down the stairs!" Riley shouted at three men who were running up the pyramid steps from below. Jax shivered all over, sensing the magic in Riley's desperate command, although it wasn't aimed at him. The man in the lead turned and bashed the second one in the head with his rifle, knocking him off the stairs. The third man, Angus Balin, put his rifle to his shoulder and fired. Jax flinched as a bullet ricocheted off the rocks above his head. Then the man under Riley's control barreled into Angus, and the two of them disappeared over the edge of the terrace.

Jax turned to look above him, worried about the other Balin shooting at them. The angle of the pyramid sheltered them, but if Balin came down after them . . .

"He won't leave Wylit," Riley said, guessing Jax's thoughts. "And he's still got Evangeline as hostage. I couldn't reach her."

Riley looked every bit as stricken as Jax about that. And as if flying bullets weren't bad enough, Jax could hear Wylit's voice above them. The crazy Kin lord was still trying to cast his spell. "What are we going to do?" Jax asked.

Riley looked around wildly and for a moment didn't seem to have an answer. Then a low chopping sound rose above the sound of shouts and gunfire on the other side of the pyramid, and he went limp with relief. "Reinforcements," he gasped. "It's about time."

Over the pyramid, a helicopter appeared. It was as ugly as a flying turkey, an old model that probably dated all the way back to Vietnam. How had Riley gotten a helicopter?

"Where's Miller?" Riley yelled over the noise.

"He went over the other way," Jax shouted. "Is he really on our side?"

"Of course he is!"

The floodlights on the Pyramid of the Sun went out one at a time, leaving them in darkness. Wylit's men were shooting out the illumination that made them easy targets from the air.

"Miller kicked you," Jax protested. "He told them to sacrifice Tegan!"

"He kicked me so Balin would think I was down," Riley said. "He handed Tegan the knife and put my instructions into her head. They were meant for you, but Balin moved you out of reach."

"This was all *on purpose*?"

"Would've worked better if the Morgans hadn't been

late." Riley looked up at the helicopter, which was making another turn around the pyramid. A searchlight swept over them, and Riley held up both hands, signaling *It's me! Don't shoot!*

"The Morgans?" Jax repeated. Someone waved a hand in salute before the helicopter banked away.

"Yeah. Congratulate me. I'm engaged." Riley twisted around to look toward the top of the pyramid. He'd traded himself for the use of Deidre's clan and their weaponry, Jax realized. He'd let Miller beat him up and offer him as a sacrifice so the two of them could get close enough to rescue Jax and Evangeline.

Another series of explosions erupted along the Avenue of the Dead. Jax's head buzzed as intuition combined with magic. "That's the Crandalls, isn't it?"

"And Donovan. He joined up with us to get his daughter back." Riley grinned briefly at Jax. "They crawled here through tunnels A.J. and I learned about on TV." Jax nodded his understanding. Tegan had screamed for her father because she knew he was here. "It's only a distraction," Riley said, "but it keeps them guessing how many people we have—and where."

Jax squirmed in worry as the helicopter circled again, shooting at the lower levels of the pyramid. "I don't know where Tegan went."

"She's under the table." Riley glanced upward again. "It's safest there. The Morgans aren't supposed to fire on the summit unless I okay it. That's part of the deal I made with them."

Light streaked across the sky again, longer and farther than before. It snaked across the purple heavens, breaking into branches and widening. A wind rose around them, swirling tiny pebbles. Jax half expected the sky to shatter like glass.

"On the other hand," Riley muttered, "if Wylit keeps trying to cast this spell, the Morgans aren't going to care about our deal. They'll kill everyone up there to prevent him succeeding."

"Evangeline has no cover," Jax said. The Balins had tied her hands to the table's surface. Unlike Tegan, she couldn't hide beneath a table.

"I know." Riley twisted around again, peering up at the summit.

"Miller said he'd kill her if we couldn't rescue her."

"He won't."

"He said he would," Jax insisted.

"You don't know him. He *won't*."

The helicopter scattered reinforcements running up the Avenue of the Dead. Seeing it fly nearer to the other pyramid, Jax grabbed Riley's arm. "They've got M2s on the Moon Pyramid. They'll shoot the copter down!"

Riley cursed and stood upright, waving his arms at the helicopter. They didn't see him.

Jax held up Miller's walkie-talkie.

Riley spared him one incredulous glance, then snatched the radio. "Deidre, this is Riley. They've got anti-aircraft guns on the Moon Pyramid. Stay out of range. Over!"

Jax cringed. Was Deidre *on* that thing? It was her voice that responded. "You certain? Over."

"Our man on site confirms it. Over." Riley glanced at Jax again, and Jax realized he'd been promoted on the field from *you idiot* to *our man*.

Instead of flying away from the Pyramid of the Moon, the helicopter turned directly toward it, bearing down on the summit at full speed. Light erupted from the top of the smaller pyramid as the M2s lying in wait fired back, revealing their position. But the helicopter was on them in seconds, silencing the big guns with its own fire.

Riley stuffed the radio into his back pocket and spoke to Jax. "Quick, go around the side and cut Evangeline loose. Get her under cover before the Morgans lose patience with me."

"What are you going to do?"

"Create a distraction." Riley waved him off to the right, then scrambled the opposite way.

Jax eased around the side of the pyramid until he could see the altar on the summit. Evangeline stood out in her white dress against the purple sky. Wylit was still shouting his insane statements, trying to bully the Eighth-Day Spell into obeying him. He flinched whenever the light from the helicopters passed over him, but it didn't seem to affect him the way Evangeline's intensely magnified candlelight had done.

"I have foreseen this death from the sky. . . ." Wylit's voice carried on the wind that billowed the train of Evangeline's dress. " . . . more sacrifices to feed the power of our will . . ."

Jax caught a glimpse of Balin, gun in hand, and pressed himself into the cobblestones as flat as he could. Gripping his dagger in a hand slick with sweat, Jax gathered his nerve to haul himself up that incline and cut Evangeline free before Balin could react. *Riley would do it*, he told himself.

No sooner had he thought it than Riley *did* do it. He appeared over the crest of the summit and snatched up a fallen gun before ducking behind Wylit's sedan chair. Balin reached under the hotel table and dragged Tegan out. He twisted her arm behind her back and held her between himself and Riley.

"Hiding behind a girl?" Riley hollered. "You coward!"

Balin apparently didn't care what Riley thought of him. He forced Tegan forward as a shield and fired over her shoulder. Bits of wood, fabric, and stuffing flew in all directions, while Riley slid onto his back, hunkering down.

Jax crept closer to the summit. Riley had seconds, if that much, and cracks were still spreading across the sky.

"Go to sleep, Tegan!" Riley yelled. Tegan's knees buckled. She pitched forward despite Balin's grip on her arm. Balin tossed her aside with a curse. Riley took the opportunity to fire at Balin, winging his shoulder. Riley next aimed at Wylit, but the old man ducked behind Evangeline.

"Come out where I can see you, Wylit!" Riley commanded.

Jax could feel the force of Riley's magic from where he stood, but Wylit merely laughed. "You haven't got half the power of your father, boy. If you want to shoot me, put the bullet through *her*!"

Riley cursed and ducked as Balin fired at him again.

Ignoring the gunfire, Wylit ripped the gag from Evangeline's mouth and grabbed her by her braid. "By my will this shall be done. Say it!" When she didn't obey, Wylit slashed her other arm with Excalibur, then held the blade poised over her right eye. "You don't need two eyes to serve your purpose for me. You don't even need one. Say it. *By my will this shall be done.*"

Evangeline pressed her lips together and shook her head.

Jax clambered to his feet and surged upward, holding his dagger out in front of him. "Let her go, Fishface. Or I'll put this through *your* eye!"

Wylit laughed at the sight of Jax. "You dare threaten me, whelp?"

"Let her go," Jax repeated. He hadn't quite made it to the level surface of the summit, and he struggled to keep his balance on the incline. Pebbles shifted beneath his feet.

Wylit noticed his trouble, and his mouth widened in an ugly smile. "I'll kill her first."

"Kill me and you have no spell caster," Evangeline called out.

"I haven't run through all your family members yet," Wylit hissed. "Your brother was too weak. He died mewling. And you're too stubborn. Perhaps your sister will be the one I need."

Evangeline gasped. Jax growled, "You monster."

"My lord!" Balin left the cover of the table, his gaze fixed on Jax. The exchange of gunfire between him and Riley had stopped. Jax caught a glimpse of Riley lying motionless behind the bullet-ridden chair. Either he'd been hit or he was out of ammunition.

Or he was playing possum.

Balin wasn't certain either. He moved cautiously, keeping one eye on Riley while trying to find an angle to shoot Jax without risking Wylit. "My lord," he said, "hold very still."

Balin raised his gun, taking aim just as Miller charged the top of the pyramid, yelling like a berserker and running full tilt into Balin's side. Balin fell with Miller on top of him. Someone's gun went off.

Jax lunged forward and sliced his dagger through the twine binding Evangeline's right hand. She snatched up

Riley's blade from the altar and hacked through the binding of her other arm. Then she grabbed Wylit's shoulders with both hands and shoved him.

They tumbled past Jax, over the side of the pyramid.

38

EVANGELINE AND WYLIT HIT the stony hill with enough force to send them somersaulting down the incline in a tangle of arms and legs. Jax skidded after them, heedless of the winds still buffeting the pyramid. Wylit's headdress flew off, and he landed on his back on the fifth-level terrace. Evangeline's body struck him first before rolling off and coming to a stop inches from the edge.

Jax fell to his knees beside her. Her forehead was gashed, and her limbs were limp. "Evangeline!" He knew it wasn't good to move someone with a head injury, but that didn't apply to people fleeing homicidal maniacs, right? He slipped an arm under her shoulders and tried to lift her up.

Then her whole body jerked. She sat up, looking around wildly. "Where—?" Evangeline recoiled when she saw Wylit lying beside her.

Jax hadn't given the old man a glance in his rush to

reach Evangeline, but now he sucked in his breath when he saw what had happened. Somewhere in her tumble down the hill, Evangeline had lost her grip on Riley's honor blade—and it had ended up in Wylit's chest.

To Jax's astonishment, Evangeline reached out and grabbed the dagger as if Wylit were trying to steal it from her. It didn't come easily; she had to tug twice before she managed to pull it out of his body.

"You two all right?"

Jax looked up to see Riley limping down from the summit. He was bloodied, but his injuries looked more like grazes from flying debris than bullet holes. As he descended, he slammed a new magazine into the grip of his pistol with the palm of his hand. "Get back," he said grimly, extending his arm and taking aim.

But it wasn't necessary. Wylit stared sightlessly at the sky, the blue of his eyes already dimmed. Riley lowered the gun, his shoulders sagging in relief as he realized he wasn't going to have to make his first kill after all. Jax sucked in a lungful of air and looked up, only to discover that the heavens still seemed seconds away from shattering into a thousand pieces. "Evangeline," he whispered in horror.

"I see it." She wiped the Pendragon dagger clean on the train of her dress and then turned it around and offered it to Riley hilt first. "Thank you for the use of your blade."

Riley didn't take it. "You can hang on to it if you like. I want *this* one." He bent and picked up Excalibur.

Evangeline watched him examine the ancient relic. "Wylit didn't complete his spell," she said, "but it's activated."

"I know." Riley gave her a sideways glance and said in a low voice, "Spell casting's not my thing. I don't know how to fix this."

A figure appeared at the edge of the summit. Riley whipped around, Excalibur in one hand, the pistol in his other, and Jax stood in front of Evangeline, shielding her.

A.J. Crandall waved at them and called to someone behind him, "They're here!" Then he turned to Riley. "The pyramid's secure. The rest of the complex not so much, but Deidre's men are cleaning up."

"Tell Riley to get up here, *now!*" There was no mistaking Mr. Crandall's bellow from the summit. A.J. turned, looking worried, then ran out of sight. Riley sprinted uphill after him.

Jax turned to Evangeline. "Do you want me to get you to a lower level, if it's safe?"

"No, I need to get to the top." She eyed the sky again, loose strands of hair whipping around her face in the wild wind.

Jax took her hand and helped her mount to the summit. In the center of the platform, two people lay on the ground next to each other: Balin and Miller. Both Crandalls were crouched beside Miller. Near the altar and the table, Thomas and his father were trying to rouse

Tegan. Michael patted her cheeks anxiously to no avail. "Pendragon!" he hollered.

Riley was headed toward Miller, but he diverted his steps enough to bend and brush his fingertips across Tegan's head. "Wake up, kid. You were very brave."

Tegan's eyes flew open, and her father nearly crushed her in a hug. Jax watched only for a second, then followed Riley with Evangeline still holding his hand. They had to step over Balin. His eyes were closed, thankfully, but his head was twisted in an unnatural way. Jax shuddered, realizing Miller had killed Balin with his bare hands.

Meanwhile, Riley was arguing with Mr. Crandall. "He said it was just a flesh wound—nothing serious. He was on his feet a minute ago."

Mr. Crandall shook his head bleakly, his hands pressed into Miller's side trying to stop the bleeding. Clearly Miller had been wrong, or lying. "Find out if the Morgans have a healer in their bunch," Mr. Crandall snapped at his son.

A.J. unclipped a walkie-talkie from his belt and took a few steps away.

"Come on, Miller," Riley said. "You've been hurt worse than this before."

Miller had lost his glasses in the fight. He seemed to have trouble focusing, but when Jax glanced at the wound again, he knew the problem wasn't Miller's eyesight. Jax's stomach lurched.

"She okay?" Miller mumbled to Riley.

"Yeah," said Riley. "She's right here."

Evangeline leaned over Riley's shoulder. "I'm fine. You saved us."

Miller closed his eyes. "Worried I was . . . too late . . ."

"Miller," growled Riley. "Stay with me. Hey!" He smacked Miller's face, like Michael had done to his daughter, but not as gently. "I *order* you to—" Riley didn't finish the sentence. Jax figured even the Pendragon voice couldn't command someone to stop dying.

"'S okay," whispered Miller. "Was tired of being here without Alanna anyway."

That was the last thing he said. A.J. and Deidre were on the walkie-talkie, ordering some vassal with healing talent to the top of the pyramid, but there wasn't any point. Mr. Crandall sat on his heels, swearing under his breath. Riley just knelt there, saying nothing.

Jax rubbed his eyes with the heels of both hands. He hadn't even liked Miller.

Evangeline put a hand on Riley's shoulder. "I'm really sorry," she said. "But you don't have time to grieve now." He looked up, and Evangeline indicated the sky. "I'm not sure how to fix this either, but I need your help to try."

Riley looked once more at his dead friend, then staggered to his feet. "Tell me what you want me to do."

Evangeline led Riley to the altar, and Jax followed. When the train of her gown caught on the foot of the table, Jax said, "I've had it with this." He grabbed up handfuls of the fabric and started cutting it off with his dagger.

"Yes, do that," said Evangeline. "He picked this stupid dress. I reject it, and him, and everything he stood for." She gripped the Pendragon blade in her right hand and held out her other one to Riley. He shifted Excalibur to his left hand and entwined his right hand with hers.

Jax hacked the last of bit of excess dress off and backed away.

Evangeline took a few deep breaths, her brow rumpled in concentration. For a moment, she looked like she had no idea how to start, but then she spoke up loudly. "I reject everything that happened here tonight. That man spoke nothing but lies."

She looked at the crate. "Niviane of the Lake was a great queen, and she was allied with two great men, both of whom are represented here tonight. The three of them together conceived a plan to stop magic being used to subjugate the innocent. I stand by what they did, even if it imprisons me for the rest of my life."

Riley watched her, looking uncertain and waiting for his cue, while Evangeline addressed the sky. *Who's listening?* Jax wondered. *Is it God or Nature or the whole Universe? Please, whoever it is . . .* He found himself praying. *Listen to her.*

"Niviane will be returned to a proper grave once the spell is repaired," Evangeline said. "We have the blade she gave Arthur to seal their alliance, which was returned to her on his death. And we are heirs to the Pendragon and Emrys lines, with full right to claim their spell as our own."

Tegan appeared at Jax's side. "We can help," she whispered. She slipped her hand into Jax's, wrapping her slim fingers around the hilt of his honor blade. Then she held out her other hand to her brother, who caught it and reached out to his father. A.J. and Mr. Crandall approached Jax's other side, and A.J. offered a hand to Jax, honor blade and all. Catching on, Jax gripped A.J.'s hand and his dagger together.

Evangeline nodded approval at them and continued, "Like the original casters of this spell, we are joined by our vassals and brave allies. A friend of the Pendragons sacrificed his life to the cause—"

"Brother," Riley said abruptly. "Miller Owens was engaged to my sister. He was supposed to've been my brother."

"Brother," Evangeline repeated. Her voice wavered. "Your brother and my brother both died preserving the eighth day."

"And Jax's dad," Riley added.

"Siblings, parents, and allies," Evangeline said, lifting her face to the sky, "all committed to keeping the eighth day where it belongs—one isolated day, one shared world, one rotation of this planet on its axis in the span of a second. By their will and by ours—this shall be done."

Jax stared at the sky. It was purple and cracked like an egg.

"You *will* listen to us," Riley shouted over the wind that whipped hair into his eyes. He yanked his and Evangeline's clasped hands into the air. "I *command* the forces of the universe to obey—in the name of the heirs to Merlin Emrys and Arthur Pendragon!"

The forces of the universe had no answer for him. Riley glared at the sky and added a few swear words to his command, but his face reflected the glittery sheen of cracks that weren't going anywhere.

"It's not enough, son," shouted Mr. Crandall. "You've got to give it something else!"

Give it something else? What else could the universe want? Jax shifted his feet uneasily. Wylit had wanted to enhance his spell with a human sacrifice. Riley had that corroded relic of an iron dagger in his hand, and Evangeline was standing there in that awful white dress, just perfect for . . .

Panic crossed Riley's face, and he looked at Evangeline.

"Man up, Riley," A.J. called out.

Evangeline stared at Riley, white lipped. "Do what you have to do," she whispered.

"No!" Jax shouted, pulling his hands free and lunging forward.

A.J. tackled him, and Jax hit the cobblestones with almost two hundred pounds on his back.

Riley swung their joined hands down and around Evangeline's back. The hand with Excalibur went behind her head, and he hooked the back of her neck in his elbow. Then he pulled her close and kissed her.

Jax would've gasped, but A.J.'s weight didn't allow him any space to breathe.

Oh, right. Melinda said strong emotions would enhance magic, too.

When Riley let go of Evangeline, she staggered backward, bumping into the altar. Her eyes were wide and startled. She and Riley stared at each other a moment, and then they looked up to see if the world was still ending.

A.J. eased off, and Jax sucked in air and rolled over. The cracks were already closing, fading to nothing in the normal purple of a Grunsday night sky.

"Dang, I think that did it!" Riley gave Evangeline the sappiest grin Jax had ever seen, still holding her hand.

She blushed pink.

And then she vanished.

Mr. Crandall looked at his watch. "Thursday. Right on time."

39

THE MEXICAN AUTHORITIES were on-site within min-utes, but they weren't very interested in getting involved. When informed that the Morgans were a private security force foiling an act of terrorism by a drug cartel, the local police backed off, leaving the Morgans to clean up the casualties and haul away the survivors.

It took both Crandalls to get Riley off the pyramid. His legs failed him halfway, and he almost took a nosedive down a staircase. After that, Mr. Crandall and A.J. kept their hands on him, and once they were on the ground, they forced him to sit on the stone steps while a Morgan vassal checked him over.

"Bruised, contused—and then he threw everything he had into one heck of a spell," the healer concluded. "He'll survive, but he should take it easy for a few days."

"I'll take a vacation in Mexico," said Riley, in between gulps of water from a bottle. "I hear that's restful."

Michael Donovan cleared his throat loudly. "I hate to be bringin' this up, Pendragon," he said. "After all, you just saved seven days of the week. But is there still an eighth day?" He looked worried. Without Grunsday, it would be a lot harder for the Donovans to conduct their family business—pilfering, safe cracking, and being a general nuisance.

Riley drained the water bottle before answering. "Yes."

"How do you know?" demanded Thomas.

"Because she's still up there." Riley and Jax said it in unison, then turned to each other in surprise. Jax sensed Evangeline's presence on the pyramid because he was her vassal, and Riley did too because . . . well, Jax wasn't sure why, but he could guess.

Riley looked at Jax. "What was all that hollering about at the end? What'd you think I was going to do? Kill her?"

Jax felt his face flush. He should've known Riley would never hurt her. *We're the good guys. Right. I forgot.* Even Miller hadn't carried out his threat, and now that Jax realized who Miller was to Riley—and who Miller had lost—he understood why Riley had trusted him not to hurt Evangeline.

"Incoming!" A.J. shouted, and Riley jerked to his feet. Jax whirled, expecting an attack by one of Wylit's stray vassals.

But it was Deidre.

She was dressed in combat gear and body armor with enough weaponry strapped to her torso, arms, and legs to take on a small army. Which, of course, she had just done. She stalked across the Avenue of the Dead, black hair flying in a ponytail behind her. "I need a word with you," she said, pointing Riley out.

"Uh," said Riley eloquently, while everybody stepped away from him.

"I understand you almost got yourself killed on that pyramid tonight," she snapped, "and then, as an encore, you saved the world with a kiss."

"Well, um," added Riley.

"The engagement's off. I have no intention of being anyone's second choice. I don't care *who* you're descended from."

"She's . . . not . . ."

Deidre put her hands on her hips. "If you didn't have feelings for her, *it wouldn't have worked.*"

Riley ran a hand through his hair and frowned, as if that hadn't occurred to him. However, A.J. and his father exchanged knowing glances, and Jax guessed it was no surprise to them.

Deidre laughed at Riley's expression. "Don't you get it? If *I* end the engagement, that lets *you* off the hook. You don't owe my mother an oath of loyalty."

Riley exhaled as her words penetrated through his exhaustion. "Your mother's going to be furious with you."

"Oh, I'm sure she'll still blame you," Deidre predicted. She turned to walk down the road toward the helicopter and shot back over her shoulder: "Stay out of her pistol range."

Riley sank down on the stone step, looking like he'd just had a pardon from the governor. He covered his face with his hands wearily.

Mr. Crandall slapped A.J. on the back. "He's cooked. Let's arrange transport and get him someplace he can rest."

Michael Donovan cleared his throat. "I happen to've recently acquired a number of Land Rovers," he mentioned, pulling several rings of keys out of his pockets, "and I'd be willing to let one go for the right price." Jax wondered when, amidst all the action, Donovan had found time to steal all the car keys.

"Take care of Miller first," said Riley from behind his hands.

"All right, son," said Mr. Crandall. "A.J. and I will get him down. Don't worry."

Everybody started moving at once. Tegan punched Jax in the arm and said, "Jerk," as she left.

"Same to you," Jax replied, knowing they both meant *Glad you're okay.*

In less than a minute, Jax found himself alone with Riley, who lowered his hands. "Jax, we need to talk."

Jax nodded. His legs were rubbery, and his head was pounding, but some things needed to be said. "This was my fault. All of it. Evangeline was in danger, and billions of people almost died, and Miller *is* dead because of me."

"Don't be an idiot. Wylit's been looking for her for years."

"But I didn't tell you about the Donovans, and they brought in Balin."

"You didn't know what was at stake," Riley said. "I kept you in the dark too long. That's on me."

Jax couldn't stand up a second longer. He dropped down on the step beside Riley and propped his head in his hands.

"You weren't going to be around for very long," Riley went on. "I didn't want you to know too much. And . . . I didn't want to end up liking you."

"Well, I didn't want to like you either," Jax muttered.

"We can't go back to that house," Riley said. "Melinda's going to get our stuff out of it, and then I have to take Evangeline somewhere else."

"Is Melinda's family really all right?" Jax asked.

"They lost their house, but they're safe." Riley sighed. "Melinda wants out. She asked me to release her from her vow. And it's the right thing to do. She's not cut out for this kind of life."

Jax tried to imagine Melinda on the pyramid with them and nodded. "I'm sorry."

"There's no hard feelings involved. Just the end of a certain kind of relationship. But I wanted you to know it was possible—to be released."

Jax lifted his head.

"You're really too young for this kind of oath," Riley said. "Even someone born into a clan doesn't pledge their loyalty until they're sixteen. And—the Balin gang aside—it's almost unheard of for Transitioners to swear to Kin."

"But—"

"Your father didn't want this," Riley interrupted him. "He was pretty specific. He didn't think you'd transition at all, but if you did, I was to give you the most basic training possible and send you back to your cousins. He didn't want you being a vassal—not to me, not to anyone."

Jax frowned. *Dad wanted me ignorant and isolated and only partly trained.* "Why?" he asked. His voice almost broke on it.

"I don't know," Riley admitted.

With a sickening feeling, Jax realized he'd probably never know.

40

THEY WERE LATE getting to the top of the pyramid because Jax's leg cramped halfway up. *I hate pyramids*, he thought, limping behind Riley. *Never. Climbing. One. Again.*

By the time they reached the summit, Evangeline was already there in that ruined white dress, still holding Riley's dagger, looking lost and alone. Then, she spotted them mounting the final hill, and her face lit up. Her eyes darted to Riley first, but it was Jax she threw her arms around, nearly knocking him over.

"Are you all right?" she asked, hugging him tightly.

"You asked me that last week, too," he reminded her. "I'm fine. But holy crap, Evangeline, look at you." He let go of her and looked her up and down. She was still bleeding from the cuts Wylit had made on her arms. Eight days later, and it had been no time at all for her.

Good thing they'd come prepared. While Riley bound up her arms in gauze, Jax handed her a plastic water bottle.

"Drink," he said. "You're probably dehydrated."

Evangeline drained the whole bottle without stopping and looked like she wanted another. Riley tied off the bandages. She eyed him sideways, shyly. "Do you want . . ." She held his dagger out on her open palm, but her gaze fell to his waist, where he wore Excalibur now.

"No, I wasn't going to ask for it back," Riley said quietly.

That was his backward way of offering it as a gift, and Jax held his breath waiting to see if she'd accept. Niviane had given Excalibur to Arthur as a symbol of their alliance, and if Evangeline accepted Riley's blade, Jax was pretty sure the meaning was similar.

Evangeline blushed and gave an embarrassed smile, then made a circle with her finger. Riley didn't know what she meant, but Jax did. He grabbed Riley's arm and made him turn around so Evangeline could reach under her dress and put the dagger away in its hidden sheath.

"We have to get you off this pyramid and away from this town. If you're ready . . ." Riley glanced over his shoulder and apparently she was, because he turned and took her firmly by one arm. Jax took the other. "Don't worry, we've got you, but *let's go*."

Evangeline started stumbling on the first set of stairs. "Sorry," she gasped.

"It's okay. I didn't make it down on my own either," Riley said, as he and Jax threw her arms over their shoulders and lifted her right off her feet. "It's a wonder you can stand at all after casting that spell."

Jax could only grunt his agreement. She wasn't very heavy, but Jax was shorter than Riley and the stupid stairs were way too narrow and deep. This was *hard*.

"Is there some reason to hurry?"

"There is," Riley admitted. "Can't conduct the level of magical mayhem we did last week without attracting attention."

There'd been Dulacs and Dulac vassals in Mexico this week, looking around the pyramid site, asking questions. They wanted to know if the threat to the Eighth-Day Spell had been eliminated and how they could assist the Morgans. They were particularly interested in discovering the whereabouts of the Emrys heir involved, expressing their "concern" that she ought to be in "protective custody" for the safety of everyone. In fact, they volunteered for the job.

Deidre Morgan had diverted them as much as she could, claiming Evangeline had been killed during the attack on the pyramid. But some of Wylit's vassals who might know better had gotten away, and no one liked the idea of the Dulacs catching up with them before the Morgans did.

"They suspect I'm lying," Deidre had told Riley. "But my mother and their clan leader currently have a truce, so they're playing nice for now. They probably think *I* have her, and if I act suspicious enough, I can lure them away from the pyramid at midnight on Wednesday. That'll give you time to escape with her. In the meantime"—here she'd included Jax in her intense gaze—"stay out of sight. *Both* of you."

The Crandalls hadn't liked that plan at all. They'd wanted Riley to leave Mexico on the first plane available, certain that if the Dulacs learned a Pendragon had survived their assassination attempt five years ago, they'd fix that mistake at once. But Riley wouldn't leave without Evangeline, and neither would Jax.

So right now Deidre was leading the Dulacs on a wild-goose chase, and all three Crandalls were circling the pyramid complex with binoculars and high-powered rifles.

Jax was panting hard and sweating by the time they reached the Avenue of the Dead. Evangeline stubbornly made them put her down so she could walk to the car herself, but she groaned when she saw it was the Balin brothers' black Land Rover.

"Yeah, I know," Riley said with sympathy. "But Donovan and I made a deal for it." He threw open the back door for her. "Donovan handed over the keys, and I didn't bust him in the nose."

"Riley." She looked up at him through her pale eyelashes, and he froze. "Thank you. For everything. Not just yesterday. But . . . everything." Her cheeks were pink, which may have been from the stairs, except she hadn't been doing most of the work.

Riley opened his mouth . . . and nothing came out.

Jax shook his head. *Pitiful.* The girl was finally willing to talk to him, and Riley had no idea what to say. Then Jax brightened. "Hey, I've got an idea. Why don't you two get in the back and chat? I'll drive."

That snapped Riley out of his stupor. "You don't know how to drive."

"I'll learn. It's Grunsday. Who's going to pull us over?"

"Get in the back, Jax," Riley growled, walking around the side of the car.

As they passed each other, switching places, Jax whispered, "Chicken."

"Shut up."

In the back of the Land Rover, while Riley peeled down the Avenue of the Dead at way too fast a speed, Jax opened up a cooler and offered Evangeline another water bottle. She took it, but she was looking at him so sadly, he stiffened.

"What?" he demanded.

"Jax," she said, then paused as if reluctant to continue. "I took you on as my vassal under emergency circumstances. I thought it would save your life, and then you ended up saving mine." Her gaze darted toward the front seat. "But I think you were probably meant for someone else."

"Who, him?" Jax pointed a thumb at Riley. "I wouldn't

swear to him if he was the last liege lord on earth."

"Wouldn't want you, squirt," Riley replied without taking his eyes from the road.

Evangeline looked back and forth between them with her brow crumpled, as if she couldn't tell if they were joking or not. "I'm offering to release you," she explained.

"I know."

This was exactly what Riley had predicted she'd do. Here she was, exhausted and wounded, and all she was worried about was giving up something she thought she had no right to—Jax's loyalty and friendship.

Riley had said he could have Jax back with Naomi in just a few days if Evangeline let him go. By fall, Jax would be enrolled in a new school. Kidnappings and pyramids and running away from homicidal Transitioner clans would be a distant memory.

He could take up trombone again. Join the astronomy club. Just like his father had wanted.

Too bad Dad never talked it over with me.

"Do you not want me around?" Jax asked Evangeline.

"It's not that. It's just—"

"Was I a bad vassal?"

"Of course not! You were brave and quick thinking—"

"Is it because I'm a Transitioner? Or a lousy cook?"

"Be serious," Evangeline said in an exasperated voice. But she was biting her lip and trying not to laugh. He recognized her expression from the pepper-spray incident.

"Okay. Seriously, then. *I decline your offer of release.*" Jax said it solemnly and formally, using the words Riley had given him to say. When he saw the relief in her eyes, he grinned and used his own words.

"You're not getting rid of me that easily."

ACKNOWLEDGMENTS

I'd like to thank my agent, Sara Crowe, and all the wonderful editors of HarperCollins who helped me make *The Eighth Day* the best book it could be: Alexandra Cooper, Alyssa Miele, Barbara Lalicki, and Andrew Harwell. I also want to thank my husband, Bob Salerni, who took me to Mexico to climb the Pyramid of the Sun; our tour guide, Alvaro Arestegui, who taught me the history of the place; and my brother-in-law, Larry O'Donnell, who helped me plan a military assault on it. I owe thanks to my daughter Gina, the very first reader for every chapter of this book, and my daughter Gabrielle, who designed Jax Aubrey's mark. A big thank-you also goes to my critique partners, Krystalyn Drown and Marcy Hatch, as well as my beta readers: Henry Becker, Gwen Dandridge, Lenny Lee, Katie Mills, Susan Kaye Quinn, Mary Waibel, and Maria Ann Witt.

A very special thank-you is owed to my reading

classes from the 2012–2013 school year. These students were "handcuffed" to me and dragged along on my publication adventure. They cheered me on through every step in the process! Thank you, Jimmy, Matt B., Isabel, Rachael, Valerie, Isaac, Joey, Miranda, Josh P., Zach R., Aidan, Angelo, Kyle, Javi, Darrien, James, Shelby, Kira, Luis, Alexa C., Matt C., Mike, Zoe, Chase, Matt H., Patrick, Laura, Katie, Savannah, Abby, Owen, Josh M., Alex, Macie, Grace, Brayden, Nathan, Chris, Karl, David, Lauren, Alexa Y., and Sabriya.

THE MAGIC OF THE EIGHTH DAY DOESN'T END THERE.

Turn the page to find out what's next for
Jax, Riley, and Evangeline in

THE
INQUISITOR'S MARK

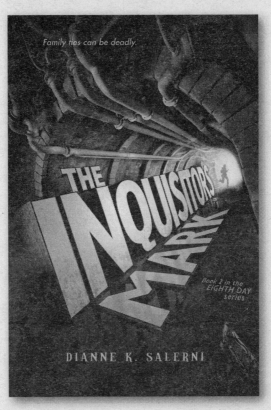

1

JAX AUBREY'S PHONE RANG at least once a day, and it was always the same number. Only one person ever called him, wanting to know where he was, what had happened to him, and when he was coming back.

I'm not coming back.

Jax didn't know how to break that news to Billy Ramirez, although Billy should have figured it out for himself by now. Especially if he'd peeked through the windows of Jax and Riley's old house and discovered it'd been emptied of all their belongings.

It did feel good to know that somebody cared. The last time Billy had seen Jax, three weeks ago, Jax was being driven away in a hearse. When Jax got back the phone he'd lost that night, there'd been a long list of missed calls and worried texts on it.

But Riley had explicit instructions for him regarding the phone. "Don't contact that friend of yours.

What's-his-name. Billy."

"I have to let him know I'm okay," Jax protested. "After what he saw—"

"Sorry," Riley replied curtly. "Too many people are looking for Evangeline."

Jax sagged. It was his fault Evangeline Emrys had been captured by vassals of the crazy Kin lord Wylit. His stupidity had almost gotten them both killed, along with billions of Normal people who had no idea the residents of a secret eighth day had plotted to destroy the regular seven-day week.

So Jax didn't argue with Riley. But he did send one text. He owed his friend that much.

```
Jax: im ok don't worry
Billy: dude where r u
```

Jax didn't reply.

It was also Jax's fault that Melinda Farrow's house had burned down. Jax had almost broken into girly tears apologizing to his magic tutor when she delivered all his stuff from Riley's old house to their new hideout in the mountains of Pennsylvania. He felt even more guilty because the horror of almost losing her family had made Melinda decide she no longer wanted to be Riley's vassal. When Riley released her from her magical vow of service to the Pendragon family, Jax felt it in his own gut.

Jax had sworn his service to Evangeline, so he knew how strong the relationship was between liege lord and vassal. It may have been an emergency that caused Jax to take the oath, but now that the bond between him and Evangeline existed, he couldn't imagine severing it.

It made Jax sad to see Melinda leave Riley's clan. It was small enough already. Riley had no living family and only the three Crandalls as vassals—plus Jax, for whom he was legally responsible. In a way, the little clan was like a family in itself, and lacking any close family of his own, Jax was grateful to be a member.

Still, it was a tight fit in the house Mr. Crandall had found for them. A two-bedroom cabin on the back side of a ski area didn't provide much space for five people, not to mention the sixth person who was present one day out of eight.

In fact, they had to put Evangeline in a room that was meant to be a large closet under the stairs. "Just like Harry Potter," she remarked when she saw it.

Riley cringed. "Sorry. I suppose we could—"

"No, it's fine. I was joking," she said quickly, as if afraid he'd take offense. After years of living alone as the eighth-day "ghost" in the house of an old woman, it must've been alarming to discover she was expected to share a small space with a bunch of almost-strangers. In Evangeline's disjointed timeline, she'd been in a car driving through Mexico only a few minutes ago, even though it had been a week for everyone else. She looked dazed by the abrupt change in location. "I only need a place to sleep," she said. "It's not like I have anything but the clothes on my back." Clothes they'd swiped from a clothesline in Mexico— leaving payment, of course.

"I bought spare clothes for you," Mrs. Crandall assured her.

Evangeline kept close to Jax all that day. He didn't blame her. Mr. and Mrs. Crandall were big and intimidating— both of them built like tanks. Their son, A.J., was just big and goofy, but Evangeline wasn't used to the company of people at all. Jax was the first friend she'd had since she'd been forcibly separated from her family as a child. She still acted a little shy around Riley, too, even though it was obvious she had a crush on him and Riley had made it pretty clear he liked her back.

But there wasn't time to let her get used to socializing with a bunch of people. Evangeline would be with them only twenty-four hours before she vanished again for a week, and they had plans to make.

"The Dulac clansmen who showed up at the pyramid were told you were dead," Riley informed her. "But the eighth day is intact, so it's obvious an Emrys heir still exists, maintaining the spell. It's a fairly well-known fact that your father had three children—and the Dulacs also know one was lost years ago."

He said it as tactfully as he could, but Evangeline

still blinked back tears. Her younger brother had died at the hands of Wylit, the same Kin madman who'd captured her.

"With only one Emrys heir left—or so they think— the Dulacs are going to go looking for your sister, to prevent any more attempts by the Kin to alter the spell," Riley continued. "And what they call 'protective custody' will really be *servitude*. They'll use her. If she's anywhere near as strong as you were up there on the pyramid, they'll use her magic for their own selfish purposes."

Evangeline nodded solemnly. She was used to being sought by unscrupulous people—Transitioners and Kin alike. Jax thought it was a terrible burden she lived with: being a key to the Eighth-Day Spell that imprisoned dangerous Kin in an alternate timeline. In some ways, Evangeline and her sister were the two most important people on the planet, and Jax, as the sole vassal of the Emrys family, felt a little inadequate for the job of protecting them. Thankfully, he had Riley's help.

"We'll have to get to Adelina before they do," Evangeline said. "Do you know where she's hiding?"

"No, but I know who does and where to find *them*," Riley said.

"The Taliesins," Evangeline guessed, and Riley nodded.

"If you're in agreement," he went on, "we can act next week—well, your tomorrow. And after we find her, we'll come out of hiding. You and your sister. And me."

"What do you mean?" Mr. Crandall broke in.

"I'm done hiding," Riley repeated, looking Mr. Crandall in the eye. "From Ursula Dulac especially. Once we have Evangeline's sister, I'm claiming my seat at the Table."

Mr. Crandall and A.J. exchanged uncomfortable glances. Ursula Dulac was the head of the Dulac Transitioner clan, and was a powerful and corrupt leader who used her magic for personal gain. She had arranged for the assassination of Riley's family because the Pendragons wielded too much influence at the Table, the council of Transitioner lords descended from Knights of the Round Table. Riley's father had thwarted her attempts to influence Normal politicians and complete shady business deals. Consequently, Ursula had not only taken action to remove *him* as an obstacle to her plans; she'd tried to wipe out his entire family. She didn't know one of the Pendragons had survived, and it wasn't surprising that the Crandalls were uneasy about her finding out. But Jax did wonder why Mrs. Crandall was now looking with concern at *him* instead of at Riley.

"I agree with anything that reunites me with my sister," Evangeline said.

"You realize this puts you both in danger," Mr. Crandall pointed out gruffly. "You'll be targets for anyone who wants to eliminate you"—he looked at Riley—"or use you as a pawn." He turned to Evangeline.

"I'm accustomed to people trying to use me," Evangeline replied simply.

"And I don't intend to be an *easy* target," Riley said, decisively ending that discussion.

Evangeline offered to instruct the Crandalls on a way to protect this house from enemies who might be looking for them in the meantime. "I could do it myself," she said, "but I think your talent is better for this type of protection."

"At your service," Mr. Crandall replied. He and A.J. were both artisans with the talent of transferring magic into craftsmanship. A.J.'s specialty was tattoos, and Jax had heard that Mr. Crandall had a knack for making honor blades. From scratch. With a forge.

The eighth day passed with them making plans for the following Grunsday and working on protection for the cabin. Evangeline vanished at the stroke of midnight, as she always did. Jax grew bored in her absence. Melinda had brought his bike, and the June weather was cool and pleasant, but the nearest town was ten miles away, and its big attraction was a strip mall and a Denny's. In between, there was nothing but woods, bait shops, ski shops, bait *and* ski shops, and one dirty bus station run out of the back of a convenience store. The cabin's TV got only local channels, and although thanks to Melinda he now had his computer back, it wasn't connected to anything. Riley had ordered cable and internet, but it hadn't been installed yet.

Mr. Crandall approved of cable but complained about the internet. "Security risk."

"Let Jax have his computer," Riley said. "He learned his lesson."

Riley knew about that too, now—how Jax had contacted a Transitioner forum online, which turned out to be a trap, which led to him getting kidnapped by a bank robber, which led to his rescue by thieves, which led to revealing Evangeline's hiding spot . . .

Jax *had* learned his lesson. But the messages from Billy were getting more and more pathetic. Shortly after Jax ignored a call on Saturday, he got a follow-up text.

```
Billy: is it something i did
```

Jax sighed. He took the phone outside, away from the cabin, and sat against a tree. What was the worst that could happen? This was *Billy*.

```
Jax: u did nothing wrong
Billy: where r u
Jax: middle of nowhere
Billy: r u in trouble with the law?
```

Jax laughed out loud. What was he supposed to say? *No, I'm hiding from murderous Transitioners and evil Kin. Who are they? Well, the Kin are an ancient race of sorcerers, including some rotten ones who tried to take over the world back in King Arthur's time. To defeat them, King Arthur and his allies trapped all the Kin in a secret eighth day, and the descendants of the people casting the spell became Transitioners, who experience the regular seven days plus the extra one. No, I don't have a head injury, thanks for asking.* Of course, now that Jax thought about it, Billy would probably believe the whole thing. He loved everything related to science fiction and fantasy.

Standing up, Jax put his phone in his back pocket, leaving his friend's last question unanswered. Let Billy's imagination run wild. It would keep him entertained.

He was headed toward the front door of the cabin when he heard Mrs. Crandall's voice through an open window. "You should have talked him into accepting her offer," she was saying. "You should have *insisted* that Evangeline release him."

Jax quickly moved up against the side of the house, where he couldn't be seen.

"It's not my place to interfere between a vassal and his liege," Riley replied.

"But you're his guardian. You promised his father you'd send him back to that Naomi woman as soon as he knew enough to survive—not let him swear on as a vassal

9

to the Emrys family. That's a dangerous position for any-one, let alone a thirteen-year-old boy!"

Jax held his breath, waiting for Riley to say, *But Jax is smart and brave and talented. He can do the job.*

Instead, Riley said, "Did you see how Evangeline stuck to Jax like glue? He's the only one of us she knows really well. We *need* him until she gets more comfortable with us. But you're right. By fall, he's got to go. He needs to be enrolled in school anyway."

"Sooner," Mrs. Crandall insisted. "Sooner is better."

Jax slid down and sat against the side of the house, feeling kicked in the gut. *Guess I'm not a member of Riley's clan after all.*

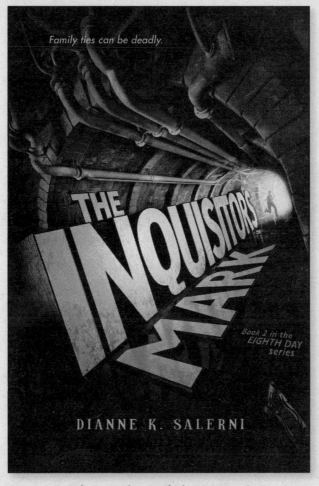